I0572185

A tale of love and lust in the old south

Dangerous Compulsion

REVISED

IMOGENE GRANT

Ocala, FL

Zeta Publishing, Inc
P.O. Box 953
Silver Springs, FL 34489
www.zetapublishing.com

This is a work of fiction. All of the characters, names, incidents, organizations, and dialogue in this novel are either the products of the author's imagination or are used fictitiously.

Ordering Information:
Quantity sales. Special discounts are available on quantity purchases by corporations, associations, and others. For details, contact the publisher at the address above.
Orders by U.S. trade bookstores and wholesalers. Please contact Zeta Publishing: Tel: (352) 694-2553; Fax: (352) 694-1791 or visit www.zetapublishing.com

First Published by AuthorHouse

Rev. Date: August 2019

ISBN: 978-1-7327914-6-6 (sc)

ISBN: 978-1-7327914-7-3 (e)

Library of Congress Control Number: 2018962423

Printed in the United States of America

Chapter 1

In memory of black men and women sold at auction, the slave block formed a disquieting backdrop behind the docks of Savannah, Georgia. A cruel reminder of a brutal chapter in American history, that is often overlooked or forgotten.

Barbarities such as mutilations, branding, chaining and murders were prohibited by law in the eighteenth century.

The limitations of the supply of Negroes led to good results, if anything can be considered good in that era. The masters paid more attention to the safety and condition of their chattel. There were three million plus slaves in 1867 in the Southern states. It was well into the next century when the United Nations committee on slavery reported that only a vestige of bondage was declining.

Nevertheless the committee found that forms of slavery effected a large number of people. These types of servitude included serfdom, peonage, and various abuses, from adoption of children and the transfer in marriage of women without their consent. The conference adopted a Convention on the Abolition and practices similar to slavery, to supplement the convention. It provided for penal sanctions against the practice.

It has been said slavery was and has led to the detriment of the black man in America.

The sun shimmered on the surface of the ocean as the wind created little wavelets in the oppressive heat of Post Civil war August, 1867. The sails of the Extreme Clipper Ship were stark white against a blue sky. The fast running vessel cut through the water with unbelievable speed. Savannah, loomed closer in a matter of minutes.

Henri Devereaux stood on the bow of the ship; his erect stance made him appear taller than he actually was. His fingers touched the silk stock wound around his throat. His green eyes surveyed the coast line on either side of the city.

"Steady as she goes!" he bellowed, with a thick French accent, then turned his attention to the busy cauldron of humanity in the port of Savannah.

The South was busy digging itself out of the devastation of the Civil War. The docks and surrounding streets teamed with black and white laborers.

Black dock workers bent down to their job; coils of muscles rippled and gleamed with sweat as they put their backs into the task of unloading a cargo ship.

They raised their voices in rhythmical sounds. "Heave ho! Hum! Lift dat bale! Ha! Tote dat rum! Ho! Dark of night, soon' 11 come! Hum! Ha! Ho!" The tune was repeated in varying cadences, while they carried the casks of rum and rolled the hogsheads of sorghum and molasses ashore. The Negroes walked with sure footing down the single planks from the ships to the dock, around the bales of cotton and lumber waiting to be transported to foreign places.

Poor whites who were overseers and others tallied the shipments as they were unloaded. Many hangers-on were stragglers and bullies, who thought it amusing to torment the Negroes, who were helpers to the merchants. Blacks were tripped or shoved off the sidewalks.

The Clipper ship dropped anchor a short distance from the harbor. A long boat was lowered along side as the sun blazed high in the sky. The workmen voices could be heard over the street noises.

Henri stepped over the side to the deck of the small craft, followed by Stephen and Jean-Claude, his men servants. The captain piloted the boat and guided the small vessel into port. Henri stood by the bowsprit. The craft glided smoothly to a stop at the edge of the dock. He and the servants, Stephen and Jean-Claude, walked among the bales of cotton and workmen. He relished the sights and sounds of the pastoral American city.

In the glare of the sun, merchants and scalawags alike ogled the Frenchman's clothing, from his fine gray hat to his shiny boots. Henri and his well dressed entourage made their way slowly along the wharf. The stench from the pigs, pinned on the pier was formidable; in addition to that of the workmen and others in the crowd.

The stragglers gathered close to Henri and his attendants. They snickered, talked loudly behind dirty hands as spittle sprayed from their mouths. Some jeered!

"Dapper Dan is comin' through!" one ruffian yelled.

Henri looked at them with disregard. As he continued to make his way through the throng of malodorous men and caged animals.

A one-eyed giant of a man with a straggly red beard blocked his path. The rogue's battered face attested that he had been knocked down, gouged, bitten and spiked into unconsciousness dozens of times in fierce brawls. Henri made his way around the hulking giant of battered human flesh.

An inhuman scream from ahead distracted the crowd as a surly drunken, bearded man slapped a young Negro woman and hurled her from the sidewalk. The woman went stumbling one way. Her bundle in the other direction. He stood weaving over her; a giant of a man.

"I told you to get on ahead! You black wench!" he yelled. "Gal, now you gonna get it!" And fumbled to get the whip off his belt. The rabble encouraged him to teach her a lesson. No Negro would dare cross or disobey their master.

The crowd formed a circle around him and the woman. "You black hearted witch! You're my property. You do what I tell ya'!" Spit dribbled into the dirty, stringy beard as he drew his arm back to beat the woman.

The crowd moved closer to see the anticipated lashing. The woman cowered on the ground with one arm raised to protect herself against the blow. August Blanc, the woman's master brought the whip forward to strike.

Henri was now abreast of the bad-tempered rogue, who was about to bit the woman.

Bracing herself against the assault, her hazel eyes mirrored her terror; nonetheless August brought his hand down to deliver the blow.

Henri reached out and grasped the whip in it's downward thrust, and held it in a surprisingly strong grip.

An eerie hush fell over the crowd as they moved hungrily in, several steps.

August Blanc, was taken by surprise. "What?! Who?!" he turned and gaped at Henri. "Well, well, what have we here? A pansy!" he said, laughing loudly. "How sweet, can you get folks?!"

"You looking at a cute one August!" someone yelled from the sideline of fair weather friends.

Raucous laughter came ·from the crowd.

"Why you sweet smelling pop-in-jay! She's my property!" August declared savagely.

"That's no way to treat your possessions, monsieur", Henri's responded quietly.

"I'll give you, a whipping within an inch of your sweet life!" August said, showing off for his cronies. His meanness was forbidding as he rushed the intruder. August's discolored teeth were bared in a sadistic grimace, as his foul breath burst from his mouth.

Henri sidestepped the first onslaught and sent a fist to August's neck. His servants scrambled back against a store front. Henri tossed his hat and cane to Stephen, then tugged gently on his fine ieather gloves.

The hooligans charge, had ended in the crowd of jeering onlookers. His foul breath repulsed even some of them.

August turned, and shook his head like an enraged bull, squaring his shoulders for another rush at the Frenchman.

His rage was formidable.

The men circled, as Henri waited poised for the hoodlum to attack.

"I have sweet smelling Dandies like you for breakfast, every day," August bragged.

The raucous crowd encouraged him on, in the battle. He charged head down like most street brawlers. Henri sidestepped again with the agility of a bull fighter.

Slamming a jarring blow to the side of the hooligan's face.

The crowd fell silent again as the drunk staggered and stumbled into the riffraff; with blood pouring from his nose.

The crowd held him up, and turned him around; then they shoved him back into the fray.

The Negro woman looked on in surprised disbelief, and frightened pleasure. Then she rolled out of the way of her stunned master, who made another charge.

Henri used a series of kicks and fist blows sending the big man floundering to his knees. Blood gushed from another cut over the bridge of his nose.

August touched the side of his face. The ruffian stared in disbelief at his blood. He roared, and turned a little unsteady with fists raised, and swung wildly. Round house blows, designed to decapitate any human being, were directed at the man causing his misery. August missed the mark.

Henri eluded the wild swings, then delivered the final barrage of blows sending the thug to the ground groggy and bleeding.

The crowd looked on with grudging respect, at the man of slender build who was unscathed, by the bully of Savannah.

The Frenchman collected his hat and cane, and brushed imaginary dust from his lapel. "Help her up and bring her over," he ordered the servants. They went to her, helped her stand, then brought her to the sidewalk.

The crowd parted in further disbelief, because no one dared help a Negro in public.

Henri gently turned her face from side to side. He looked at her delicate bone structure, and flawless black skin, then her almond shaped hazel eyes. He directed his servants, "Get her bag and take her ..."

"You can't take her, she's my property!" August said. He gulped wiping the back of his hand across his mouth. "I just bought her today! I'm taking her with me!" August staggered to his feet and stood reeling.

"How much?" Henri inquired.

"Two hundred dollars," a crafty look filled August's blue eyes.

Henri reached into his breast pocket for a money pouch, and gave the man the money. "Jean-Claude, take her to the ship and get her cleaned up. I will return when my business arrangements are completed. Stephen come with me," he directed, walking toward the shipping office.

"She wasn't worth more than a hundred," August shouted, trying to regain a modicum of dignity, to Henri's back. "We'll meet up again; you wait and see!"

Henri walked to 'Abberdeen Shipping Offices'. Inside, he went across the room to the desk. "Good morning. I'm Henri Devereaux. I'm here to see Monsieur Abberdeen."

"Do you have an appointment?" the male clerk asked. "Yes. My card," Henri replied.

The clerk crossed to a door behind his desk, knocked then opened the door marked 'John Abberdeen, President' and went inside, closing the door quietly. "Sir, a Monsieur Henri Devereaux to see you. He said you expect him."

"Yes, yes I've been waiting for him. Show him in man!

Don't keep him waiting!" John Abberdeen said, returning from the window.

The clerk scurried out and was back soon, escorting Henri into the office. John Abberdeen came from behind his desk to meet the Frenchman with his hand out stretched.

"Monsieur Devereaux it's a pleasure to see you again," Abberdeen said.

They met in mid-room and shook hands.

"Please, have a seat. Can I get you something? Coffee?" Abberdeen inquired.

"Coffee would be fine," Henri answered.

"Bring coffee," Abberdeen directed the clerk, then he said to Henri. "I saw the fight, or the whipping you gave ale August," he chuckled. "Where did you learn to fight like that?" Abberdeen asked.

"In the Orient," Henri answered. His tone of voice put an end to the next question.

"August is a mean one. You be careful, he'll try to get even," Abberdeen warned.

"Thanks for the admonition."

"How was your voyage?" Abberdeen asked, and went behind his desk.

"The Devereaux Clipper is a beauty, and quite fast," Henri replied.

"You travel a great deal?" Abberdeen asked.

"Yes, I've been to many countries," Henri answered. The clerk came in carrying a tray with an elaborate coffee pot, fine China and silver service. He poured the dark rich 1 iquid, asking, "Sugar, cream?"

"No, black please," Henri answered, while passing a packet of papers to Abberdeen. "These are the invoices for the cargo of rum, fabrics and machinery," he said.

Abberdeen took the parcel of papers.

The clerk placed the cups in front of the men and left the room closing the door quietly.

"I want to see Devereaux Manor before I leave for France," Henri said, sipping the rich brew.

The merchant opened a desk drawer and removed a package. "I know you'll like that part of Georgia. Corne I'll show you," he walked to a state map on the wal 1. Henri fol lowed.

Abberdeen pointed to the map, saying, "This area here is where the Chattahooche mountain streams run in a Northerly direction and empty into the Tennessee River system. Then it continues on to the Mississippi. Your representative picked the best place for your home, and everything is ready."

"Are there inlets along the bay?" Henri asked.

"Yes. That's beautiful country up there in Kalb Kove," replied the merchant. "It's located between Savannah and the Tennessee boarder. You'll love that part of Georgia," Abberdeen said.

"I'll have to go there soon," Henri answered. "The work on your home was done according to your instructions," Abberdeen said.

"Yes. I'll study this as soon as the cargo is unloaded," Henri said, and walked to the desk and picked up the papers.

"I took the liberty of arranging transportation to Devereaux Manor.

I also, extended invitations for dinner so you can meet some of the businessmen and plantation owners up there; I hope you don't mind?" Abberdeen asked.

"That was kind of you. It should work out splendidly.

Before my return to France," Henri said.

"The pleasure was mine. I included a list of house and field servants," Abberdeen answered, pleased with himself.

"The plantation has overseers and laborers as I've directed? Pay scale everything?" Henri asked. After pausing a moment, inquiring, "The silk wall covering arrived intact?" "Yes, I was there as I said, the mansion was in the final stages of completion right down to the oak tree lined drive. There's a good overseer: a Negro named Seifus, trained him myself. Business is slow now, but it's picking up."

"It would seem you have done your job well," Henri said. " 'Devereaux Manor' of Kalb Kove, Georgia, the name fits perfectly," Abberdeen said proudly.

Henri shook Abberdeen's hand, turned and left the office.

"It's beautiful, absolutely beautiful," Abberdeen said loquaciously, following him out.

"I'll be looking forward to doing business with you in the future Monsieur Abberdeen. Come Stephen," Henri said. As he pulled on his gloves, and left the building, with his servant.

John Abberdeen hooked his thumbs into his suspenders, grinning with pride. He went to the window that overlooked the harbor, rocking back and forth from heel to toe with his chest out. He watched Henri and his attendant make their way toward the pier. Farther out in the distance, the graceful lines of the extreme 'Clipper Ship' rode at anchor in the bay.

The ships mate, said, "Monsieur Devereaux it's bad luck for a woman to be aboard ship! Men are hard to handle even if she is as black as the night," as Henri went below deck. "That's nonsense," Henri answered. "She's a human-being and she stays until I find a better place for her."

The mate stood with his hands on his hips, and watched as Henri walked to his cabin. The man shook his head and turned toward another compartment. "She probably has a heart as black as she is," he muttered.

Henri entered his quarters and removed his gloves, hat and coat, then poured a goblet of wine. He was about to sit for supper when he become aware of the girl, staring at him. He saw her frightened eyes, in the shadows behind the bed.

She hid her face when he turned to look at her. He set his goblet aside, and went to her, gently helping her up. "Don't be afraid I won't hurt you little one," he said, and led her to the seat near the porthole and sat her down. His servant had cleaned her up and dressed her in an over-sized white night shirt. A belt cinched it around her slim waist. Her features rivaled any Egyptian Princess he had ever seen.

He looked at her anew; she was tall with a small rounded head on a long graceful neck. Her hair was closely cropped and fitted her head like a skull cap. The hair was tightly curled, not woolly as one would expect of someone of African decent. Her body was graceful, slim as a young sapling, with cone shaped out thrusting breasts.

Her skin was like black velvet. He glanced over her long ebony thighs, only half-concealed by the night shirt. The garment accentuated her slender curving hips, and a waist as small as a child's. Her small nose served to balance her face along with her slightly slanted, half-closed eyes, that smoldered yellow brown under thick lashed lids.

"You are, beautiful," he said, softly and reached out to touch her cheek. She continued to cower, and moved to the farthermost end of the seat. "No one will hurt you here little one," he persisted. "What is your name?"

"Ymani sir," she answered in a thickly accented, throaty voice.

"That means 'faith'," Henri chuckled, saying, "You're not showing much faith now. Come I won't harm you. Eat, there's plenty for both of us."

"You know, my country?" she asked hesitantly.

"I've traveled to North West Africa and a few others places in that country. I have seen many in your nation, but none as lovely as you," he responded. Fascinated, he reached out to touch her skin again. She moved farther away, "I didn't think it possible, but you are as beautiful as any woman I have ever seen in any country," he repeated.

She relaxed a little as he poured a goblet of wine for her, and served her some food. Ymani reluctantly relaxed across from him and ate hungrily. Henri sat, sipping his wine, watching her consume the food.

Ymani stopped when she discovered he wasn't eating, she turned away ashamed.

"When did you eat last?" he asked.

"Two days sir," she answered, hesitantly and continued to avert her face.

"You'll always have enough to eat as long as you're with me. I'll take care of you," he said softly.

She smiled bashfully revealing small white teeth. Her face was briefly transformed from lovely to beautiful.

"Now, the sleeping arrangements," he said, and slapped both hands on his knees and stood.

Her smile disappeared as quickly as it had occurred. Her eyes grew wide with apprehension. He noticed and walked to an alcove, and pulled back a curtain to disclose a couch against the wall. Then he found a warm coverlet, "This is where you'll sleep while on board. Take your meals in here, don't go on deck until night. The men think it's bad luck having a woman on the ship. I'll see that you have suitable clothes to wear," he said.

She had difficulty understanding everything he said.

Turning, he shrugged into his coat and left the cabin.

Ymani stood in the shadows after night fall, near the rail, wrapped comfortably against the ocean breeze. She gazed in desolation out to sea. Ymani didn't see the moonlight as it shimmered on the water. Her memories were of her homeland, Africa.

A sailor crept closer, from one shadow to another and spun her roughly around. When she started to scream, he covered her mouth with a gnarled hand. She could smell his fetid breath through his battered lips. As his face descended toward hers, she could see his yellowed teeth. Ymani struggled to get out of his iron clutches, but her efforts had no effect against his strength.

Henri came on deck while the ruffian was pressing her backward against the rail. "You there!" he roared.

The sailor shoved her to the deck and disappeared into the darkness.

Henri started to follow, but decided against it. He helped Ymani to her feet and then below. "There will be a better place for you at Devereaux Manor," he said.

The Savannah River rose in North Georgia and South Carolina, flowing past the cities of Savannah and Augusta. The two Georgia colonial settlements whose lives were tied to the river.

The Georgia Belle moved very fast toward the landing. At the right moment the captain ordered the wheels reversed.

The big wheels turned in the opposite direction as the river had slowed and the water boiled white. When the wheels slowly turned forward again the river boat came to a smooth stop, alongside the dock, nestling up to the new pier.

The captain took the cigar out of his mouth, and barked, "Run out the plank!"

Two giant Negroes with deep throated grunts pushed the canopied, rope-strung plank, used for passengers to board or leave the vessel.

"You're here, sir. I'll be back within a week, to pick you up for the trip back," the Captain said.

Henri nodded walking ahead of Jean-Claude, Stephen and Ymani, to the pier.

Workmen from the steamboat carried their luggage to the dock where men from the plantation stored it in a small wagon.

Seifus waited beside the open carriage. "What are you called?" Henri asked.

"Seifus sir," the young man bowed, and looked nervously at Ymani and quickly away.

"Ymani will ride up front with you, Seifus," Henri said, as he and his servants climbed into the cushioned seats behind the driver's perch.

Seifus helped Ymani to the driver's seat. She drew the light cape around her and sat with her back half-turned to the driver, her head bowed. As he drove along Seifus stole quick furtive lances at her from the corner of his eye.

In the background, the Captain of the Georgia Belle pulled the bell cord, it clanged loudly. The plank was lifted from the pier and pushed inward to the forward deck of the river boat. Two white clouds of smoke belched up from the stacks. The side wheels slowly turned once, twice, three times then the familiar beat became steady. The water boiling beneath the paddles.

The carriage ran smoothly along the stone path to the Manor; the view was magnificent. Coats of white wash gleamed in the sunlight. The Columns stood slim, tall and dazzling in the bright daylight. A veranda swept across the front of the mansion, as Devereaux Manor nestled in a way where one had a view of the bay leading to the ocean on one side. And on the other a pleasant walk along a river path to a grove of weeping willows, with perennial wild flowers along the creek that emptied into the river.

The stone pathway was bordered by fragrant jasmine. It curved gracefully around the corner of the manor to reveal well-laid, terraced gardens of roses, lilies and honeysuckle. The lane continued on through a line of magnolia trees. Then past the terraced gardens to a road leading to the back entrance of the plantation. The drive leading to the front door was lined on either side with transplanted great oaks.

In the gardens the smells of oleander, lavender, crepe myrtles and gardenia mixed among the acacia and magnolia.

In the distance a creek lined with weeping willow trees blew gently in the wind, and a veritable plethora of wild flowers accentuated the feeling of warmth. The over hanging balcony in the rear of the manor outside the master bedroom, had ironwork as delicate as lace. The carriage approached the cooks' kitchen house.

"Seifus, stop here,;' Henri ordered. "I want to talk with Mama Jo a moment. You and Ymani come with me."

The brick kitchen house was in use. It's fireplace was fourteen feet across with trivets, pothooks, game spits and kettles on trivets. The ovens, with the hollowed-out tops had live coals, waiting for Mama Jo to bake fresh bread while she hummed softly under her breath.

Mama Jo was a large, not overly fat mulatto, with blue eyes; freckles dotted her nose and cheeks. She had a sunny smile, and was a pleasingly plump voluptuous woman, who always wore one of many colorful scarfs on her head.

"Mama Jo?" Henri asked, as he went into the kitchen followed by Seifus and Ymani.

She stopped humming and turned, saying, "Yes sir, I'm Mama Jo."

"I'm Henri Devereaux, it's good to see you have everything well in hand," he said looking around the kitchen.

"Do you like your work place?"

"Yes sir," she answered.

"I have another chore for you, in my absence," Henri said.

"Yes sir, Mama Jo will do it."

"I want you to take care of Ymani, while I'm in France," he stated, then took Ymani's hand and brought her forward.

"Yes sir. I take good care," Mama Jo said, putting an arm around the young woman's shoulder.

"You stay with Mama Jo, she and Seifus will care for you," Henri spoke good-heartedly. "Seifus will move both you and Ymani into the house in the willows."

Ymani's hazel eyes grew round with fright. She shivered uncontrollably as tears spilled down her cheeks.

"Don't be frightened, you'll be cared for here. You stay at Devereaux Manor with Mama Jo and Seifus," Henri said, touching her shoulders lightly.

"I'll take care, you'll see. Mama Jo will take good care of you," she said, comforting the young woman.

Henri started toward the door then turned. "Mama Jo, I'm having a dinner party for the businessmen and their wives. Think you can handle that?" he asked.

"Yes sir," she replied.

"I'll be back later to tell you what I want."

"Yes sir."

"Seifus come with me, we'll finish our tour," Henri ordered, and left the kitchen house followed by the overseer, back to the carriage.

Ymani tried to break away to follow them. "You stay with me, you'll see. Ymani will be just fine," Mama Jo said, holding her to her bosom.

The young woman stared longingly after the carriage then clung to Mama Jo, her only protector in a cold and foreign land.

The carriage went over a path to a hillside, along a wagon trail leading to the sugar mill where the machinery for crushing sugar cane was going full blast. Henri stopped to watch for a few minutes as wagons left in the direction of the slow moving barges along the river inlet.

August Blanc dismounted in a grove of trees atop a knoll overlooking the plantation. From that vantage point he had a panoramic view of Devereaux Manor, the slave quarters and surrounding fields. Henri never saw'the hulking figure of his, now, arch enemy.

One of August's eyes was swollen shut. A dirty bandage covered his forehead; his nose was flattened and bruised.

"I'll see you in hell you pansy son-of-a-bitch!" August said vehemently, and drank from a bottle of whiskey. He shook a ham-like fist at his unsuspecting nemesis. Then watched while the open carriage disappeared around the front of the mansion. August led his horse further into the woods, then swung astride and galloped away.

CHAPTER TWO

Henri entered through a massive oak door that opened into a foyer, leading past a magnificently hand crafted, circular staircase to the second floor. The wide hall went past spacious rooms to a sun-porch breakfast room in back.

The unequaled cabinet makers of Europe had worked with the finest woods, teak, hardwood, oak and mahogany, shaping and polishing until the grain of each piece shone through.

Yrnani, a fast learner, eagerly helped Mama Jo in the cook house along with Kitty and Sassy, young women who had duties, errands and other tasks. They giggled and frolicked until Marna Jo would have to stop their antics.

Marna Jo admonished them, saying, "You Kitty! Sassy! Stop that nonsense and get to work. You hear me! Get back to your chores!" Then she'd return to her baking. The young women snickered behind their hands, but would go to work.

Seifus was always underfoot. Standing to one side of the stove sampling food as it came out of the oven. He would surreptitiously steal glances at Yrnani, who ignored him completely.

"Seifus, you stay too much in the cook house, go out, do some work," Mama Jo scolded. "Stop making cow eyes at my little girl," she said, shooing him out the door.

The sun went down slowly behind the horizon, coloring the sky with every hue of orange, yellow and gold.

By night the manor was spectacular, lights burning bright. Crystal chandeliers were ablaze as businessmen and their wives arrived for supper with the master of the manor.

Outside on the curving drive, servants opened doors to coaches and helped guests down. Field hands would guide carriages away to the stables where every horse was watered and fed.

Music was played by an ensemble from Savannah. A rarity in the eighteen hundreds, especially in the South. The musicians were slaves who had been taught to play various instruments and tunes.

Guests arrived by one and two couples at a time.

Jude, the butler opened the massive oaken door. Visitors assembled in small groups, while the music played softly in the background. A few early arrivals danced on the newly polished floor.

High on the wooded knoll in the darkness, August Blanc drank from a bottle of whiskey. His eye was less swollen. He was able to see through a narrow slit. A sore reminder of his lost prestige after the beating by Henri. He sat brooding as he watched the guests, and listened to the music. His horse made quiet snorting sounds as it grazed on the tender grass.

August stared transfixed at the activities below. He sat to attention, when Ymani walked across the lighted space between the cook house and the manor.

"You gonna hear from me, you pansy bastard," he spat, and drank from his bottle. "Took my property from me," he muttered. Then he staggered to his horse, swung into the saddle and cantered off into the night.

As the guests arrived, their thin formal smiles vanished. Henri, a master of comportment, put them at ease with his good looks, and refinement. The daughters of the South were captivated by his continental elegance. They simpered coyly behind their fans as he touched his lips to their hands. The men took Henri's extended hand and firm grasp. They saw wealth and the possibility of making money.

Ymani watched his every move longingly from the shadows, knowing she could never hope to be a part of his life in this world. Her regard for him could never be acknowledged. She turned and ambled away toward the cook house. Her movements were not unnoticed; Seifus watched her from a distance like a love sick puppy.

Many guests entered the formal living room, ablaze with lights from opulent chandeliers.

One such couple was Dr. Edwin Gordon and his wife Myrna.

Her wrap and his hat was given to Mona the maid.

"Doctor and Meestress Gordon, sir," Jude announced.

"Welcome to Devereaux Manor," Henri said, and went forward and made a courtly bow to Myrna, and shook the doctor's hand.

Servants mingled with trays laden with delicacies, and fine wine.

"Your home is so lovely! Myrna said, as she looked around in wonder.

The knocker sounded again, and Jude was in his place by the door, opening it to admit three couples: Price Bigelow and his wife Margaret, Ralph De Vaughn businessman with his wife Agnes Diderli-De Vaughn, entering with Vincent Holmes and Mrs. Stella Morrissey-Holmes.

The maid took the ladies' wraps and disappeared into the cloak room. Jude showed the couples to the ballroom.

"Mister and Meestress, Ralph De Vaughn, Mister and Meestress Vincent Holmes, Mister and Meestress Price Bigelow," Jude announced.

Henri welcomed them as the knocker sounded again. "That's Scott and Jillian. I saw them drive in behind us," Ralph voiced, in a thick Southern drawl.

The couples followed Jude inside. "Scott! Jillian! I thought that was you! This is our host, Henri Devereaux," Vincent said loudly pronouncing Henri as 'Henry'.

All the guests were in the ballroom, wine was served along with hot hors d'oeuvre, and little sandwiches.

"This home is extraordinary! Your wife must be proud!" Agnes exclaimed.

"There is no Mrs. Devereaux yet," Henri answered. "You'll find one soon, she's gonna 'love this place'!"

Stella remarked in a sultry Southern voice.

"Perhaps. I travel widely and haven't had the time to find a wife. I leave for France in a few days so you see, there is so little time," Henri said, and raised his hands appealing for understanding.

"When will you come back to Georgia?" Jillian asked. "Nine months at the most," he answered.

"Supper is served, sir," Jude announced from the doorway and bowed. The couples filed into the formal dining room with candelabras placed along the center of the table. The silver and fragile China settings were impeccable. Servants stood waiting to serve the courses.

"The population seems more than my reports would indicate after the war ended," Henri said.

"We have a growing middle and upper-class," Dr. Gordon answered.

"My patient load is up in the last year or so. I had to put on another doctor."

"Some of the new folks are a bunch of cutthroats," Vincent added. "I've had some of my best slaves and field workers lynched in the past few months."

"It's happening all over," Scott interjected. "The story goes, the hangings have gone on for years. Negroes were a dime a dozen a while back."

"Not anymore, there's been a drastic drop in slave trading. Most of the blacks smuggled into the South in the last few years are used as low paid servants," Price reasoned.

"Enough of that kind of talk!" Jillian interrupted. "This is a welcoming party for Mr. Devereaux. Let's talk about getting you married off. We have to get those gorgeous green eyes reproduced," she said, leaning over and grinning at Henri devilishly.

"You're right, today is for celebration," Henri laughed. "Jude we'll have coffee now and brandy for the gentlemen."

"Now that we're gonna be neighbors, why not make this on a friendlier, first name basis?" Edwin said.

The coffee and brandy arrived and was served.

"Here! Here! A toast to good friends," Ralph said and raised his glass in a toast.

"Mr. Devereaux would you mind if your girl Mona, showed us your lovely home?" Myrna asked.

"Please, address me as Henri, and yes Mona will," he turned to her. "Mona, show the ladies Devereaux Manor."

Mona curtsied and led the group of chattering women out of the dining room and up the winding staircase.

The men took their brandy into the library.

"What is this about slaves being lynched?" Henri asked. "It's a bunch of night riders wearing white sheets, and burning crosses. They call themselves 'The Knights of the Brotherhood'," Scott answered.

"They come riding out of the darkness killing what they consider to be uppity Negroes, Price said. "Their purpose they say, is for the purity of the white race or some such nonsense."

Jude went among them refilling their glasses. A shadow of a man who served, but was seldom seen and never heard.

"Scares the hell outta the slaves." Vincent continued, "Suppose to keep them and the towns people in line, always the threat of death or great bodily harm."

The wives could be heard upstairs.

"There should be something the planters and businessmen can do," Henri said. "We're loosing good manpower."

"Take it from me I lost some damn good ones several months ago," Edwin admitted. " Believe me when I say I keep a close eye on my help. Especially now that I have to pay 'em," he said, and drank from his glass.

The wives came into the study.

"Your home is so beautiful!" Stella said excitedly, her Southern accent distinctive.

"Thanks so much for letting us see this lovely, mansion!" Myrna said. "Your bride will love it."

"I expect to see you and a wife when you come back from France. Otherwise I'll have to find you one," Stella joked. Henri smiled indulgently. "Darling we have to go," Stella reminded Vincent.

"Yes Henri, after that remark we can't over stay our welcome," he chuckled. "We enjoyed everything, especially the Napoleon Brandy." He drained the last swallow from his glass and made a noise of pleasure.

"You would, you devil," his wife said poking him in the ribs. The guests went noisily into the hall where Mona, Jude and other servants helped with their coats and wraps.

Later that night, in a valley between two hills, a group of rabble held a meeting. One well dressed man stayed in the shadows of the trees. The crowd was made up of red necks, poor white trash, brawlers, killers, hate mongers, rogues, thieves and drunken ne'er do wells. The female followers were as tough as most of the men.

One side of August's face was an angry purple, that extended across his battered nose. He stood on a flat rock that put him above the crowd, raising his hands for quiet.

"We gotta take a stand for ourselves and our white race!" he shouted. "They got a nigger overseer on that new Devereaux place! A white man's job!" he finished with indignation.

Shouts and angry curses erupted from the crowd.

August raised his hands again, "Now we can't go running off half cocked. We need a plan and backers." He paused, to look around the crowd, saying, "I' ll be meeting with some important people in a few weeks, they have money to help us!"

The rank and file yelled their pleasure with that announcement.

"Lay low for a few months. No more raids, nothing," August spoke calmly. "I have to go up north of here close to the Tennessee border. When I come back I'll have some good news in our favor! Now drink up! Our time will come, soon!"

The well dressed man in the shadows mounted his horse and rode into the darkness.

Everybody got down to some serious drinking. The women matched the men drink for drink. The raucous gathering resulted in an orgy that lasted through the night.

August drank from his bottle and cautiously ran his fingers over his broken nose. "We'll see about you Mr. son of-a-bitch Devereaux," he mumbled, then tapped the cork into the bottle, and laughed uproariously when he jumped down from his rock and joined the hullabaloo.

CHAPTER THREE

In France months later, Henri and his friend Andre de Ruffenac were having after dinner Brandy and cigars while watching the dancers and gaiety of an impromptu celebration from the balcony. There was unexpected excitement from the door of the Bistro. The patrons in the balcony jostled Andre and Henri to get to the rail to see the Prince of France and his entourage. The people were true Royalists and watched the Princely retinues' graceful entry, dressed resplendently. The landlord and attendants bowed to his highness. A royal visit always meant more business for his establishment. Waiters stood at attention as the imperial flock turned their coats and wraps over to attendants.

"The Prince and all his little followers," Andre said dryly, with a bored expression on his face.

Henri's glance passed on to two young women who laughed and talked animatedly. They were dressed in silks and richly colored brocade, with little bunches of curls that bobbed over their shell like ears.

"The Prince and all his entourage has arrived," Andre repeated. "They're all here bowing and scraping." He pointed, "There's that old geezer, de Lafayette tagging along with the young crowd."

Henri wasn't listening, his eyes had swept past the royal gathering to the two women entering last.

"That's General Villere, he's looking this way. Oh Lord, he's going to make a speech!" Andre continued. Then he noticed his friend's attention was directed some place else.

"Who is that?" Henri demanded, as his fingers gripped Andre's arm.

Andre pried Henri's vice-like grip from his arm and rubbed the painful spot. He stared in the direction of Henri's gaze, saying, "You have an eye for beauty. They're the loveliest, most sought after young women in France."

"I didn't ask about the others in France, just her; hair like night cascading around a face out of God's heaven."

"I hadn't suspected it but you're a poet too!" Andre said, looking with amusement at his friend.

"Good God! I ask the man the name of the woman I intend to marry, and he talks about poetry," Henri retorted.

"Wait a minute. Her name is Mademoiselle Lizzette Roget and her companion is Arlet Mamaneaux. They're related by blood to the royal family!" Andre replied.

"Good breeding. I like that," Henri smiled, nodding his head with satisfaction.

"Also every man of note in France has asked for one or the other's hand in marriage either for himself or for a son or some relative," Andre answered. "I would suggest you try someone less difficult. Say, the crown Princess of England. The lovely Lizzette, I'm told, is egotistical and an insufferable tease and you can't imagine her selfishness."

Henri never heard a word his friend had said. He was taken with Lizzette's loveliness.

"I should also suggest, it's rude to stare, Andre said, looking at him and shaking his head.

"Your suggestion is well taken my friend. You'll present me tonight," Henri announced.

"Here?! Tonight?! Andre laughed. "You're a commoner! And she's with the crown Prince? That my friend would be the height of being boorish," he stopped exasperated.

"You said by blood? Is that a distant cousin or something equally removed?" Henri asked.

"You're a wealthy man and have a lot of friends, in business and political circles of Paris. Your interests are similar. But to some royalists, is that enough? Socially you're a babe in the woods," Andre said pointedly.

Henri moved into a position, to Andre's exasperation, to study the beautiful Lizzette, as she engaged in an animated conversation with her female consort.

"And what does all that drivel matter?" Henri broke his concentration of the fair Lizzette long enough to stare momentarily at Andre.

"If you'll take my counsel. I believe later, might be better: although many have tried for the hand of the charming lady and failed. I can truly say, none have been quite like you," Andre replied.

"You're right old friend. I'll go slowly," Henri said, arching a brow impishly with an amused glint in his green eyes. "But I'll wager anything you like, that I marry the lady." He laughed and started to turn his attention back to the group below.

"Done. This is in spite of my warning," Andre said grinning. They shook hands then turned back to the festive gathering.

Henri's half-closed eyes found Lizzette. Her attention was captured by one of the most eloquent spokesman of France. She looked up, and for a brief moment their eyes met. The pink of her shell like ear lobes deepened, and the color mounted in her face as well. Lizzette averted her eyes quickly, he continued to stare.

Andre turned to him as the speech ended. "Henri! Please!" he exclaimed.

Henri turned to face him as the Prince swept out of the Bistro with his followers.

On a sunny afternoon days later, crowds of the French populace sauntered through the park. Henri let his eyes wander over the throngs of people dressed in their finest clothing; silks, linens and other materials from foreign places. The women's curls danced over delicate ears as they strolled through the park. Their subdued laughter could be heard as they ambled along the flower lined paths, twirling their beribboned parasols.

Henri's gaze went past the horses and coaches to a special open carriages with the Royal crest on the side. He and Andre made their way past the chattering people. As they came abreast of the carriage, Henri tipped his hat and Andre bowed eloquently. Lizzette nodded stiffly, Arlet waved and smiled, transforming her lovely face to radiant, causing the soft cluster of curls to sway about her youthful face.

"What on earth are you doing, Arlet?!" Lizzette demanded as the young woman turned around in her seat and looked in the direction Henri and Andre had taken.

"Nothing," Arlet said innocently.

"Tell the truth Arlet, you're making a spectacle of yourself again," Lizzette persisted.

"That man with Andre, he's as handsome as the Noblemen in the stories we read as children," Arlet swooned.

"Arlet! He's a commoner!" Lizzette made it sound like a dirty word, then tapped the back of the driver's seat. "Get us home! Quickly!" she ordered.

The carriage whizzed out of sight.

Henri and Andre walked along the avenue for some distance then turned into a tree lined drive.

"I'll have to leave you now. There's someone I must see," Henri said as he climbed into his carriage.

In the book lined library of Monsieur de Lafayette, an emissary appointed by the King of France. Henri sat across from his host sipping a very rare Napoleon Brandy, saying, "Monsieur de Lafayette I have a great favor to ask of you."

"Just ask my friend, I'm at your service," he replied. "I need an introduction to someone in the royal family." "Tell me who, and it's done, Monsieur de Lafayette answered.

"It's a young lady," Henri responded.

"An affair of the heart? But of course Monsieur, tell me who?" Monsieur de Lafayette asked.

"Mademoiselle Lizzette Roget, she scorns me wherever we meet," Henri said.

"Yes, a lovely young lady. As a matter of fact I can take care of that sooner than you imagined. Prince Phillip is downstairs, come with me," de Lafayette invited.

They left the library and walked along the broad hallway and down the circular stairs, into the lower hall of the spacious chamber.

The Prince stood by the fireplace staring into the flames. He turned when they came into the room, and said, "Monsieur de Lafayette a pleasure to see you again so soon and this is? No don't tell me," he thought a long moment. "Ah yes, Monsieur Henri Devereaux. I've read and heard of your business acumen." They shook hands, and sat in high back chairs before the fireplace.

"You flatter me," Henri answered.

"The truth must be told Monsieur," the Prince smiled. "Phillip, Monsieur Devereaux has a small dilemma involving a young woman, and only you can correct it," Monsieur de Lafayette chuckled.

"Just name it," Prince Phillip said.

"An introduction to the enchanting Lizzette." "Not a problem, it's done," the Prince answered.

At that moment Lizzette, and Arlet whirled through the door with gleeful laughter. She was busily removing her gloves.

Phillip went to meet them, and said, "Ah my lovely Lizzette and the beautiful Arlet. Come I want you to meet a friend of mine. Monsieur Henri Devereaux has honored us with a visit, show him every courtesy."

His arms went around their shoulders, guiding them over to Henri. Lizzette's smile froze on her lips when she looked into Henri's face. A frown creased her brow momentarily. Her steps dragged as the Prince conducted them across the room.

"Henri, this is my little Arlet," Phillip said.

Henri smiled into her warm brown eyes, then touched his lips to the tiny gloved hand. "Mademoiselle Arlet," he said softly. She swooned.

"This, is Lizzette Roget," Phillip said, leading Lizzette forward as he made the introduction.

Henri, stared into her shockingly beautiful and surprised blue eyes, fringed with black lashes.

"A pleasure Mademoiselle Roget," he whispered, then touched his lips to her delicate hand.

"Henri you must join us for the next royal ball, and bring a friend," the Prince invited.

"That would be a pleasure your highness," Henri said. "We must go now, but I'll expect you to join us next week. Our friend here will tell you where, Phillip said bowing as he started for the door, saying. "Come little ones, we have many things to do tonight." The young women preceded him out the door.

Henri and Andre were included in the Royal party during the following months. There was a whirlwind of parties, teas, riding to the hounds, group walks along the promenade, open carriage rides along the Champs-Elyses and the Opera with the Queen's court. Lizzette became comfortable with Henri, accepting him in her circle.

"You will be my wife," Henri said softly on the dance floor one evening as he looked into her eyes.

She shuddered in his arms, saying, "Oh Henri, that's impossible."

"Nothing is impossible little one," he said, whirling her around the dance floor at a dizzying pace. When he took her back to the Prince's table, she was out of breath.

"My head is spinning after that dance!" Lizzette said, fanning herself with a tiny lace handkerchief. There was a strange look in her eyes while watching the confident Henri surreptitiously from behind ebony lashes.

One of his eyebrows rose ever so slightly. A slow knowing smile touched his lips when he returned her stare. She turned quickly away groping for her fan, uncomfortably trying to regain her composure.

In the afternoon before the grand ball, Henri and Andre walked along the Champs-Elyees. Young women watched with artfulness, giggling when the two richly dressed men strolled along.

"Their tongues are wagging about you and a certain Mademoiselle Lizzette Roget," Andre said excitedly.

They ambled on, passing an occasional coach. The occupants in open carriages greeted them with familiarity.

"Henri you have arrived! You're the most talked about businessman on the continent. You have the ear of Prince Phillip! And the royal family for God's sake!" Andre declared.

"I don't know my friend, that kind of recognition could become an encumbrance," Henri said, with a touch of doubt.

"I don't know how you pulled it off!" Andre went on as if he hadn't heard.

"I'll tell you sometime, right now let's enjoy today," Henri said laughing, casting an eye on Andre.

"Do you realize your life is no longer your own!

Everything you do will be watched and talked about, and even imitated!" Andre said, still excited.

" Is that bad?" Henri chuckled.

"You'll have to watch your step! Every marriageable female will be planning to trap you," Andre warned.

"They will waste their time," Henri answered.

"I'm sorely aware that the Lovely Lizzette will marry you now. Not even she can resist the temptation of being a great lady of France. Marriage to a self made, wealthy, handsome scoundrel, who has the approval of the royal family," Andre said expansively.

"That's an over statement my friend," Henri said. "I only hope she makes you happy," Andre murmured.

"She will, don't doubt it old friend," Henri declared.

They walked along the avenue until the street was nearly empty of carriages and deserted of people. The homes seemed closed for the day, the quiet was complete.

The night of the grand ball, Henri and Andre entered through a wide facade. In the vestibule they surrendered their cloaks, then made their way upstairs to the spacious ballroom, where crystal chandeliers glittered above their heads. Around the walls in niches, stood statues; and paintings filled the spaces in between.

The Prince's entourage overlooked the ballroom floor. Honored guests were situated in box seats along the ornate walls, with a select view of the gaiety in the ballroom below. Henri's love for Lizzette blossomed.

She was ambivalent in her feelings, and constantly weighed the benefit to her. His attention was flattering. She wasn't sure she loved him enough, or at all. He was certainly good looking; because Arlet and others in her circle were enthralled when he appeared. It was common knowledge he was wealthy. A self made man and the catch of the season.

Henri and Lizzette swayed rhythmically on the dance floor while he gazed down into her eyes. Her provocative perfume floated up from her dancing curls. His nostrils flared. He took her hand and led her out to the balcony over looking the vast gardens. The night was clear and the sky was sprinkled with stars, while a thick slice of moon shone in the night sky.

Despite her inner opposition to his background, she couldn't resist Henri's touch that sent her senses reeling. She found herself questioning, was it love? He was certainly handsome and his green eyes sent tremors through her. Henri held her by her soft rounded shoulders, saying, "God you're beautiful! I love you more and more every day." "Monsieur this is too fast!" she said. The determination to resist his advances dissolved with his nearness. "We'll be married as early as it's feasible and soon after, we sail for America. You'll love Georgia," he said enthusiastically about his chosen land.

"You spoke of that before, but what would I do so far from home, my France?" she asked with uncertainty. Lizzette realizing it was hopeless, knew she would marry Henri and live in that far off country.

"You'll be mistress of Devereaux Manor. It's there, ready and waiting for you. Your beauty will shine over the whole of Kalb Kove, and people will bask at your feet" he promised. She tried to conceal her ambivalence as Henri painted a glorious picture.

Henri drew her to him. Their bodies touched and molded together, then he kissed her soft, red lips.

After the ball, Lizzette pirouetted into their suite of rooms followed by Arlet. She went straight to the full length mirror and looked closely at her flawless skin. She moved back to gaze at her slim figure, turning and scrutinizing herself from all angles, smoothing one hand over her flat abdomen. Her examination was a cold and clinical appraisal of her best assets.

Arlet watched with bright eyed innocence, saying, "Lizzette, he actually kissed you on the lips?"

"Yes you silly girl where else would he kiss me?" Lizzette answered absentmindedly continuing her inspection.

"Oh I think I'd faint if someone like him kissed me, and asked me to marry him!" Arlet said enthralled.

"He didn't ask, he told, me I would be his wife," Lizzette corrected.

"So masterful and romantic, how beautiful! He has such gorgeous green eyes!" Arlet exclaimed, then fell back on the Chaise Lounge with a sigh of delight.

"Arlet, you're a silly romantic. I can't marry him!" she said. Arranging her skirt one way and then another.

"Why not? Her majesty will give consent," Arlet said. "I doubt that, he's a commoner. I on the other hand am high born," Lizzette replied.

"If he asked me I'd say yes, in a second!" Arlet said.

"Don't be a foolish child, Arlet. There's a difference between an evening of fun and gaiety and a life time in a far off, God forsaken place called Georgia!" she said vehemently.

"Don't you love him, just a little?" Arlet asked.

"I don't know, sometimes I think yes and then another time I really am not sure. I like having him around," Lizzette said, as she swayed and whirled around, her ball gown billowing around her ankles.

"He's not a poodle on a leash, Lizzette!" Arlet cried. "He is the catch of the season. I don't know, maybe

I will marry him and go to that awful foreign place in America," Lizzette said. Her words were spoken with distaste. She sat on a silken bench to examine her nails, and said.

"He promised, people would bask at my feet in America." "With him there I wouldn't need other people basking at my feet," Arlet responded.

Lizzette frowned and stopped the investigation of her hands long enough to stare at her cousin. She stood and walked over, then with a forefinger and thumb under Arlet's chin she searched her cousin's face. At that moment she realized Arlet was in love with Henri. "You love him don't you?" Arlet tried to move away but Lizzette held her face in a surprisingly strong grasp. She repeated, "Admit it, you love him, don't you?"

"And why not? He's beneficent, honest and kind. He has breeding and is more nobleman than any of those pop-in-jays you've ever been with!" Arlet finished defiantly.

"How do you know he's honest?" Lizzette asked. "He loves you doesn't he?!" Arlet snapped in return. "That's more honesty than you'll, ever know!" Then she slapped Lizzette's hand away, jumped to her feet and ran crying to her room, slamming the door behind her.

Lizzette could only stand in the middle of the room aghast. The moment lasted only seconds before she went back to the mirror and resumed the inspection of herself.

The wedding was a gala affair in 1868. Andre arrived in time to be best man. There were members of the Royal family of France, continental businessmen, bankers and foreign dignitaries, the Devereaux family and close friends. They wore gowns of silks, brocades, linen and materials from foreign lands. Lizzette's wedding gown was of the purest white silk and reams of imported lace. The train required six people to carry it. The best seamstresses in France had toiled for weeks for it to be just right. The brides maids and men in the wedding party were a plethora of beautiful people, in dress as well as body. The best man and the entourage rivaled any, including the royal court.

Before the reception, Henri and Andre dressed in the north wing of the Palace with the assistance of valets.

The ruffles on their silk shirts stood out rigidly from the men's broad chests. Their suits were identical in every respect down to the mother of pearl buttons. Their boots were polished until they reflected the light from the chandeliers.

"You're shaking," Andre observed, when Henri poured a glass of wine.

"Of course, one doesn't get married every day. But I'll carry this off, because it means everything to me. Corne, it's time," Henri said, setting the glass down.

In the ballroom, Andre and Henri took their places.

"Why all this? The people you have invited are insufferably stuffy. To go through all this trouble and expense is beyond me," Andre spoke softly.

"You're wrong my friend this is not for them, my bride expected it. Afterward the rest can drown themselves in the nearest ocean. I'll have Lizzette," he said stroking the stick pin briefly.

Lizzette appeared at the top of the stairs, breath takingly beautiful from her coifed hair to the creamy silken gown. There seemingly was an intake of breath and a sigh from the men in the room, while she stood at the top of the stairs. The pause hovered in the air as an endorsement to her loveliness.

Henri moved part way up the steps to meet her, his face was awe inspired. He detected a fleeting hesitation and fright in her eyes as she stood poised on the top step. Then she moved down the rest of the way and took his hand. The festivities began with delightfully cool wine and gastronomic delicacies, the jollity was infective.

Lizzette danced until her head spun. Her laughter was heard as she and Henri danced by. When it was over she was slightly drunk. Henri carried her to bed and tucked her in for the night. He paused momentarily to stare at his new bride, then lovingly moved a tendril of hair from her forehead. Lizzette asleep, appeared exquisite and angelic.

CHAPTER FOUR

In the days that followed Lizzette spent shopping and feinting exhaustion. Henri by day transacted his business and at night he slept in a guest room, allowing her the freedom to prepare for the voyage.

Colleen, her maid, was kept busy packing and making arrangements for the journey to America. Servants gossiped.

"Was the marriage consummated?" Adele giggled.

"Of course not, this one is a man teaser too high and mighty for a real man," her friend said.

"She's passionless, no lovemaking for the great cock teaser, and him so handsome too. I could give him quite a frolic, I could," Adele said, looking longingly upward.

Colleen came into view and they turned to the packing.

The honeymoon took place aboard the Devereaux Clipper.

The ship was equipped with every comfort.

Winds blew down from the trees and fanned out over the water. Little wavelets slapped the sides of the Clipper ship while it rode at anchor in the bay. Shimmering moonlight toped the water with silver. White fleecy clouds were caught by the wind and spun into lacy wisps so thin the stars could be seen by the watcher on board.

Henri swept Lizzette up in his arms so her silken slippers would not touch the ships deck. He carried her across the surface and down the companion way into his suite, where he stood her in the middle of the massive state room. "Lizzette I've loved you sinc.e the moment I saw you," he whispered.

"And I you. Henri, it is so far away this, America." Lizzette's voice had a trace of a quiver. "I won't know anyone there," she said, lifting her face to his, close enough for him to smell her heady perfume.

"You' 11 have me, and I 1 ove you more than 1 ife, eventually you'll have our children, then you'll grow to love Georgia. It's a wild and beautiful country," he said with true enthusiasm.

"Henri hold me, don't let me go. I'm so frightened," she said, and moved closer into his arms, tears formed in the corners of her eyes. Her ardent kiss was mistaken for eagerness on her behalf. He held her soft pliable body to his and smothered her face with kisses. In the past, Lizzette had been adept in the art of seduction; although her kisses had never gone to the point of no return, this was the real thing. He swept her up and carried her to the canopied master bed. Her warm moist mouth drove him on, as he undressed her, and himself between kisses. "Henri be gentle with me," she whispered. Then moaned in pain during their lovemaking. When his strokes became forceful she felt as if her insides were being torn out. She wanted to scream and run away, but where would she go, there was no path to turn back. Afterward with his arms holding her against his chest, she could hear his heart beat like a muffled drum as he slept. Lizzette rolled away to the far edge of the bed and cried herself to sleep on her wedding night. As a young woman there had been stories of the wedding bed. Her friends spoke behind their fans of such things, with nervous snickers.

The voyage to America was rough, as the ocean rocked the Clipper ship savagely. Winds blew as if the devil himself were guiding the course. Lizzette didn't fair well in the following weeks. Sea sickness gripped her the first day out. Colleen, along with Henri's valets, were kept busy tending her needs. Lizzette would lie, listlessly and nauseous for days, pale and too weak to lift her hand.

Colleen slept in the alcove to be near her mistress. Henri moved to other quarters. When he came near, Lizzette turned away with bad temper. She wouldn't allow him to touch her not even in sympathy; blaming him for all her misery.

Devereaux Manor at twilight waited in anticipation of their arrival. Two servants stood on the levee, one held a shot gun to signal the masters return. Then finally the coach came into sight around the bend; drawn by sleek roans, that trotted along at a moderate clip. The carriage turned into the tree lined lane to the Manor.

The servant on the levee signaled their arrival. At the sound of the shot, laughter and shouts of joy burst from the domestics on the gallery and those gathered on the lawn. The instant the coach stopped, the driver climbed down from his high perch importantly and opened the coach door.

Henri climbed out, extending his hand into the dark interior. The servants fell silent, as a slim white hand took his daintily, then Lizzette stepped down the half step. The servants moved closer, all eyes on the carriage door.

Lizzette was fearful when she saw all the black faces staring at her. In France she had never seen African people as close as this.

"Speak to them, they came to see you," Henri whispered. "Good evening, my people," she managed feebly.

Mama Jo's full smiling face came into view. Lizzette clutched her husband around the neck burying her face under his chin.

The air was filled with gales of laughter and chatter.

The servants formed a semi-circle around the porch and on the lawn. Henri carried her through the cheering throng onto the gallery and into the broad hall, then up the sweeping stairs to the master bedroom.

In the shadows of the great oaks, Ymani lingered apart from the rest. Her hazel eyes glowed sadly in her velvety black face as tears escaped down her cheeks; always on the outside.

Mama Jo went to her, and said, "It ain't no use you pining away. You Negro servant girl. Come on, we go to the cook house. I got something nice for you," she put an arm around Ymani and led her away.

The arrival was observed by other, more hostile, eyes. August Blanc stood on the little knoll that overlooked the manor; a cleaner better dressed man. "Now is the time you bastard. I'll destroy everything you've ever loved or owned and that's a promise," he said bitterly. Then he mounted his recently acquired stallion. His harsh laughter wasn't heard when he galloped away.

Lizzette had changed since coming to Devereaux Manor. She sat moody and brooding for hours, while staring at the bay. She refused to go outside because of her fear of black people. Her fright worsened, and she clung to Colleen.

Henri made it an evening ritual to go out early and stay late into the night. He was an unhappy and lonely figure as he rode away. He threw himself into his business interests and worked long hours. The Manor was quiet, no parties nor laughter. All this was gossiped about in Kalb Kove.

Lizzette, realizing she was no longer the center of attention, devised a plan to recapture Henri's adoration. Knowing he wanted a son and heir for the Devereaux fortune, she and Colleen worked long hours bathing, coifing and dressing her in her most alluring gown.

That evening after supper Lizzette, in an act of grandiosity, moved close to her husband as he was dressed to leave.

"Why go out? Stay home tonight," Lizzette invited.

"Is there something special?" Henri answered, laying his gloves and hat aside.

"No. I want you here to discuss our future and to consider the son you've al ways wanted," she explained.

"You hate my coming near you. In my arms you tremble like a scared rabbit, frightened almost to death," Henri said holding her gently by the shoulders.

She looked away an instant from the concern on his face. "Oh Henri, I have been trying to change. I .. I want to be a better wife for you," she said looking at him. "A son with a mop of dark hair like yours, and your eyes with all this determination." She moved closer, "I am frightened in this new and strange land but I know your love for it is from your heart. I want to make you happy," she said softly.

His eyes softened as he gently held her close. His arms tightened ever so slightly, wanting desperately to believe. Inadvertently her body stiffened. In her frigidity she was not able to feel sensual desire, no matter how much she wanted to please her husband.

"Holy Christ! Am I such an ogre?" Henri asked. Lizzette turned away as tears flowed down her cheeks,

"It's alright, go if you must, I'll understand," she whispered.

"No I shan't go, not tonight," he said, her tears touched his heart.

She hugged him gratefully, and his arms stole around her waist. Using her old wilds she stood on tip toes and kissed him ardently on the lips. Her soft yielding body and compliant warm wet mouth worked it's old magic. The lingering kiss became all-powerful and he pulled her hungrily to him molding their bodies together. His senses were reeling, as the fire of passion spread to his loin. He effortlessly swept her up into his arms carrying her to the canopied bed.

Afterward it was the same, the trembling and frightened sobs.

Henri climbed out of bed without a word.

"Henri, please don't go! I'm sorry," she sobbed. "Yes I'll go!" he snarled over his shoulder. He dressed quickly and strode out of the room. The heels of his boots were heard loudly on the stairs. The slamming front door marked the finality. Minutes later his stallion thundered out of the tree lined drive.

The drought returned with a vengeance. As the weeks went by, heat hovered over the land. The sun burned down on Henri while he rode and worked in the fields to save his crops. He toiled beside workmen on the acreage. The back breaking labor went agonizingly slow, but the task was almost finished when summer neared autumn.

Lizzette would stand in the window and stare at the cane fields where the stalks were brown and dry because of the drought. Henri was always there for days on end, riding his great white horse. She could see the stark white of his shirt against his face. His skin was baked brown by the unrelenting sun. He rode recklessly, as if the heat did not exist, pushing himself and the field hands. They worked like mad man to get the crops to market. Lizzette's heart was like lead in her chest. She watched and was powerless to fight for his affection.

Ymani waited. Longing to be near him. She carried crocks of cool water into the fields for him to drink. He would gulped the water down and acknowledge her with a nod. He seldom spoke. She would stare after him as he rode away, wishing she could end his suffering.

Henri was rarely home anymore. Lizzette saw him for short periods at supper. He rarely spoke except in monosyllables, but to Lizzette he was always polite. Most of the time he nodded his head, then would be on his way, astride his beloved stallion. For months he bathed and dressed, then rode away to Kalb Kove, to the newly built Country Club that had been constructed to his specifications. It had become the gathering place for the cream of Kalb Kove.

Tongues wagged about the Devereaux's, because there were no parties given at the Manor. Towns people were curious about the new wife they had never met. The gossip never got back to Henri, because of the wealth and the prosperity he had brought to the region. Young women of the town looked at him with longing, then spoke of his wife with envy and spite.

The first weeks of autumn brought coolness. Lizzette walked in the back gardens overlooking the cook house. When Mama Jo came to the door, Lizzette turned abruptly, then the weakness and nausea swept over her. She had noticed the same feeling several times in the morning. Today the feeling overwhelmed her. She took a step forward then stopped, swaying. The blackness was crowding out the morning light. "Mama Jo!" she managed to call out when she felt her knees buckling, the trees were spinning. "Mama Jo!" Lizzette screamed, as the ground came rushing toward her.

On the first cry Mama Jo and Ymani came running across the short distance between the mistress and the cook house. They caught her and eased her down on a nearby bench.

Lizzette had thought the older black woman had an evil look about her. In her world in France she had never seen African people except at a distance. She had always thought they were savages and that belief had frightened Lizzette. The idea of being near or touched by a Negro had chilled her. Now, however, she clutched the cook for dear life.

"Ymani go for the master, hurry t " Mama Jo directed and cradled Lizzette's head on her ample bosom.

Ymani ran swiftly to the fields.

House servants came to assist, helping Lizzette to stand and walk.

"You take it easy mistress, we take you where you can lay down," Mama Jo said soothingly.

With one arm around the mistresses waist, she helped Lizzette into the house. The other servants hovered around to help if they were needed. Colleen met them in the master bedroom and helped undress Lizzette. Her companion bathed her face with a cool cloth.

"I'll bring you something, make you feel better," Mama Jo said.

"Thank you. Oh Mama Jo I am so sick," Lizzette whispered. Perspiration moistened her face and her breathing was labored.

"You're going to have a baby. That time will do that to you. The master is glad I bet," Mama Jo chuckled.

Henri came rushing into the room; crossing to the bed he sat beside his wife, then gathered her in his arms, and never heard Mama Jo's last words.

"Master Devereaux it'll be a fine boy. You'll see, Mama Jo knows," as she and Colleen left the room.

"Oh Henri, I feel so ill: They heard Lizzette saying as she clutched her husband while he cradled her against his shoulder. Colleen closed the door softly.

Ymani left by the back door of the manor. Seifus walked toward her, and her method of eluding him was maddening. She would look right past him as though he didn't exist. Walking on by with a queenly strut. And because of his bashfulness he would amble away disheartened.

That night in the glen between two hills 'The Knights of the Brotherhood' held it's first serious and deadly meeting in months.

A well groomed August Blanc, hopped upon a flat rock, and held up his hands to quiet the cat calls and loud rabble rousing from the crowd.

"Where you going all gussied up, August?" one yelled.

Raucous laughter and knee slapping followed.

August laughed and held up his hands again for quiet. "We have all the backing we need!" he said. There was more hooting and yelling. August waited for quiet. "Everybody here will have a job of importance in 'The Brotherhood'!" he promised. The cries of happiness were ear splitting. August held his hands up for silence. "The plan is set. You'll know in advance when a raid is to happen and which plantations and businesses to attack!"

There were yells and whoops of joy.

"I'll have a second in command, a sergeant at arms, the list is here,,, August continued above the din, then held up a sheaf of papers. "Each commander will have his own group and seconds in control. We'll hit from all directions. They won't know what happened to 'em. We'll strike fast and get out just as quick!"

"When do we get started, August?" a voice roared.

"We start in two nights! The people on this list will meet now. They'll choose their own folks. Cut down on your drinking, this is serious business. No more swilling of booze on the night before and the night of the raid; we need clear heads. Our white race is in danger! We got to keep our women and families safe! Are you with me!" August shouted.

An ear splitting clamor went up from the grinning, boisterous bevy of hooligans.

August stepped down from his rock and the men and women gathered around congratulating him, along with slaps on the back. Most had no education and wanted to be near him. They considered August their champion and benefactor. He was a changed man, one with a new and deadly purpose.

CHAPTER FOUR

In the days that followed Lizzette spent shopping and feinting exhaustion. Henri by day transacted his business and at night he slept in a guest room, allowing her the freedom to prepare for the voyage.

Colleen, her maid, was kept busy packing and making arrangements for the journey to America. Servants gossiped.

"Was the marriage consummated?" Adele giggled.

"Of course not, this one is a man teaser too high and mighty for a real man," her friend said.

"She's passionless, no lovemaking for the great cock teaser, and him so handsome too. I could give him quite a frolic, I could," Adele said, looking longingly upward.

Colleen came into view and they turned to the packing.

The honeymoon took place aboard the Devereaux Clipper.

The ship was equipped with every comfort.

Winds blew down from the trees and fanned out over the water. Little wavelets slapped the sides of the Clipper ship while it rode at anchor in the bay. Shimmering moonlight toped the water with silver. White fleecy clouds were caught by the wind and spun into lacy wisps so thin the stars could be seen by the watcher on board.

Henri swept Lizzette up in his arms so her silken slippers would not touch the ships deck. He carried her across the surface and down the companion way into his suite, where he stood her in the middle of the massive state room. "Lizzette I've loved you since the moment I saw you," he whispered.

"And I you. Henri, it is so far away this, America." Lizzette's voice had a trace of a quiver. "I won't know anyone there," she said, lifting her face to his, close enough for him to smell her heady perfume.

"You'll have me, and I love you more than life, eventually you'll have our children, then you'll grow to love Georgia. It's a wild and beautiful country," he said with true enthusiasm.

"Henri hold me, don't let me go. I'm so frightened," she said, and moved closer into his arms, tears formed in the corners of her eyes. Her ardent kiss was mistaken for eagerness on her behalf. He held her soft pliable body to his and smothered her face with kisses. In the past, Lizzette had been adept in the art of seduction; although her kisses had never gone to the point of no return, this was the real thing. He swept her up and carried her to the canopied master bed. Her warm moist mouth drove him on, as he undressed her, and himself between kisses. "Henri be gentle with me," she whispered. Then moaned in pain during their lovemaking. When his strokes became forceful she felt as if her insides were being torn out. She wanted to scream and run away, but where would she go, there was no path to turn back. Afterward with his arms holding her against his chest, she could hear his heart beat like a muffled drum as he slept. Lizzette rolled away to the far edge of the bed and cried herself to sleep on her wedding night. As a young woman there had been stories of the wedding bed. Her friends spoke behind their fans of such things, with nervous snickers.

The voyage to America was rough, as the ocean rocked the Clipper ship savagely. Winds blew as if the devil himself were guiding the course. Lizzette didn't fair well in the following weeks. Sea sickness gripped her the first day out. Colleen, along with Henri's valets, were kept busy tending her needs. Lizzette would lie, listlessly and nauseous for days, pale and too weak to lift her hand.

Colleen slept in the alcove to be near her mistress. Henri moved to other quarters. When he came near, Lizzette turned away with bad temper. She wouldn't allow him to touch her not even in sympathy; blaming him for all her misery.

Devereaux Manor at twilight waited in anticipation of their arrival. Two servants stood on the levee, one held a shot gun to signal the masters return. Then finally the coach came into sight around the bend; drawn by sleek roans, that trotted along at a moderate clip. The carriage turned into the tree lined lane to the Manor.

The servant on the levee signaled their arrival. At the sound of the shot, laughter and shouts of joy burst from the domestics on the gallery and those gathered on the lawn. The instant the coach stopped, the driver climbed down from his high perch importantly and opened the coach door.

Henri climbed out, extending his hand into the dark interior. The servants fell silent, as a slim white hand took his daintily, then Lizzette stepped down the half step. The servants moved closer, all eyes on the carriage door.

Lizzette was fearful when she saw all the black faces staring at her. In France she had never seen African people as close as this.

"Speak to them, they came to see you," Henri whispered. "Good evening, my people," she managed feebly.

Mama Jo's full smiling face came into view. Lizzette clutched her husband around the neck burying her face under his chin.

The air was filled with gales of laughter and chatter.

The servants formed a semi-circle around the porch and on the lawn. Henri carried her through the cheering throng onto the gallery and into the broad hall, then up the sweeping stairs to the master bedroom.

In the shadows of the great oaks, Ymani lingered apart from the rest. Her hazel eyes glowed sadly in her velvety black face as tears escaped down her cheeks; always on the outside.

Mama Jo went to her, and said, "It ain't no use you pining away. You Negro servant girl. Come on, we go to the cook house. I got something nice for you," she put an arm around Ymani and led her away.

The arrival was observed by other, more hostile, eyes. August Blanc stood on the little knoll that overlooked the manor; a cleaner better dressed man. "Now is the time you bastard. I'll destroy everything you've ever loved or owned and that's a promise," he said bitterly. Then he mounted his recently acquired stallion. His harsh laughter wasn't heard when he galloped away.

Lizzette had changed since coming to Devereaux Manor. She sat moody and brooding for hours, while staring at the bay. She refused to go outside because of her fear of black people. Her fright worsened, and she clung to Colleen.

Henri made it an evening ritual to go out early and stay late into the night. He was an unhappy and lonely figure as he rode away. He threw himself into his business interests and worked long hours. The Manor was quiet, no parties nor laughter. All this was gossiped about in Kalb

Kove.

Lizzette, realizing she was no longer the center of attention, devised a plan to recapture Henri's adoration. Knowing he wanted a son and heir for the Devereaux fortune, she and Colleen worked long hours bathing, coifing and dressing her in her most alluring gown.

That evening after supper Lizzette, in an act of grandiosity, moved close to her husband as he was dressed to leave.

"Why go out? Stay home tonight," Lizzette invited.

"Is there something special?" Henri answered, laying his gloves and hat aside.

"No. I want you here to discuss our future and to consider the son you've always wanted," she explained.

"You hate my coming near you. In my arms you tremble like a scared rabbit, frightened almost to death," Henri said holding her gently by the shoulders.

She looked away an instant from the concern on his face. "Oh Henri, I have been trying to change. I .. I want to be a better wife for you," she said looking at him. "A son with a mop of dark hair like yours, and your eyes with all this determination." She moved closer, "I am frightened in this new and strange land but I know your love for it is from your heart. I want to make you happy," she said softly.

His eyes softened as he gently held her close. His arms tightened ever so slightly, wanting desperately to believe. Inadvertently her body stiffened. In her frigidity she was not able to feel sensual desire, no matter how much she wanted to please her husband.

"Holy Christ! Am I such an ogre?" Henri asked. Lizzette turned away as tears flowed down her cheeks,

"It's alright, go if you must, I'll understand," she whispered.

"No I shan't go, not tonight," he said, her tears touched his heart.

She hugged him gratefully, and his arms stole around her waist. Using her old wilds she stood on tip toes and kissed him ardently on the lips. Her soft yielding body and compliant warm wet mouth worked it's old magic. The lingering kiss became all-powerful and he pulled her hungrily to him molding their bodies together. His senses were reeling, as the fire of passion spread to his loin. He effortlessly swept her up into his arms carrying her to the canopied bed.

Afterward it was the same, the trembling and frightened sobs.

Henri climbed out of bed without a word.

"Henri, please don't go! I'm sorry," she sobbed. "Yes I'll go!" he snarled over his shoulder. He dressed quickly and strode out of the room.

The heels of his boots were heard loudly on the stairs. The slamming front door marked the finality. Minutes later his stallion thundered out of the tree lined drive.

The drought returned with a vengeance. As the weeks went by, heat hovered over the land. The sun burned down on Henri while he rode and worked in the fields to save his crops. He toiled beside workmen on the acreage. The back breaking labor went agonizingly slow, but the task was almost finished when summer neared autumn.

Lizzette would stand in the window and stare at the cane fields where the stalks were brown and dry because of the drought. Henri was always there for days on end, riding his great white horse. She could see the stark white of his shirt against his face. His skin was baked brown by the unrelenting sun. He rode recklessly, as if the heat did not exist, pushing himself and the field hands. They worked like mad man to get the crops to market. Lizzette's heart was like lead in her chest. She watched and was powerless to fight for his affection.

Ymani waited. Longing to be near him. She carried crocks of cool water into the fields for him to drink. He would gulped the water down and acknowledge her with a nod. He seldom spoke. She would stare after him as he rode away, wishing she could end his suffering.

Henri was rarely home anymore. Lizzette saw him for short periods at supper. He rarely spoke except in monosyllables, but to Lizzette he was always polite. Most of the time he nodded his head, then would be on his way, astride his beloved stallion. For months he bathed and dressed, then rode away to Kalb Kove, to the newly built Country Club that had been constructed to his specifications. It had become the gathering place for the cream of Kalb Kove.

Tongues wagged about the Devereaux's, because there were no parties given at the Manor. Towns people were curious about the new wife they had never met. The gossip never got back to Henri, because of the wealth and the prosperity he had brought to the region. Young women of the town looked at him with longing, then spoke of his wife with envy and spite.

The first weeks of autumn brought coolness. Lizzette walked in the back gardens overlooking the cook house. When Mama Jo came to the door, Lizzette turned abruptly, then the weakness and nausea swept over her. She had noticed the same feeling several times in the morning. Today the feeling overwhelmed her. She took a step forward then stopped, swaying. The blackness was crowding out the morning light. "Mama Jo!" she managed to call out when she felt her knees buckling, the trees were spinning. "Mama Jo!" Lizzette screamed, as the ground came rushing toward her.

On the first cry Mama Jo and Ymani came running across the short distance between the mistress and the cook house. They caught her and eased her down on a nearby bench.

Lizzette had thought the older black woman had an evil look about her. In her world in France she had never seen African people except at a distance. She had always thought they were savages and that belief had frightened Lizzette. The idea of being near or touched by a Negro had chilled her. Now, however, she clutched the cook for dear life.

"Ymani go for the master, hurry t " Mama Jo directed and cradled Lizzette's head on her ample bosom.

Ymani ran swiftly to the fields.

House servants came to assist, helping Lizzette to stand and walk.

"You take it easy mistress, we take you where you can lay down," Mama Jo said soothingly.

With one arm around the mistresses waist, she helped Lizzette into the house. The other servants hovered around to help if they were needed. Colleen met them in the master bedroom and helped undress Lizzette. Her companion bathed her face with a cool cloth.

"I'll bring you something, make you feel better," Mama Jo said.

"Thank you. Oh Mama Jo I am so sick," Lizzette whispered. Perspiration moistened her face and her breathing was labored.

"You're going to have a baby. That time will do that to you. The master is glad I bet," Mama Jo chuckled.

Henri came rushing into the room; crossing to the bed he sat beside his wife, then gathered her in his arms, and never heard Mama Jo's last words.

"Master Devereaux it'll be a fine boy. You'll see, Mama Jo knows," as she and Colleen left the room.

"Oh Henri, I feel so ill: They heard Lizzette saying as she clutched her husband while he cradled her against his shoulder. Colleen closed the door softly.

Ymani left by the back door of the manor. Seifus walked toward her, and her method of eluding him was maddening. She would look right past him as though he didn't exist. Walking on by with a queenly strut. And because of his bashfulness he would amble away disheartened.

That night in the glen between two hills 'The Knights of the Brotherhood' held it's first serious and deadly meeting in months.

A well groomed August Blanc, hopped upon a flat rock, and held up his hands to quiet the cat calls and loud rabble rousing from the crowd.

"Where you going all gussied up, August?" one yelled.

Raucous laughter and knee slapping followed.

August laughed and held up his hands again for quiet. "We have all the backing we need!" he said. There was more hooting and yelling. August waited for quiet. "Everybody here will have a job of importance in 'The Brotherhood'!" he promised. The cries of happiness were ear splitting. August held his hands up for silence. "The plan is set. You'11 know in advance when a raid is to happen and which plantations and businesses to attack!"

There were yells and whoops of joy.

"I'll have a second in command, a sergeant at arms, the list is here,,, August continued above the din, then held up a sheaf of papers. "Each commander will have his own group and seconds in control. We'll hit from all directions. They won't know what happened to 'em. We'll strike fast and get out just as quick!"

"When do we get started, August·?" a voice roared.

"We start in two nights! The people on this list will meet now. They'll choose their own folks. Cut down on your drinking, this is serious business. No more swilling of booze on the night before and the night of the raid; we need clear heads. Our white race is in danger! We got to keep our women and families safe! Are you with me!" August shouted.

An ear splitting clamor went up from the grinning, boisterous bevy of hooligans.

August stepped down from his rock and the men and women gathered around congratulating him, along with slaps on the back. Most had no education and wanted to be near him. They considered August their champion and benefactor. He was a changed man, one with a new and deadly purpose.

CHAPTER 5

Seifus stood trembling beside Ymani, tonight she turned and looked at him, then spoke to him at last. "You slave," she said hurtfully. The words were spat at him, then she turned and walked away swinging her hips like a queen.

He caught up with her, turning her around to face him. "You be my woman and I'll be your man."

Ymani spoke in the mixture of French and English she had acquired since her capture. "You no man!" she said. "My man tribesman to make slave. He's warrior 'fight' no slave! Even woman in my tribe, 'no slave' die first, kill self no slave!"

"You servant girl now like me, you be my woman!" He shook her by the shoulders.

August and his band of cut throats rode through the woods along the fence. He had a view of Seifus shaking Ymani.

"No bow down!" she shouted. "Ymani, Princess of my tribe! Make bow down I kill me!" She disengaged herself and stormed away.

Seifus walked along beside her frowning, she had no right to say that about him and make him feel like an animal that's owned by somebody. He grabbed her shoulders again.

August burst through the hedges from the upper terrace followed by his men; blood curdling cries issued from their mouths. August lashed Seifus with his whip and dragged him to the ground. Ymani stood transfixed in horror when August struck the overseer repeatedly.

Most of his men rode to the slave quarters, except for the cottage hidden in the grove of weeping willows. They set fire to the cabins, then bludgeoned and killed everybody that tried to escape. Old men, women and children alike died amid screams of terror. A mother tried to rescue her toddler in the path of the marauders and despoilers of human life. The woman and child were trampled to death.

While back on the edge of the quarters. "Come here, gal! You belong to me!" August barked.

His shouted words mobilized her into action. She turned and ran screaming toward the manor. Her outcry allowed Seifus to escape into the darkness of the scrubs. "The nigger's getting away August!" one man shouted.

"Well what we waiting for? Let's get 'im!" Adrenaline flowed and the smell of blood was in the air. They swerved their horses with wild hoots and hollwers, charging into the bushes.

Seifus ran ahead, bent over, tripping over roots. He scrambled to his feet, running deeper into the underbrush.

August and his men were in close pursuit, beating the bushes, coming closer to their prey.

Seifus would have to run across and open meadow bordering on the bottomland, that way would lead to his freedom. Gasping for air, he took the chance and started running as fast as he could across the wet grassland, fleeing for his life.

"There he goes! I'll get 'im!" The man said raising his rifle to shoot. August knocked the barrel down where it discharged into the ground.

"No! He's mine!" He yelled when they surrounded the slave. August used his whip with a snap to encircle Seifus' ankles and drag him to the ground. He climbed down and use his whip to beat Seifus until his back was bloody, then kicked the fallen man into semi-consciousness. The Knights tied Seifus' hands to a length of rope and led him at a staggering run as August galloped deeper into the trees. One Knight tossed a rope over the limb of an oak tree. The other end of the rope was knotted about the exhausted slave's neck.

Seifus fought desperately for his life but his strength was not enough against the raiders. They hauled him kicking and screaming off the ground. His cries were abruptly stopped when the rope tightened around his neck. His body twitched in death, then slowly twisted in the gentle breeze.

"Die you black son-of-a-bitch!" "You won't take a white man's job in hell!" August roared. Wild laughter followed as he and his men rode across the knoll overlooking Devereaux Manor. They stopped to inspect the devastation the raid has caused.

Henri worked along with the servants that were left. They battled in the darkness to get the fires under control; live stock made noises o f pain in the background. Women cried as they cared for the wounded. A bucket brigade was formed. The process was painfully slow as they labored through the night until all the blazes were out.

The Knights Of The Brotherhood struck at four major plantations within a perimeter of fifty miles. They burned houses, barns, murdered men, women, children and slaughtered live stock. Crosses burned around Kalb Kove county. The sheriff and his deputies were out of town on a trumped up search for escaped indentured servants.

The next morning at day break, Seifus' dead body was found hanging from the oak on the edge of Devereaux land. His dead body swayed gently in the wind. Jude looked up at the once robust young man. A tear escaped down one black cheek as he cut the body down, then transported the remains to the burned out quarters.

Henri stared down with mixed emotions at the dead body of his overseer. "Jude get the runners, I have some messages to send." he ordered. The servant ran toward the manor, then to another domestic, "You, bring sheets to wrap the bodies." He said as exhausted field hands removed Seifus' body from the wagon.

The house of the overseer was in bad shape, but with some clearing out would have to accommodate the dead. Between wailing cries the woman washed and wrapped the remains to have them ready for burial. Funeral services had to be held by night fall, because as the blazing sun rose high in the heavens the charred bodies were getting ripe. Male servants sweated profusely as they dug the graves. When the sun reached its pinnacle in the sky, the task was almost done.

The responsible men of Kalb Kove gathered that night. Merchants, businessmen, planters, all representatives of the community. John Abberdeen, Doctor Edwin Gordon, Price Bigelow, attorney, Ralph De Vaughn, Vincent Holmes and Scott Rappaport.

"I've used care to keep the meeting secret." Henri said.

"We need to do something about this band of cut throats before our businesses are wiped out!" Abberdeen yelled.

"Needless to say that's what this meeting is all about," Doctor Gordon said sarcastically.

"I lost a lot of my best workers in that raid!" Vincent protested.

"Maybe we could meet with them and find out what they want. We don't want to rile 'em too much. My business was just recovering." Scott said.

The argument lasted late into the night.

Henri rode the energetic stallion along the rows of burned out cabins in the servants quarters past mid-night. The only one left standing was among the willows, the house with a breeze way, where Mama Jo and Ymani lived. It was occupied now by the female domestics. He rode past and left some distance between him and the cabin. Stopping in the shadows of the weeping willows, he sat waiting. The silence was broken by little sounds of the night.

"I'm here," a quiet accented voice with the familiar rasp came from the shadows.

Henri waited.

"We have the perpetrators under surveillance awaiting your instructions," the voice stated.

"Did you check the names on the list?" Henri asked.

"Yes, and you have some very interesting associates." the voice chuckled.

"Tell me about them?" Henri questioned.

"It's in my report. One is not trustworthy; moreover he furnished the money to put the other planters out of business. There's one whose interest is only money, the rest are shaky but reasonably honest. It's all there in the report." The voice stated. A white packet glowed in the thin streak of moonlight.

"The funds for your 'Network' has been set up in the usual way. Payments will go directly to your organization. Adjustments will be made as needed. Is that satisfactory?"

"As usual you have been thorough, how did you set it up so fast?"

the voice asked.

"On my last visit here, I had a suspicion there would be a need for such a contingency plan as ours." Henri answered.

"I'll meet you her the same time next week." The voice replied.

Henri rode off toward Devereaux Manor.

Throughout the fall the heat returned to penetrate the backs of the workers on the plantation. Work went on, on the employee quarters. Henri toiled as usual with the field hands. In the evening he sad beside his wife's bed, his brow furrowed with worried on his expressive face.

Mama Jo had become a constant fixture in Lizzette's room. His wife cried if the older woman was out of her sight for too long. Henri was helpless and could only watch Lizzette's fitful sleep. He would fall into bed late at night exhausted, and be up at dawn the next morning.

The weekly meetings took place with Henri and the Network; he gathered information about the carriage trade of Kalb Kove County, along with the towns people from the northern border to Savannah.

Doctor Gordon visited regularly, worrying about Lizzette's weakened condition. The heat was a hardship on the young woman, her health was delicate by nature. The seizures of nausea and fainting were unending. She was not able to walk in the early mornings because of her swollen feet and legs. Lizzette spent most of the long hot days in bed, the servants bathed and changed her gowns when the perspiration soaked through. Because of her great vanity she cried endlessly about her swollen, misshapen body and the never ending queasiness.

Henri persuaded his wife to take a drive in the cool evening breeze in the fall of 1869. The comfortable carriage moved smoothly over the lane, then turned into the drive to the Manor when the first pain struck. Suddenly Lizzette doubled over crying out in agony.

"Take us to the Manor and hurry!" Henri ordered the driver, holding Lizzette.

The driver cracked the whip, and not being used to the crop, the horses sprang into a fast gallop.

"Don't kill us, just get us there in one piece quickly!" Henri barked.

Slowly the frightened animals calmed down and trotted at a fast clip to the front door of the manor. Henri leaped to the ground and reached back into the carriage. Lizzette sank into his arms and clung desperately to him, while he carried her into the manor and up the stairs to the bedroom.

Mama Jo stood to one side in the doorway. "The bed chamber is ready sir, water is boiling. I take good care of mistress you'll see," she said while he laid his wife on the bed.

Henri stood baffled at the complete preparations. Mama Jo chuckled and beckoned the maids to help her undress the mother to be. Lizzette stretched out her hand to Henri as he knelt beside the bed. His face drawn, the pallor made his eyes stand out starkly.

"Don't worry so Henri. Mama Jo will take good care of me until the doctor comes." Lizette said, her face contorting with pain.

Henri was surprised with the force of her suffering; he stood apprehensively. "Colleen, tell Jude to ride for that damn doctor!" he exclaimed.

"Doctor sent for already. Need Colleen to get hot water." Mama Jo answered and pushed him aside.

Henri strode through the door and shouted. "Jude! Take the fastest mount and meet Doctor Gordon!" he ordered. "Get a move on, man!" he bellowed. Henri went back and sat on the bed and held his wife's pitifully tiny hand in his. Lizzette seemed to drift into a restless sleep and periodically muttering gibberish.

"Rest quietly my love, you must conserve your strength." Henri whispered. Colleen stood anxiously by, a quiet ghostly figure.

The doctor arrived two hours later. Henri couldn't conceal his impatience after the long wait. Doctor Gordon was filled with good humor and confidence. Therefore, it was easy to relax a little. "Henri my boy, I can guarantee you a fine healthy son. But I can't work with you pacing up and down the floor. I know you have Bourbon. Right?" The doctor asked.

Henri nodded.

"Good, go and get deliciously drunk and stay out of my way. I'll need a woman to help me, not one who's faint-hearted." The doctor replied.

"Mama Jo is here." Henri said.

"Come Mama Jo, let's get to work. Henri I want you to wait outside." The doctor said and smiled broadly when he hustled him out the door with Colleen.

The examination took an eternity while Henri paced outside, listening to his wife's cries of agony. The doctor came out finally. Henri took three strides to cover the distance between them.

Doctor Gordon's face was grave, "I'm staying for as long as it takes. Send a boy to tell my assistant that I'm here. I'll need a change of clothes, also my instruments. Give him this note," he said, scribbling hastily.

"It's that bad?" Henri asked.

"Yes it's that bad and could get even worse." The doctor said.

"God almighty." Henri cried.

"She's not developed for child bearing; moreover, Lizzette is built narrow in the flank and the baby is unusually large. If she survives, I must caution you there will be no other children." Doctor Gordon replied.

"If, she survives?!" Henri exclaimed.

"Yes, and you have to get a grip on yourself, she needs your strength. Now, is there a place for me to change?" The doctor asked.

"Colleen, show the doctor to the east wing, supply him with anything he needs." Henri ordered.

Throughout the night the doctor slept at intervals. Lizzette's suffering was disturbing to watch. Henri went to her bedside hundreds of times, her pain had etched a grimace around her delicate mouth. He could only stay for short minutes because of her distress. When he was away from her, he cursed himself with all the foul words he could think of. At her side he prayed to the blessed virgin to preserve, and keep her and their precious baby. He knelt there holding her fragile hand, dark shadows circled her eyes. Henri closed his eyes for a second and Lizzette shrieked, a blood curdling scream. Dr. Gordon rushed into the room, Mama Jo ran over and shoved Henri away while the doctor examined his patient.

"Wait outside, Henri. This is a dry birth it will be touch and go from now on. Your son seems impatient to get here and I mean right away." The doctor said.

Henri held Lizzette's hand momentarily, then reluctantly went toward the door. The two slave girls stood nervously in the corner to help when needed.

"Go now! Henri! I haven't a moment to lose." the doctor said impatiently, then turned to Mama Jo. "I need you right here to help her bare down when I say. Understand?"

"Yes sir." Mama Jo answered and stood exactly where he wanted her.

"Mama Jo, we have bloody show and rapid swelling. I don't like the color of that drainage either. I have to take the baby. Have you seen that done?" The doctor asked.

"Yes sir." Mama Jo replied.

"Good, just give me a minute." The doctor said. He went to the basin filled with warm soapy water, thoroughly washing his hands and up his arms. He dried them on a pristine white towel, finishing with his preparations quickly. The young servant girls huddled in the shadows frightened.

Henri paced the hall as scream after scream rented the surrounding quiet. His body stiffened with each out cry as if he physically felt the pain. The servant girls came out slamming the door and ran in opposite directions down the hall, then returned with sheets, towels and blankets.

Colleen sat prim and straight in a chair, her eyes closed, clutching Rosary beads.

Suddenly there was an eerie quiet, Henri stopped in stride. There was a slap and an angry baby bawled. Henri turned toward the bedroom.

Doctor Gordon abruptly opened the door and came out into the hall. Henri tried to see around him but the doctor gently pushed him toward the stairs saying. "You have a fine healthy son." He looked at Henri's tortured face. "Come with me. Mama Jo and the girls are cleaning Lizzette up. She wouldn't want you to her now anyway." The doctor led Henri down the stairs and into the study. "Sit down, I need a little libation and so do you." Then he walked to the liquor cabinet and poured two stiff drinks, gave one to Henri, then sat beside him and crossed his legs.

"How is …?" Henri started to speak.

The doctor shushed him. "Have a drink then I'll tell you." Henri opened his mouth to speak again.

The doctor held up one finger and said. "Uh, uh, drink your drink."

Henri complied grudgingly and waited.

"It goes without saying, Lizzette had an arduous pregnancy and her labor was pure hell." Dr. Gordon said. "You have to be gentle and understanding with her in the months to come."

"Will she be alright?" Henri asked.

"In time, it'll take a lot of care. You'll need a wet nurse in the mean time. You probably have some women on the plantation that can do the task." The doctor replied.

"And my son, Etienne?" Henri asked.

"Best paid of lungs I've ever heard," the doctor said and chuckled, then drained his glass.

CHAPTER SIX

Henri watched helplessly as Mama Jo applied a cool wet clothe over Lizzette's forehead and eyes. His wife had a stressful night. Now she complained that her eyes hurt.

"You best get the doctor, mistress got child bed fever bad!" Mama

Jo urged.

This mobilized Henri instantly. At last he had something he could do to help. He cast a last look at Lizzette's flushed face and hurried out.

Everyone at Devereaux Manor spoke in hushed tones as the days passed. They tipped around for fear of disturbing the mistress. Henri haunted her room where she lay feverish, clinging to an ethereal thread of consciousness. Doctor Gordon was a permanent fixture for the two weeks it took to get her through the fever and delirium.

Marna Jo prepared teas, aromatic salves and poultices. The wise older woman coerced Lizzette to drink broths and when she grew stronger, gruel and thick soups.

"I'll take Mama Jo with me anytime, the woman has worked miracles," Doctor Gordon remarked.

"Mama Jo is my treasure and she stays right here," Henri laughed.

"Well, be that way. But, if she wasn't a slave, she could be a midwife. I've always thought some Negroes could be professionals," the doctor said.

"Seifus was one, he was worth more than his pay," Henri answered.

"It's too bad. I never had a stomach for slavery anyway, a waste of human minds," he said, sipping his brandy. "What's the decision on the Knight's?"

"We're working on it. Eventually that kind of servitude will be gone," Henri said.

Jude came to the doorway, "Supper is served sir." He bowed and left the room, followed by Henri with an arm about the doctor's shoulder.

Lizzette's color improved; although she had none of her old vigor and her gleeful laughter was gone. Long days of depression ensued when she would gaze out over the bay. She appeared a forlorn lost being at times, and would have nothing to do with her son nor Henri, staring at them with distaste.

Doctor Gordon recognized the manic-depressive psychosis and was surprised the hallucination manifested itself during the manic delirium phase. It tended to resemble illusions rather than clear cut hallucination. The doctor arranged for an around the clock watch on Lizzette, especially at night. She avoided all activity and any joy of living. Her life was spent as if she were dead. There was a persistent absence of emotion following the birth of Etienne. At first there were tearful denials and angry protests that this was not her country while longing for France.

When she was able, she walked around the plantation with slave girls in attendance. She spent most of the time on the rocky cliffs overlooking the bay, where she would stare out across the water. In

Lizzette's troubled mind she believed her life was in danger. Mama Jo was the only person who could bring her out of her tearfulness.

Henri spent long periods with his son Etienne, and went to the Country Club, when it was too much to bare.

Months went by and paranoia occurred in Lizzette's psychotic states. Her notions of persecution were not based on logic. Because she was high born, she believed the masses were plotting to kill her and the baby.

In the night when Colleen fell asleep. Lizzette, ever watchful, slipped out of bed and tipped surreptitiously down the hall to the baby's room, where for the first time she took Etienne in her arms. The night nanny slept soundly on her cot in the shadows.

"I'll save you, come with me," she whispered, then looked furtively around, her eyes bright with a certain kind of madness. Lizzette ran down the stairs bumping into Jude on the way to the front door. She had difficulty getting the heavy door open. Jude ran to Henri's study and knocked loudly on the door. "Sir, sir! Mistress Devereaux took the baby and run off to the cliffs!" he cried.

"Get Mama Jo, quick!" Henri yelled, chasing after Lizzette. "Get moving man!" He saw the white dressing gown in the moonlight as she ran to the ridge. Etienne's screams were heard in the distance, as Lizzette ran up the incline.

Lizzette's voice was maniacal, saying, "Stay away!" hysterically. "I'll jump!" she hissed, backing to the edge.

Henri stopped, hands raised, "Lizzette, come down you might hurt yourse 1 f," he coaxed.

"No!" she shouted, over the baby's screams.

"Please let me help you, give Etienne to me. You don't want to hurt Etienne your child, our son?" he pleaded.

"The voices told me, this is the time. I can't wait any longer. Soon it' 11 be too late! Don't you see!?" she said as her eyes widen with dementia.

Mama Jo ran up the hill gasping for air followed by Jude, Colleen and Ymani. Other servants were on the way up as well.

Lizzette moved threateningly toward the precipice and looked wildly around holding the baby above her head on the edge of the bluff.

Mama Jo walked slowly toward her and kept her gaze hypnotically on the deranged woman's eyes. "This is Mama Jo, you don't want to hurt that child," Mama Jo admonished. "I don't want you to hurt yourself either," she said soothingly as she moved closer to Lizzette.

The older, wiser woman came alongside her and gently took the baby. Henri quickly took his son while Mama Jo coaxed Lizzette down the hill, talking all the way. Ymani followed close behind.

"Will you help me, Mama Jo?" Lizzette asked, under the cook's spellbinding voice.

"Yes child, I'm here to help you, and your family. You go with me and I'll make you something special," she said.

"Oh could I have a cool glass of wine? It'll help me to rest. I need to rest," Lizzette's eyes were childlike.

"Yes, child. I'll go get it myself."

"Oh Mama Jo, you're so good to me. You won't take too long, will you?" Lizzette said, clinging to the servant.

"Yrnani will stay in the manor for a while to help Colleen with Etienne," Henri directed quietly.

"Yes sir," Mama Jo answered, and continued down the hill, talking softly to Lizzette who was charmed by the cook.

"Ymani, pack some of your belongings and come to the manor tonight to sleep in Etienne's room," Henri ordered.

"Yes sir," she answered, in her throaty voice, then went toward the house in the willows.

Ymani stayed close to the child as the months passed.

Other servants took care of Lizzette. Life at Devereaux Manor never returned to normalcy.

It was midnight in a bare room, the only light was from an oil lamp that cast deep shadows. The four captives wore white sheets as they sat blindfolded, tied to straight back chairs. The Knights made guttural noises through the bandanas over their mouths while they struggled to get free.

They were being studied from the shadowed perimeter of the room, the leader, approached the weaker of the bunch. He whispered in a rasp, saying, 'Quiet! I want your leader and the person financing you?" He paused, "Your gags will be removed, one by one you' 11 answer my questions."

The first man sat with his mouth tightly closed, this happened with all of the marauders.

"Take one, two and four," the voice instructed.

Hands with garrote swiftly wound thongs around three of the men's throats. They kicked and tried to scream while their faces turned purple, and their eyes bulged from the sockets. The choking sounds stopped but the muscles twitched and moved from one group of muscles to another for several agonizing minutes. The fourth man sat speechless. Totally intimidated after the assassinations, words spilled from his mouth. "I don't know him! August knows his name!" he swallowed. "But I can show you where he lives! If you just don't kill me! I'll get outta Georgia and never come back in my lifetime, honest to God!" he groveled.

"Show us, then we'll put you on a barge down river," the voice rasped. "If you're seen in this territory you get the same treatment as they did," he said indicating the dead men.

"No! Just let me go! You won't see me again!" he said. That night three bodies were dumped at the doorway of

Scott Rappaport. He sold the family holdings, and in a fortnight moved away under the cover of night.

The sheriff of the time was a known sympathizer who practiced shadow law, always a mile away when he was needed most. The Knights controlled Kalb Kove's office of Jim Crow justice.

Henri waited astride his white stallion.

A rasping whisper came eerily from the shadows of the weeping willow trees. "We've taken care of four from each band of marauders."

Papers were extended to Henri. "I heard about the message sent and the antagonist who moved, we'll meet as needed," Henri said, riding toward the manor, where later he read the reports and locked them in a drawer of his safe.

Etienne at a year old was taking his first steps. His being there had changed everything at Devereaux Manor. Life on the plantation was geared to revolve around him. Ymani watched his every waking moment and was on her feet at the slightest whimper, even in his sleep. Colleen who was well versed in French and other languages started to teach the child little songs and words as soon as he could speak.

Ymani, always in the background, learned with Etienne.

He was a handsome boy and everyone told him so. He had reached back among his ancestors for his dark good looks.

His complexion was golden and would later in life tan beautifully in the sun. His inky dark hair curled in masses over his forehead. When he stared fixedly at a visitor his father's green eyes stood out starkly. People would gasp with astonishment that his eyes were even more striking in contrast to the darkness of his skin and hair.

Henri would watch Ymani while she rocked the baby and sang little songs in her rich throaty voice. He had forgotten how lovely she was. Her golden eyes glowed in her velvety black face. She had not changed with all the work that had been required of her to do. When she stood to put the sleeping child to bed, her carriage was so proud. He had to tear his eyes away from the young woman leaning over his son's bed.

Colleen spent long hours with Lizzette, mostly at night.

Doctor Gordon had taken temporary residence in the east wing for the on going objective: Lizzette's health. Henri stayed home and spent restless nights in his study.

Lizzette was miserable, and weak from refusing to eat; her mind was troubled with imagined disservice.

"I doubt if she'll survive much longer, she's too frail physically," Dr. Gordon whispered to Colleen one evening. "God knows her reason is one of our major problems, and there hasn't been any fight for a long time."

"We should get Henri," she said.

"Good idea," they went out of the room and down the hall to the study. There was no answer to their knock.

Colleen opened the door and entered the study. Henri had his head pillowed on one arm atop his desk, an empty Brandy decanter stood at one elbow. The strong smell of liquor permeated the room. Henri raised his head when Dr. Gordon shook him by the shoulder. His face was chalky white with dark shadows around his eyes. He sank back in his seat and frowned with a look of defeat.

"Henri?" Dr. Gordon said quietly.

"Yes, Doctor," Henri answered, bleary eyed.

"Lizzette is worse, there are grave complications. You should be with her now."

"I'm not so sure of that, only the blessed mother can help her. She hates me!" Henri lamented.

"I think you're wrong there. I believe she loves you in her own way. She's dying of this sickness and heart break."

"Dying! You say she's dying?" Henri cried, and bound to his feet.

"Yes, she needs you, go to her Henri and stay with her no matter what," Dr. Gordon encouraged.

"I have tried, but she will have nothing to do with me," Henri said, adjusting the ruffled shirt front. "But I'll try again," then he was gone.

In the bed chamber Henri bent over the still form of his wife, then sat on the edge of the bed and held her hand.

Doctor Gordon and Colleen stood in the doorway, unnoticed. "Soon I'll be at peace Henri," Lizzette whispered. "There is much to be said," he said faltering.

"There can only be truth between us now," she said grasping his hand.

" I promise that," Henri said.

Lizzette's mouth widened into a sad ghostly smile. Her words were so low he had to lean close to hear. "Thank you for our son, take care of him," she uttered.

"I will, sweetheart."

"I'm not afraid anymore, and I have no fear of dying. I know you and our son will be alright," she murmured.

"No you can't die! There's too much for us to do!" he exclaimed in anguish.

"I am afraid I must, there's no longer any doubt," she spoke the words with strength and clarity.

Henri started to speak but changed his mind. The look of death was there, on her face. He gasped with the realization, and touched his lips to her hand then buried his face in the pillow beside her. She lifted one hand and stroked his hair.

In the doorway Colleen wept silently.

Lizzette closed her eyes; three days later and slipped into unconsciousness and died quietly in the night.

Ymani continued to spend every waking hour with Etienne. August watched her movements from the shadows of the woods on the knoll overlooking the manor. Several times she saw him and ran to Mama Jo.

"You be careful child, that man is up to no good," Mama Jo cautioned. "He steals gals he's drawn to, and you one. I can't help you when a white man got the hankering for you. I can only bind your wounds," she held Ymani to her bosom.

One evening at twilight Ymani walked leisurely toward the Manor along the lower terrace in close proximity to the knoll that overlooked the mansion and a large portion of the plantation. August was perched on the hillside in the shadows. He watched as she came within yards of his vantage point. The graceful movement of her lithe body under the cotton dress accented her small waist and flaring hips. Her out thrusting breasts strained against the material of her clothes; his eyes devoured her. He led his horse from the shadows down the hill and cut her off, then tried to touch her. Ymani backed away in fear, "I won't hurt you. You're pretty for a black filly." His eyes roamed hungrily over her body as he moved toward her. "You really belong to me and I'm taking what's mine!" August said and grabbed her. Ymani struggled against his strength and managed to break free.

She ran screaming to the house with the breezeway. August followed on horseback. He caught her near the front of the house as she stumbled up the steps to the porch. He dismounted and chased her into the breezeway.

"Please sir, don't hurt my child," Mama Jo pleaded, holding Ymani.

"Get away from her, you ole witch!" he shouted and pushed Mama Jo away.

The screams alerted the field hands who gathered to see what the ruckus was. One ran to report to Henri.

August hurled Ymani off the porch. She fell sprawling on the grass. "You got a lotta fight for a black gal. I 1 ike 'um like that, full of fight," his grin showed discolored teeth.

Ymani crawled back toward the front porch; Her hazel eyes glowed with terror. He grabbed her wrist, dragging her

to her feet and clutched her waist crushing her body to his. He fumbled with the top of her dress and ripped the front away, exposing her ripe breasts. Henri galloped toward the fray.

"I'm coming back for you. I'll get you next time!" August said, and shoved her away. He swung into the saddle and whipped the horse savagely. It reared and lunged into a fast pace, kicking up dirt and grass as he galloped away.

"Who was that!?" Henri asked, reigning the stallion to a stop.

Ymani tried to cover herself.

"Big mean man, August Blanc," Mama Jo answered. "Try to take my Ymani. He always watch my little girl, sometime day and sometime night. Mama Jo see him all the time." She held Ymani, rocking her in her arms.

"You stay in the servant quarters in the manor until we take care of this problem. No walking around at night!" Henri ordered. Both women nodded in agreement.

Henri met with the Network in the weeping willow grove, saying, " I want the August matter to be disposed of."

"You' 11 hear of it," was the whispered answered. "Is everything else under control?" Henri asked. "There are some loose ends but nothing major."

"Take care of this problem," Henri said, and rode off toward the manor with gentle urging of the stallion.

CHAPTER SEVEN

Henri went to Ymani's room that night, she moved toward him shivering and afraid. He touched her smooth black face, cradling her in his arms. He smelled the musk of her warm body. "You'll be alright now," he said softly.

He had an overpowering urge to kiss her full sensuous mouth. Having been deprived for so long the kiss got out of hand, as he planted bruising kisses on her throat and lips. She returned them with the same ardor. Her supple young body molded to his; her arms tightened around his neck. He guided her to the bed and in the heat of mutual need they undressed each other. The lovemaking was from shared desire, their kisses were warm and lingering. She moved her body into a position to receive him and gasped when he entered her. He uttered a pleasurable sound. Henri was gentle to start then his thrusts became more forceful as their sweaty bodies slapped together with each stroke. Ymani moaned with delight. His breathing was erupting in gasps when they reached climax.

They were satiated for the moment, but later made love in the early hours of the morning. Afterward he lay spent beside her. In the future, many nights were spent in Ymani's room to her absolute delight. Their lovemaking was slow and sensual at times and at times the urgency was overpowering. It was obvious she was pregnant as the months passed. Early one morning she was taken to Savannah to a Creole doctor. "I want her to have the best of care, all her needs must be met," Henri directed.

The doctor nodded his agreement and understanding,

"If I'm not mistaken I heard two heart beats. I think you're about to have twins in about four months," he said.

"Is she strong enough to carry and have two babies?" Henri asked.

"Yes, this is no delicate woman. She'll be fine for many more children," the doctor said.

On a moonlit night, August raced through the dense woods between the two hills. He could hear his pursuers and pushed his sweaty horse beyond endurance. The stallions breathing was labored. The animai tripped on a root and screamed when one of his legs was twisted grotesquely. August was thrown free and jumped to his feet. He grabbed the rifle from the saddle. And in a moment of kindness, put the animal out of it's misery by putting a bullet in the horse's brain. Then he ran bent over into the bush, the chase was closing fast.

His pursuers found the dead animal. "He's on foot. Take to the bush!" a pursuer roared. "We got him cornered, that trail leads to a dead end!" August disappeared without a trace. The raids of 'The Knight of the Brotherhood' trickled to a stop without it's leader.

Ymani was moved into the house by the river again.

Field hands were put on duty to watch over her and Mama Jo. Her time passed without incidence until she was taken to the doctor in Savannah for delivery. That day in 1872 the baby boys came into this world with lusty cries. They were the image of Henri, cafe ole complexions with mops of tight curly black hair and his green eyes. Henri was so pleased with his new sons he started to make plans for their future.

He spent many nights and some evenings at the house in the willows. The lovemaking had reached heights never imagined, their spirits and bodies entwined. A carriage with a back seat was built special for her to rest when on long trips. Mama Jo slept with the twins in a small bedroom across the breezeway porch. Ymani was Henri's constant companion when he traveled the countryside and abroad. The boys were taken to Europe for tutoring as soon as they could be left with a governess and teacher. It was decided the twins would stay in the South of France. Their lovemaking went on as before.

Ymani and Henri were spoken of in the community in hushed tones and with knowing winks.

Doctor Gordon stood in the doorway} one late afternoon watching Etienne at twelve across the table from a servant's son. Carlton was a Mulatto and Etienne's constant companion. Their playing cards were fanned out in their sticky fingers.

Carlton's furrowed face was more fair than Etienne's. "Deal me another one" he said.

"I'll bet two tea cakes." Etienne said. "Done," Carlton answered.

They played on until there were five cakes on the table.

Each boy had four cards on the table face up. Etienne had a good run of cards three jacks and a queen showing. Carlton had three tens and an ace. Etienne turned up his cover card giggling loudly "Pay up I win!"

Henri had joined the doctor in the doorway to watch.

"I gotcha, Etienne!" Carlton said, grinning from ear to ear, then slapped his last card down. "I got four of a kind!"

Etienne glared at the two hands, then, with all the force he could muster, slugged Carlton in the jaw, sending him tumbling backward. Before Henri and the doctor could cross the room, Etienne had Carlton down and was pounding his face with both fists. Henri and the doctor pulled him off, but before he could be dragged away Etienne placed a well aimed kick that sent Carlton sprawling.

"Etienne stop!" Henri shouted. "Now get down and pick up the cakes and give them to Carlton."

Etienne was sullen but complied. "Does this apply to my black mother and brothers, am I the servant now?" he sneered.

Henri stiffened as his face reddened. "Then get up to your room. I'll talk to you later! Carlton, go and let Mama Jo look at that eye," Henri said, Carlton ran crying from the room.

"He is getting more difficult, and spends an inordinate amount of time trying to see how much he can plague everybody. He doesn't dare challenge me yet," Henri said, as they walked to the front door.

"You must have patience. The boy will grow up in time, and learn the way of the South," the doctor said.

"You should know. How many in your brood now?" Henri chuckled.

"Too many, we've had our last one."

"If you say so," Henri said, as they reached the door. "Remember next week, Etienne's twelfth birthday."

The doctor nodded his head.

"You and your crew will come?" Henri asked. "Yep, we'll be here," the doctor said, and left.

Henri looked upstairs and shook his head, then slowly started to climb toward the bedrooms.

The years passed, and in 1890 Etienne was twenty-one.

His birthday dawned sunny and clear, guests started to gather from all the plantations and parts of the city. Businessmen, professionals and traders came from as far away as Savannah. Henri's philosophy and beliefs were looked down upon by Southerners. But because he was the man with the most wealth and power, they dared not criticize him in or out of his presence. If Henri said jump, one would ask, when? And how high?

His business affairs included cotton, sugar cane and his own sugar mill, international banking and trusts, the arts, newspapers, hospitals that cared for many races, freighting, and passenger trains with his own elaborate accommodations and other new and budding enterprises.

Young men and women came by carriage and horseback. The halls of Devereaux Manor echoed with their voices and laughter. On the lawn of the manor, tables were laden with food fit for a king and his court. Etienne sat regally at the head of the table.

Carlton stood in livery just in back of Etienne to fulfill his every beck and call. He didn't smile much anymore. He had learned his lesson early and well at twelve. When he had gone to Mama Jo for her to look at his bruises, given in the beating at the hands of Etienne, she held him in her arms, and said softly, "Child, we can't win by fighting them. They're too strong. We have to be clever like the wily ole fox. Etienne tell you to do something, do it quick from now on. Do it better than anybody else. Learn to read, write and to figger. You can outsmart him.

Carlton, grow up strong in body, like in your mind. The day will come and you can be shed of Etienne. I'll help you when the time is right."

At twenty-one Etienne watched the activities with contempt. It was only when Henri's gift was led around, did he straighten up. His green eyes brightened in his handsome face when the stallion pranced into the center of the lawn. He sprang from his seat and examined the magnificent animal, as the horse snorted and pawed the ground.

"You must thank your guests first," Henri whispered.

Sullenly, Etienne said, in both English and French. "I thank you one and all for your kindnesses."

"Can we ride him, Etienne?" an acquaintance asked.

If a look could kill, Etienne frowned at the questioner and said in a cold and deadly voice, "If you touch him, I'll kill you." Whirling he strode into the great hall. Henri quickly had wine and other delicacies served.

The orchestra members tuned their instruments, getting ready for the evening of gaiety.

Rene Doucet, Etienne's only real friend, walked into the ballroom filled with laughter. A vivacious woman drew Etienne's attention, her laughter rang above the others. "Who is she?" he asked.

Rene turned to look in that direction, saying, "Caroline Ravel!, daughter of Jake Ravel!?"

"The industrialist out of New York?" Etienne asked. "One and the same. I understand she's the apple of his eye, and I might add she's chased by bachelors between here and New York, as well as other places," Rene replied.

"She's got my vote and apples too. I want to get to know her. I believe this could be the beginning of something extraordinary," Etienne said.

"I'll introduce you," Rene said, and started across the dance floor. Etienne hesitated momentarily. Rene looked around waiting, "Come on, don't get cold feet now, that dance is almost over." They made their way across to the couple as they finished the dance and strolled toward the French doors.

"Roger, Caroline. Allow me to introduce our host, Etienne Devereaux," Rene made the introduction.

Etienne shook hands with Roger, "Roger, welcome to Devereaux

Manor." Etienne bent over Caroline's small hand and touched his lips to her fingers, then found himself looking into warm beautiful brown eyes. "I'm so glad you came, " he said softly, turning to Roger, he asked, "May I have this dance with Miss Ravell ?"

"You didn't ask me," Caroline interjected. "My permission is more important than Roger's," her voice was husky. Its warmth thrilled and fascinated Etienne.

"Sad but true," Roger chuckled. "A woman who makes her own decisions."

"You may dance with me, sir," Caroline said, being not as diminutive as most women of the day. She fit just right in his arms for dancing and probably anything else. They whirled around the dance floor throughout the evening. The balance of her stay in Kalb Kove was spent in the company of Etienne. They dined and went horseback riding. She rode astride her horse like a man with the wind in her hair. A party on the Devereaux Clipper set the turning point in their courtship. Caroline was a tease and deliberately provoked his lust. Their kisses were becoming more intense.

His frustration was evident at the manor. He was horribly abusive toward the servants and took his sexual desires out brutally against the women. His stallion felt the brunt of the whip for the first time. The horse was frightened and would rear up on his hind legs and try to run.

Etienne would reign him in savagely. The bridal cut into the animal's mouth. He tried to stay away from Caroline but the urge to touch her and just to see her was a compulsion. His craving was never equated with love, but a powerful lechery and the need for mastery over her.

His kiss, aboard the Devereaux Clipper became so aggressively demanding she had to struggle to push him away. "Etienne! You can't have me until we're married. Do you love me enough for that?" she asked.

Etienne answered in a husky, lust filled voice, saying, "Of course I love you, and only you, Caroline." He gently embraced her and took his leave. "Until tomorrow my love," he turned on his heels and swung into the saddle, then with a courtly salute galloped away.

Caroline likened that bit of gallantry with love, when she floated inside on her self-imposed cloud nine.

The wedding was the gala event of 1891. There were many bridesmaids, best men, the church overflowed with people from as far away as New York. Caroline's father arrived at the last moment from Europe to give his daughter away.

The ceremony over, they danced. As Etienne whirled her around the floor, the gaiety of her laughter filled the air.

Henri mingled with the throng. Ymani watched from a secluded, vantage point in the balcony. Etienne was safely married. The episodes in his past were put just there, in the past. Henri believed his son was in a more responsible position. The management of Devereaux holdings was in the hands of competent general managers. He and his new family could travel on the continent and other far away countries. He and Ymani had four children and most of their time was spent in France where their living arrangements were not an issue. His attachment to his children was to watch them mature. His only girl, Denise, was the apple of his eye, but Robert was the most serious, and brilliant, of all his offsprings. Robert would later in life make a number of scientific breakthrough's in blood studies.

CHAPTER EIGHT

The honeymoon started aboard a Devereaux Industries train, the "Classic Express". The family car had been out fitted with a canopied bed and other comforts. The second car was for dining and food preparation, then the servants' quarters.

Etienne staggered drunkenly when he carried his bride over the threshold, and to the elaborate four poster bed. He planted wet kisses over her face and neck, then dropped her on the bed, and thought it hilariously funny. The champagne was iced and waiting. He stumbled over and sloppily poured two glasses and brought one to Caroline, gulped his down and went back for another.

Repulsed, Caroline sat quietly on the bed realizing too late that this was not going to be a pretty night; dread filled her eyes. "Etienne please be gentle-hearted with me," she said quietly.

"You've teased me for months, it's time to come through.

I married you, you're my wife now," Etienne slurred, then reeled over and pulled her to her feet. She jerked away.

Angered, he roughly whirled her around and pulled her young lissome body to him, bending her backward, crushing his slack wet mouth on hers, holding her by the shoulders. His eyes were filled with filled with drunken lust, as his gaze traveled over her ripe pliant body.

Caroline tried to fight him off but her strength was nothing against his. Etienne ripped the front from her once lovely gown, then proceeded to tear the rest of her clothes off. In his excitement he shed his clothes between lip bruising, sloppy kisses.

Caroline turned her face away in shock and disgust, her naked body was literally tossed to the head of the bed.

Etienne entered her forcefully without regard for her comfort or sensitivity. Brutally his piston-like, grinding thrusts caused her to cry out in pain. Her hands gripped the head of the bed gasping while he drove himself into her.

Etienne mistakenly believed her cries meant she was enjoying his brutal act of carnality. When it was over he rolled away and immediately fell into a besotted sleep. Caroline curled into a fetal position as far away from her snoring husband as possible. Her body ached as she shook with sobs.

By the end of the trip to New York she needed several drinks before each sexual assault. They sailed for Europe on their honeymoon cruise around the world. Caroline found she needed a drink earlier every day throughout the trip and back. She started to carry a flask, and was caught by the worst gossip, several times taking sips from her bottle. At times she laced her tea with drollops of brandy. By the end of the day she would fall into bed drunk.

Etienne stayed at the gaming table until late into the night. He would look down at Caroline while she slept, her face appeared angelic in sleep. His lust for her was barbaric and his taking of her sexually was akin to the worst kind of rape. She would awake to him tearing into her night after night. Then there were the times she would just lie there and endure the cruel punishment.

Days before the honeymoon couple returned, Mama Jo called Carlton to her. She hugged the straight young Creole, then stood back and looked proudly at him, saying, "Etienne is corning back in a few days. I told you when the time come I fix everything. The time is now. You go tonight by the light of the moon." A look of fear crossed his face. She hugged him again and rocked him gently to her bosom, "Don't be scared, God will go with you all the way." Then she reached into her pocket. "Take this money the master gives us for work and you be alright. You learned lots of things from Colleen, now your way will be clear." He nodded his head when she shoved the home made money belt into his hand. Marna Jo squeezed his hand shut around the pouch. "Keep this hid under your clothes.

Come here let me help you tie it around your waist and don't show no heap of money 'too dangerous'. Keep just a little bit in your pocket." He stood passively while she wrapped the belt around his middle then tied it securely and tucked his clothes in around him. She bent behind the door for two bags to sling over his shoulders. Her instructions continued, "One is for warm clothes and a heavy coat. I hear tell it's cold up North, and this one's got your food. Use it careful. Mama Jo fixed everything. You go through the marshland when the moon is high," she said, pointing in that direction. "Hayman knows what to do. I talked to him, he paid already. Don't you show your money before nobody. You hear me?" Marna Jo repeated emphatically.

"Yes ma'am," Carlton answered.

Later Mama Jo watched as Carlton surreptitiously moved from one shadow to another to the marshes. She had given her blessings and prayers. Now she stood in the darkened doorway, as tears washed her cheek. She saw him disappear into the bottomland, then turned to go inside drying her eyes. "Go with God child," she whispered.

On the other side of the swamp hours later Carlton was whisked away in an old wagon that took him North past the next two plantations. The pathway had been planned and carried through without complication many times in the past.

In two days the newlyweds arrived with much fanfare from the servants. Caroline pleaded exhaustion and went to bed. Etienne was angered and strode through the manor,

"Where's Carlton?!" he shouted. "Have him saddle my horse! I'm going into Kalb Kove!"

"Carlton not here, sir," Jude said.

"What do you mean Carlton's not here?! Where is he?!" "A few days now he not here. Just gone," Jude shrugged his shoulders.

"Get the men together and bring the dogs. I'll find him and beat every inch of hide off his back! Get moving, before I take the whip to you!" Etienne said, but he would never touch any of the servants except Carlton for fear of Henri's wrath. Carlton had been his companion since childhood.

Men searched the marshes, as the horses' hoofs sank into the putrid mud while darkness was stealing down rapidly. "We'll get off and lead the horses," Etienne ordered, turning to Jude. "You said he was last seen going this way?"

"Yes, sir. We need more light in here. It's bad, a lotta muck and mire under the brush," Jude said. Etienne waved his finger and two servants galloped off. They were back shortly with pine knots to use for torches;

they ignited them passing them around.

The tracker searched for signs, saying, "He went this way, gimme his shirt for the hounds to get a whiff." He shoved the garment under the dogs' noses, "Here boys, take a good sniff of this shirt." The dog keeper took the lead, moving as quickly as possible through the sodden bog. It was difficult keeping up with the dogs, because the underbrush tore at their clothes. The tracker stopped to look over the ground, saying, "He's headed North, it took a lotta guts to come this way." He looked closely at broken branches where someone had fallen into a bush, breaking the limbs. Beyond them the wet grass had been torn up by running and stumbling feet. The ground under foot was a greenish ooze that made sucking sounds as they searched.

"Damn fool," Etienne grumbled, when they arrived at the river bank and looked out over the fast flowing water. It was forbiddingly black with the odor of rotting wood, dead fish and small animals.

"This is as far as we can go tonight," the tracker said. "You'll have to get somebody to trail him wherever he's going up North."

"How long would it take?" Etienne asked.

"Week or two, maybe longer. He's had several full days start," the tracker answered.

"Get the men you need to help and start at sunrise!" Etienne said angrily, then lashed his horse ferociously. The animal cried out in pain, reared momentarily and galloped away, his horses hoofs' tore up clumps of wet grass and mud. The other searchers followed at a single-footed slower pace.

Etienne didn't stop until he reached Kalb Kove.

The stallions breathing was labored, his coat was frothy with sweat. Etienne reined the animal viciously to a stop in Rene's courtyard. He climbed down and tossed the reins to the groom. "Cool him down first, water and feed him later!" Etienne snapped, and strode into the residence.

"What's the bridegroom doing out at night?" Rene asked. "Carlton ran away, and this marriage business is not all it's supposed to be. I might add, it's not for me," Etienne said, then sprawled in a chair before the fireplace.

"Have a drink. From your appearance you can use one," Rene said. After crossing the room to pour two hefty drinks, he took one to his friend. "Come with me tonight, I have a special place to show you," Etienne started to protest. Rene said hurriedly, "You'll like this place. Change your boots, you can ride one of my Arabians," he offered.

Etienne stood and drained his glass, saying, "Okay let's get this show on the road. I need something different tonight!" he walked out in a more jovial mood.

Rene led Etienne through Kalb Kove up a tree lined lane to an imposing house on the outskirts of town. It was ablaze with lights while the sound of music and laughter floated into the street. "Not much to look at from here," Etienne complained.

"It doesn't compare to Devereaux Manor, wait until you see what's inside," Rene answered.

They went through the foyer and entered ornate double doors, surrendering their hats, gloves and coats to a young Mulatto woman. Rene paid the admission, then they went into the ballroom, stopping inside the door. Overhead chandeliers glimmered against the ceiling. The dance floor was magnificently polished and the dancers were graceful. The men were white planters, professionals and businessmen out for a night of recreation and relief from the wife. The young women were statuesque and ranged in color from blonde blue eyed, redheads to cafe ole and dark hair.

"The women are lovely, aren't they?" Rene asked.

"I don't have a taste for dark meat, what's so enjoyable about this?! All of you planters have been busy in the slave quarters trying to create a more acceptable Negro," he said.

"You haven't seen anything yet. Don't make your judgement in haste. They've forgotten more about lovemaking than our women will know in a lifetime," Rene bragged.

"Okay, let's make the rounds. We can't just stand here!" Etienne said with ill-temper.

The two richly dressed men moved around the dance floor of laughing men and women. A number of older men were there from other towns and nearby plantations. The young women watched the new arrivals from behind their fans, commenting on the gentlemen when they walked by. Etienne stopped, his fingers tightening like a vice on Rene's arm. His gaze had settled on a ravishing quadroon descending the stairs. "I see what you mean about them being beautiful," he said. The others in the room need not have existed in her presence. She was statuesque, almost as tall as he. Her skin was a flawless golden tone and her hair was burnished auburn with lighter strands for highlight. Etienne ascended the first few steps to meet her and took her hand, saying, "Understand this, you're dancing with me."

She turned toward him without saying anything, her clear blue eyes widened momentarily. "You must ask my mother, sir." Her voice was husky and rich as it flowed from her wine red lips.

"To hell with your mother, you're dancing with me tonight!" he said vehemently. A smile touched her mouth as his eyes wandered over the low cut gown. It barely covered her breasts. Frills of fine lace fell from her shoulders. The bodice clung to every inch down to her slim waist. He swung her away from the stairs, onto the dance floor. Her forehead touched his chin. The heady perfume made his thin nostrils flare. He looked down at her closed eyes as he whirled her around the floor. Her lashes seemed to change color with each turn from golden auburn to black in the shadows. Etienne swung her from the dance floor and out to the veranda. In the different light of the moon he held her at arms length. The light caught in her hair and her lashes. Her beauty took his breath away. "My God, you're lovely!" he said as he drew her to him. Her face lifted to his as her full red lips parted softly. He lost himself in her kiss, leaning her backward against the balustrade, aware of every point of contact. The warmth of lust spread to his loin, she felt good in his arms. His head was whirling when she shoved him away. "You will belong to me," Etienne's voice was husky.

"Sir, I'm Myriah Vander Voort, I was born a free woman. My father, Edgar Vander Voort cares for my family," she said.

"I am Etienne Devereaux and the arrangements can be made. You'll belong to me, no one else can have you!" he said, grabbing her shoulders roughly.

She freed herself without difficulty. "No! I belong to no one! I am free, sir! No matter who you are, any arrangements will be by my father's choice," Myriah snapped, then walked away majestically.

He had never had anybody speak to him in that manner. Etienne stood there not able to move, his brain was still spinning from her taste. He started to go after her but he didn't dare cross her father, his mind raced. "There's a way! I'll devise a plan to have her. Then she'll know who the master is!" he said, adamantly, slamming his fist against the banister.

Etienne stayed out of town, but Myriah's face was etched in his memory. He couldn't stop thinking about her soft body against his. Her musk and the way she tasted. It infuriated him that he couldn't forget her. He prowled the plantation, and fantasized about how he would take her down a notch or two. Then he agonized over what was taking Rene so damned long to make the arrangements? A multitude of fears coursed through his mind. What if something went wrong and he couldn't make the necessary agreement? Her father was an influential man in Georgia. Vander Voort mining was a force that couldn't be trifled with. Maybe he wanted marriage for Myriah, after all she was his daughter. Never in Etienne's life had he been refused or had to wait for anything, but protocol required he wait.

Caroline was concerned about his preoccupation. He drank alone and brooded for long hours in his study. She realized she missed his attention, not out of love but out of selfishness. He seldom came near her in the last days and answered in monosyllables. He was changed, it was more than Carlton's running away. At supper one evening she was anxious to tell him something. "I have good news, " she said.

His preoccupation was impenetrable. "Etienne!?" she prodded.

"Yes, Caroline?"

"We're going to have a child. I thought we could have a little dinner party to make the announcement," she said.

When Jude entered with a note just then, Etienne said absentmindedly, "That's fine," while he read the note. He laid his napkin aside and left the room without another word. Her news made little or no impression on him. Caroline heard his stallion shortly afterward thunder off toward Kalb Kove; not to return for days.

Soon he arrived in the flagstone courtyard that surrounded Myriah's new home, with fragrant flowers, ferns and other hanging plants. French doors opened to the courtyard and balcony. It had taken time and money to seal the transaction. He tossed the reins over the rail and strode into the house, slapping his riding crop against his boot.

Myriah waited dressed in another breathtaking gown. He was not sure how to proceed and sat in the chair she indicated.

"Please, have a seat I'll serve you," she said, then walked across the room. It was maddening to watch her and not touch her. The wine was served then Myriah went about serving supper. The meal was set in the formal dining room that opened onto the courtyard. Fragrance from the plants wafted in on breezes as they ate in silence. He was fascinated with her coloring in the candle light that danced over her hair and face. Etienne felt the warmth of desire spreading over him.

"Would you like coffee in the courtyard, sir?"

"This has gone on long enough!" he said heatedly. "The niceties are over! You know what I'm here for, so let's get to it now!"

"No need to be so tasteless about it, we can go to the bedroom if you wish," she replied.

"That's more like it and I wish it." Etienne was up and out of his chair instantly following her upstairs and into the master bedroom. Once inside he kicked the door shut and whirled her around and ground his mouth on hers then reached for the bodice of her dress to rip it away. She disentangled herself with flashing eyes, her hands on her hips. "No! You will not maul me nor tear my clothes," she said fiercely. "I'll teach you how to make love to me."

"What? You! Will teach me?!" he said taken aback. "Yes, it seems you need some guidance in the matter." Etienne raised his hand to slap her.

She looked him levelly in his eyes, squared her shoulders and said, ominously, "That's no way to treat a lady, and especially me. I'm no slave and will not tolerate a beating from anybody!" She paused, "Now if you will stand near the bed 'I'll undress you' and show you my way."

Something in her manner suggested he comply, she was in control for now. Etienne raised his hands in submission.

Her warm wet mouth worked sensory magic as her tongue flicked between his lips tantalizingly, while she undressed him slowly, fondling his erogenous zones. Myriah removed her clothes seductively, and due to his low boiling point the warmth of desire spread to his viscera as she revealed her golden young body. With a concerted effort, he held himself in check, while his hands flowed over her smooth skin.

"Now I'll show you my way," Myriah whispered and sat seductively astride his lap facing him, her pliable breasts pressing against his chest. She placed little kisses on his neck and face, every touch of her warm ripe mouth sent shocking thrills through his body. Her perfume was heady, intoxicating, pleasurable and maddening. His arms encircled her slim waist as the nipples of her breasts hardened against him. Softly her lips caressed his sending him wild, his loins ached. He held her hips roughly to him and kissed her throat, tasting her breasts, then crushed her mouth with his.

"I can't wait," Etienne said, breathing fast.

"Yes you can, it'll be worth it," she whispered hotly.

The ache in his loin was almost too much to bare. At last they rolled into bed their bodies meeting like two magnets. His senses were reeling when she allowed him to penetrate her. An audible sigh escaped his lips when he sank into her warm moist enclosure, soothing him. He was tempted to quicken his movements, but she slowed his urge to do so. "Slowly take your time," she coaxed. "You're a good lover, I need to feel the same release along with you, take your time sweetheart, slowly," she whispered into his ear.

The minutes seemed like hours but passed deliciously as her movements quickened and his thrusts became hammer-like. She moved her body to receive his every jarring stroke, sending their senses to dizzying heights. Her cries of pleasure drove him on while her fingernails dug into his back. Their agile young bodies slapped wetly together during the mating. At climax he made a resounding cry of discharge, then remained poised momentarily above Myriah before settling his body on hers. Finally when his breathing was under control, he rolled away, only to rise up on one elbow to look at her in a kind of amazement. "How does someone so young know so much about making love?" he asked.

"We're told how to please our men," she replied coyly.

They made love through the night. He became smooth and sensual for mutual pleasure. Etienne realized his mating before tonight was just coupling. Someone else's pleasure had never been uppermost in his mind, nothing in his life could equal his feelings now. While they lay in bed he had one leg across her thighs. There was an urge to touch her and smell the perfume of her after making love. If this was enchantment she had him under her spe1l. " It was worth every excruciatingly painful moment you made me wait," he whispered, gently kissing her swollen lips.

Etienne stayed for days, seldom did they leave the bedroom except for food, bathing and linen changes. They made love all over the house, both were unquenchable. Myriah was ready and could give equally of herself. The two young savages were rarely satiated for any length of time. He was not able to stop the lust that had turned to a covetousness he had never known. He understood his father's feelings for Ymani. Myriah lay beside him while he kissed her ear. "What're you thinking lovely, Myriah?" he asked. She smiled but didn't answer, just snuggled closer. There was a hidden part of her, an ethereal little something that was her territory alone. He could not and would not intrude. It was distracting for Etienne when she wouldn't allow him to enter this bit of herself. He wanted total possession, but could never reach into that little niche.

Reluctantly he returned to Devereaux Manor and had voiced every excuse he had ever used not to go, but none would be convincing.

The announcement party at Devereaux Manor took place, one year after the wedding. Supper was served in splendor. The best tableware was used the food was prepared to a turn. Etienne was inattentive, the object of his thoughts was far away and the conversation lagged. Caroline, from the first glass of wine ate very little, but drank with every course, her laughter and conversation was forced.

When Etienne spoke to her it was a quiet rebuff.

"Caroline I think you've had enough to drink."

"Do you really think that my husband?" she asked.

The guests were ill at ease while the evening wore on.

It was obvious they wished the supper was over and they could leave. The wives were embarrassment for Etienne. The husbands were glad their wives didn't have a drinking problem.

"You are, having a child," Etienne said pointedly. "Our child, Etienne!" Caroline snapped.

"Jude, Mrs. Devereaux will not be having anymore to drink tonight, or any other time Is that clear?"

Jude bowed and moved the wine.

Dinner was over and Caroline clamored for a drink. "I'll get my own drink," she announced, then opened the decanter. Etienne took it from her, locking it away.

" It is time for you to go to bed, " he said through clinched teeth.

"Yes, my Lord and master," Caroline said as she teetered toward the stairs waving her empty glass. He followed her into the hall and to the stairs. Their guests were busily shrugging into their wraps, gloves and coats. Halfway up the stairs Caroline turned and dropped the wine glass, trying to focus her bleary eyes. 'Shall I wait up for my nightly bang? Or will you be going out again tonight?" she asked laughing hysterically, as she staggered upstairs.

There was an audible gasp of surprise and self-consciousness from the guests as they left hurriedly.

Etienne angrily paced the floor of the study late into the night. When he went to the master bedroom Caroline slept, her face contorted in drunken stupor. He closed the door and went to a guest room and plopped down on the bed fully clothed. Sleep never came because Myriah's face hovered above him. Her perfume and the taste of her lingered. He remembered the day they parted as she stood in the door. The sun behind her shown through the gossamer gown that outlined her slim silhouette. He wondered, as he had over the past few days, what she was doing? Who visited when he was away? "Who!? Who!? Who!?" Was there another man? Whose hands are touching her? Was his mouth kissing and tasting her body? He rolled over to shake the image.

France in 1892, Jean-Claude and Jean-Pierre were in their twenties, they entered the dining room for dinner. They were erect, tanned and slightly taller than Henri. Their hair was done in the style of young men of the time. An older Henri and Ymani had watched with pride earlier in the day when their sons had graduated with honors.

"Good evening Mama, Papa," they said, in unison.

Henri stared at the young men, his sons who were a golden version of him. If pride could burst his buttons this moment would have.

The door burst open again and his daughter Denise squealed all the way across the room to Henri. He held her in his arms and kissed her delightful little face. Robert quickly followed and went to his mother. Ymani hugged him close. Denise had her mother's hazel eyes and the classic beauty of the Egyptians. The children were a cross between Ymani and Henri. Their family gathering lasted into the night. When Henri finally carried his sleeping daughter upstairs to her bed. He sat and marveled at her trusting innocence and childish beauty.

Summer in Georgia and Caroline's pregnancy was the most miserable time of her life. The weather was sultry and the mosquitoes seemed to search her out to dine on. She lied and was abusive to the servants, except Mama Jo whom she showed a modicum of respect. Mona and the other house servants felt her wrath, because they had orders from Etienne and couldn't bring her wine or bourbon to drink. She tried to break the glass doors to the liquor cabinet and threatened suicide, to throw herself off the cliff into the bay. There were around the clock vigils to make sure she didn't kill herself. She bribed, coerced and forced the more frightened servants to bring bootleg whiskey or anything alcoholic. Caroline hoarded any she found and she had her way by using any means necessary.

Etienne spent more time in Kalb Kove. One late evening as he rode through the residential area where Myriah lived, his spirits were exuberant. Suddenly he reined his horse to a halt in the shadows of the trees. Myriah was carrying on an animated conversation with a young man. The gentleman hugged her shoulder with one arm then walked away. Etienne stiffened because the man had touched her. Jealousy churned inside him while he hastily rode the rest of the way. In the courtyard he tossed the reins over the hitching post, slapping his riding crop angrily against his boot, and went striding into the house.

Myriah started toward him, delighted that he had come, but stopped confused, because of his fierce look.

"Who was he? The man you were talking to?!" he asked angrily.

"What man?" she inquired. "At the gate moments ago!"

Myriah was bewildered, then she understood, and burst out laughing. Her hilarity lasted several moments. Etienne shook her, and shouted. "Who was he?! I'll beat every inch of skin off your back!"

She dried her eyes, saying, "That, was my little brother Allan. He'll be glad to hear you thought he was a man."

That bit of information was like cold water thrown in his face, he knew she had brothers.

Her demeanor changed and her blue eyes glared. "The day you beat the skin off my back, be prepared to kill me. I am not chattel to be ill treated, nor do I like being spied on. You don't suppose in your wildest dream, that I sit here everyday waiting? I'm a young woman with spirit. This is an arrangement. You don't own me!" she said with fervor.

Her harsh words like a fist to the solar plexus. She twisted out of reach. "I was mistaken, I apologize." he said.

She turned seductively to show off her slender form.

"I know, I'm last on your list but you can't control my every breathing second. This is my body to care for. It's here for you only. I love your use of it, but you won't abuse it!" she said hotly. "I'm young, don't think I'll be lonely and yearn for you. My family, will visit when you're away."

He went to her contrite, gathering her in his arms, kissing her throat and shoulders, then gently her full soft mouth. He felt the warmth of her through her garments. "And what would you do if I beat you? No man ever spoke to me the way you just did, ' he said softly, letting his 1 ips trail down her throat to her shoulder.

"My dear lover, I have three brothers and you don't want to know what I'll do; besides there's something better for us to do," she kissed him letting her tongue taste his through parted, lips and like all their kisses it was soon lengthened and out of control. He carried her to bed and in the heat of their mutual desire they undressed each other.

In Rene's study later, Etienne stood before the fireplace with a drink in hand. Rene chortled, saying, "I see you're getting into dark meat. Excuse the 'I told you so'."

"Believe me I've been sorry for that remark."

"The lovemaking alone is compensation enough, everything else is gravy," Rene said.

"I can't stay away from her. She's in my every waking thought and has the guts to be sassy with me. It's as if she's the one in control," Etienne replied.

"I told you that. So she screwed your brains out, this too will pass, it's pure lechery my boy," Rene laughed.

"It's as if I'm under a spell. I can't eat or sleep without her. The way she talked to me, standing there unafraid and I took it. I'd kill a man for less," he said.

"This is beginning to sound serious," Rene said. "You'd better slow down and think about this, and your wife. Take this girl to my Villa for a month and screw your brains out, get her outta your system."

Etienne continued, as if he didn't hear, "I saw Myriah talking to a man. I wanted to strangle him, especially when he hugged her shoulders. Turned out he's her younger brother. I checked and felt more than a fool, these are the lengths I've gone to."

"I can see you do have a problem, and I feel partly responsible because I took you there," Rene replied.

"When I'm at Devereaux Manor I prowl the halls and the grounds. As a matter of fact I've seen more of the plantation in the last few months than in my whole life," Etienne responded, then they were quiet, each to their own musing.

CHAPTER NINE

There was loud knocking on the door, and moments later an aging Jude was escorted inside. "Mistress Devereaux's time done come," Jude said. "The doctor is on his way, Mama Jo said you come quick!"

Etienne arrived at the Manor. In 1892 his son had made his premature entry into the world. Marna Jo wrapped him in warm blankets and held him up for Etienne. "Your son come too soon. He's a little bit, but Marna Jo will put some meat on that little body, you'll see," she promised.

Etienne was not inclined to touch the shriveled red bit of humanity and strode down the hall to the master bedroom. Then he walked to the bed to look down at his wife. He stiffened when he smelled the liquor on her breath. She slept in a drunken stupor, not aware she had given birth.

In the months to follow, the parents didn't stay in the room with little Nicholas Devereaux. Colleen and Marna Jo nurtured the infant and a wet nurse fed him. Nicholas flourished.

Once Caroline had her figure back, the servants packed a small traveling trunk at her command. She was anxious to go and wanted nothing as a reminder of Devereaux Manor. Etienne found her dressed and ready to travel; pulling on her gloves.

"So you're leaving? What about Nicholas?" Etienne asked. "I'm not the mother type. I was never sure if you wanted a son but you have one now, to carry on the Devereaux name, that is if he lives," she said, waving her hand in dismissal.

"You're his mother, for God's sake!" he exclaimed. "That kind of appendage I don't need. There's a life waiting out there for me, and I'm going to find it and enjoy," she said and walked to the window, then came and stood in front of him. "Sleep with your Negro chippy and the both of you be damned. She'll give you lots of half-breed brats!" Etienne stiffened. "Oh give me some credit. You were followed," she laughed, saying. "It was obvious, always mooning around, the absences. I knew you were mounting somebody all the time."

A coach man came and carried her luggage away.

She continued, "I must go now, just remember Nicholas was your last big bang with me, and probably your best. He's yours to raise as you will. I never want to see either of you again in this lifetime."

"Have you seen him?"

"Once or twice, now I'm free of the both of you and this damned plantation," she said, leaving the room, laughing all the way.

He stood at the window watching the carriage disappear in the oak lined drive, carrying Caroline away from Devereaux Manor. A sense of relief stole over Etienne when he entered his son's room, and for the first time held his child in his arms. Nicholas' thin face had a healthy color at last. "Nicholas, it's you and me now," Etienne said, while he stood in the filtered light of the sun. Nicholas opened his eyes, revealing the Devereaux distinctive green eyes and smiled a toothless grin.

After her father's death, Caroline became the belle of many balls in New York, Europe and other places in the world. She partied, swore, drank like a man and slept with those men who pleased her. There was money to burn, and it streamed in endlessly. Ole Ravell's will had specific language as to what would happen to anyone who attempted to cheat his daughter, or those who stole from the company; a system of checks and balances. Caroline proved to be adept at finances with the help of her lawyers and trusted management. She demonstrated that she was the wrong person to cross or double deal with in business matters. Caroline cared lavishly for her male companions, but when she tired of them she threw them over without a backward glance.

One hot afternoon weeks later, Etienne found Myriah dancing vigorously in the court yard. She jumped, whirled, gyrated and undulated to a pagan rhythm. He stood there, his face red from the sun. His clothes were dusty from the ride to Kalb Kove. "Myriah! Have you lost your senses!?" he demanded.

"I'm so glad you're here," she answered, brightly and mopped her face with a towel. "I have so many things to do before the baby comes."

"That wild dancing can't be good for you nor the baby! What if you had fallen!?" He could smell her warm fragrance.

"I'd get up and try that step again. I won't break and the baby is as healthy as a little colt," she said, placing his hand on her swollen abdomen, he felt the baby kick.

"Hey. That's my boy," Etienne marveled.

"Besides I need the exercise. It's good for me and the baby," she said, and walked to a table in the shade of a magnolia tree for a cool drink.

"My dear sweet Myriah, your duty to yourself and my baby is safety. You will be careful in the future?" he asked. "Etienne, sometimes you're impossible." She went to him dancing with her arms around his middle, nuzzling his neck.

"We could exercise another way,•' she said softly. "How?" he asked.

"Take me to bed. I've got the hots for you," she said. "You're so naughty. I can't, I might hurt you.

She put a finger to his lips to shush him and led him to the bedroom. "You love this naughty body, you won't hurt it," she whispered kissing him hungrily. With mutual desire they undressed each other between lip bruising kisses. The trail of clothes was strewn across the room. They lay in bed as tongues flicked between open lips tasting and touching erogenous zones. Then he gently held her voluptuous breasts in both hands and took first one, then the other in his hot wet mouth, arousing, and titillating her desire.

Etienne's loin was near bursting when she sat astride him. When he entered her, he uttered a sigh of delight then gently held her swollen belly between his palms. Their mating was slow, sensual and sweetly passionate while she rocked smoothly back and forth. Het t e r e d pleasurable groans and she gasped when they reached climax together. He was shaken visibly when it was over and kissed her mouth gently. Etienne had never known a woman who could control him so completely, and make him like every nuance.

Savoring every minute, he discovered his inner most feelings for her and wanted to take care of her. He held her while she slept. Myriah's warm breath was on his chest. It was as his father had told him many times, that caring knows no color. Then he felt a sharp kick from her naked belly. He smiled to know his son had the nerve to kick some sense into him too. Drawing her closer, he fell asleep.

In the brush filled glen the newly organized 'Knights Of the Brotherhood' met and threatened eliminations by cold blooded murder. The oath of secrecy was the decree in the South. The leader bellowed, "We're gonna get that nigger loving son-of-a-bitch tonight! I want volunteers!" Hands were raised and he made his selection.

The sheriff acted like private cops for whites.

On his way to Devereaux Manor, Etienne rode along the oak lined drive toward the mansion. Shots rang out and he was thrown side ways in the saddle. But he managed to hold on, and later staggered into the front hall where he collapsed.

The servants rushed around getting him to bed and his shirt off. Mama Jo cleansed and was dressing the wounds when a rock crashed through a window.

Doctor Gordon arrived to find Etienne in the living room pacing the floor. He was naked to the waist, one arm in a sling and a tight bandage around his flank.

A messenger had been sent for the constable. Etienne was worried as he read the note several times. The legend of the note, "You nigger loving son-of-a-bitch. I'll see you in hell. The bitch is next!"

Henri's last words to the Network were, "Watch over the Devereaux clan no matter who. Take any measures you deem necessary." After the bushwhackers had shot Etienne they rode to Kalb Kove. The Network members had witnessed the shooting. One stayed to make sure Etienne knew he would be avenged.

Others followed the Knights into Kalb Kove.

Outside Myriah's house one man stood in the shadows while their leader moved stealthily from one shadow to another toward the house. Out of the night the one who waited was garroted from behind with the skill of an experienced assassin. The body was lowered to the ground and a special knot was tied. There were furrows on his throat where his fingernails had gouged the soft tissue as he tried to save his life; the body twitched in the darkness.

They caught the leader as he searched for a way into the courtyard, men from the Network, one took him high and the other around his legs. The Knight kicked and scratched and tried to get away before his neck was broken expertly. His remains were carted away to join the other dead man. The bodies were dumped in the glen for the others to find. That faction of the Knights was not heard from for some time.

In 1899 at the turn of the century. Marna Jo was propped up in bed. Her white hair framed her full face. Everyone on the plantation paid her visits and cared for her through the day. Colleen arrived in the afternoon. The old servant's eyes were closed and her breathing barely moved the coverlet. "Mama Jo?" Colleen whispered.

"Come on in chile, Mama Jo awake," she answered in a feeble voice.

"Is there anything I can get for you?" Colleen held her friend's hand.

"No chile, I was just thinking. I won't see my boy Carlton again." She squeezed Colleen's hand. "If I don't see my boy, tell him I love him and my heart will always be with him," Mama Jo said softly.

"I know you loved him. Mama Jo, who were his parents?" "He's my grandson. My daughter was killed by that man

August Blanc. Stole her in the middle of the night, and Carlton was the outcome. She died giving birth, but August killed her sure enough," Mama Jo said, then closed her eyes and drifted off to sleep. Colleen sat with her for a while, then covered her hand gently and tipped out of the room.

Mama Jo died quietly in her sleep two days later.

People from plantations near and far came to give their last respects to the beloved Negro woman, who had helped to deliver a number of their children. Etienne did one thing she had ask for during her life: Six white horses pulled the carriage hearse with her casket to the graveyard.

Myriah was taken to Savannah for the birth of her first child. Etienne was as nervous as any soon to be father. She delivered in a short time. His second son made his appearance with a lusty cry. Etienne burst through the door after the first howl. Myriah's well being was uppermost in his mind.

His eyes devoured her face as he gently touched her hair. "Can I see the baby?" she whispered.

"In a while. You rest, I'll be back." Etienne stayed to see the baby washed and wrapped in warm blankets. Then he watched the little Creole doctor's every move while he took care of Myriah. "How is Myriah, doctor?" he asked.

"This is a strong woman. She'll have many babies." "And my son?" Etienne asked.

"Of all the Devereaux children I've delivered, this is by far the most magnificent," the doctor answered.

Etienne and Myriah later had two girls, the image of their mother with auburn hair. Long lashes fringed their wide green eyes. As little girls, his daughters had ripeful mouths. "I'll have to get a shotgun to keep the boys away; none of this arrangement business either," he added.

"If you say so," Myriah laughed.

When the time came to take his family to France, the Devereaux Clipper was anchored in the bay in sight of the Manor. All of his children, Roger, Danielle and Julianna were educated in France. The family enterprises flourished.

Etienne, as his father, settled in the Devereaux compound in the South of France. He married Myriah on the continent where such connubiality was overlooked.

Nicholas Devereaux, in spite of his rocky entry into this world, survived his low birth weight, thin body, poor eyesight and respiratory problems. But, although he was a brilliant boy, the heir to the Devereaux fortune couldn't run and play with the other children.

He was the joy of Colleen's life, the scholar she had searched for over the years. Tutors were summoned. As a boy he read voraciously, and seemingly absorbed knowledge.

He was the first at an early age to compile the history of 'The Devereaux Legacy' and graduated early from the lower grades. He went to France to study international law and graduated in record time. Nicholas was so painfully shy he proposed marriage by telephone to Elizabeth Ashley-Samuelson. Surprisingly she accepted because she loved him too; it was a marriage made in heaven. Nicholas and his wife both were intellectuals and found happiness. They had a son Aaron and daughter Abigail. The children were well loved and pampered by Nicholas and Elizabeth.

Caroline was in her Manor in the year 1927. In Paris one day, she read in the news that her son, Nicholas Devereaux was staying at 'The Regency Hotel' with his wife and children. The following day she sent him an invitation to visit her.

Because of her alcoholism, Caroline had developed liver disease. Her physicians gave her partial answers and pills. Her abdomen was painfully swollen, the one thing that vexed her most in view of her past pride in her figure. As she looked back on her life she remembered the fun she had and her regrets.

The day her son arrived, Caroline was as nervous as a school girl and needed three drinks to fortify herself; much to her nurse's chagrin. Nicholas was shown into her sitting room where she sat before the fire. He could see she was a sick woman. Pale and drawn with little spidery blood vessels that spoiled her nose, she wore too much makeup. Her bird like fingers held the coverlet over her swollen midsection, but there was a certain bravado in her manner.

He felt sorry for this withered bit of humanity who had given him birth. However, there was something in her demeanor that suggested he could like her.

"I'm sorry I can't stand to greet you, I've been a little under the weather lately," she said, breathing with short gasps for air.

"No need to get up ma'am. I've wanted to meet you as far back as I can remember," he said. His voice had the last vestige of a French-

American accent.

"Sit there, I want to look at you," she indicated a chair across from her. " You grew into a handsome man, if I do say so myself." There was pride in her eyes, "I left you as a baby, and I'm sorry I did that. After I had gone, there was no turning back, but 'I did live my life with style'," she said, without contrition.

"I'm not sure I understand, but I forgave you long ago." Nicholas had grown to manhood, an attorney-at-law. She looked at him, saying, "You' re a handsome man, tall, a sensitive mouth, and the famous Devereaux eyes behind those gold rimmed glasses," she enumerated his assets.

He was uncomfortable under her unblinking scrutiny. When she changed the subject. "So, I've read you're a brilliant attorney, and that's from people who know, I've checked.

Of course my son could do no less," she said, smiling. "Thanks, Ma'am."

"We would get along better if you dropped the ma'am. In spite of my life style, I kept abreast of your upbringing and education." She stopped and gazed into a far away place. Then repeated, sadly, "The only thing I'm sorry for is leaving you in the hands of others to raise."

Nicholas didn't know how to address this woman who had abandoned him in his infancy. He had never known what to say to women, and meeting his mother was a most unsettling situation. She continued, "I'm glad you're a lawyer, because you'll need that skill to handle the Ravell holdings, which you'll soon acquire." He opened his mouth to make an objection but she raised a thin hand; the gesture stopped his comment. "You're my heir and when I die, all this, everything will be yours as my only living relative," she said tiredly.

"But, ma'am," he started to protest.

"No, no, no," she admonished breathlessly. "I would like you to try, and call me 'mother' just once. I know I don't deserve it, just please try."

"I guess I could address you in that manner, but the word is so foreign to me," he answered.

Her voice seemed to find some inner strength. "Yes I'm aware of that. Just think about it, and try." She paused. "Enough of that for now, the necessary papers will reach you soon after my demise. They're in order. Believe it or not I'm a thorough business woman," she said, stopping to look at him, then smiled wanly. "I don't want to be rude but I tire easily and I must rest now. Come and visit me again before you leave Paris, and bring your family, my grandchildren."

"I'm sorry. I'll come again soon," then he hesitated, "Mother," she closed her eyes. Nicholas had another sad look at the pitifully fragile woman. He touched his lips to her forehead and tipped out after adjusting her lap covers.

Caroline died the next night, a thin smile on her lips.

Her funeral went unnoticed in death. She was a forgotten individual who had played a minor roll in her lifetime. Her power was yet to be felt through her son. The only person in attendance at Caroline's funeral was Nicholas, who said a silent prayer at the grave side. Following his visit to France he became one of the wealthiest and most powerful men in that era, a power he wielded with firmness and a modicum of mercy. Nicholas was the youngest elected judge in Georgia.

Colleen couldn't have been more proud of him than if he were her son. She died as she had lived, quietly in her sleep. She had carried her spinster-hood with grace to her grave. Nicholas had attended two funerals in a short period; although Colleen's was the most significant for him.

During that time 'The Knights Of The Brotherhood' raised it's ugly head and proliferated. Some grew to be professionals and minor level politicians, modest farmers and merchants. Their facade had changed but the rhetorical beliefs were the same. They regrouped and met without secrecy, everything was done openly and boldly, still spewing the same swill, save our white race and protect our white women, and the end justified the means. They never stopped the lynching of Negroes and any Jew or Carpetbagger who might be near by. They pillaged, reeking havoc on the country side, plundering, stealing and literally raping, producing numerous mixed breed children. The United States is filled with a diversity of Creole, Quadroon's and Octaroon's.

August Blanc had disappeared not to be seen again. He never knew Carlton was one of his many children.

Carlton had escaped to the north and had struggled to live in the harsh winters of Philadelphia. He had educated himself, and survived the hardship to become a noted orator and teacher.

The beatings and burning of Negro churches escalated.

The Brotherhood was arrogant and had no fear of the law, arrests were seldom.

Carlton ventured back to Devereaux Manor years later and knelt in pray at Mama Jo's grave. He had prospered and educated his children, and watched his grandchildren grow.

Nicholas' daughter Abigail Devereaux grew to be a lovely woman with a long mane of flowing black curls. She went on the stage and achieved some success as an actress. His son, Aaron Devereaux studied law and eventually assumed the bench as a judge in the lower court system of Georgia.

Judge Aaron Devereaux was a mixture of Henri for a certain kind of fairness, Etienne for ruthlessness and his father's brilliance. He was handsome, aristocratic, elegant and his carriage courtly. During his youth, scandal followed him. He was a notorious womanizer who had affairs with show girls; in addition it was rumored one was pregnant by him.

Servant women were not safe around him. Nicholas was continuously getting him out of a series of predicaments. Aaron had to be sent to Paris for tutelage and refinement.

The Network Organization changed along with the community around it. Nobody knew about this body of people who blended into the fabric of the community. It was essential for the organizations revitalization and secrecy.

Aaron Devereaux in 1949 met and married Laura Coultier-Devereaux of New Orleans, the home of jazz, swing, ragtime, and seafood suppers one could die for. Laura was statuesque, blonde, beautiful and loved partying and festivities of all kinds. Swingers were not known then, but she and Aaron had a grand time together.

Her family was land poor, and her father tried to marry his daughters into the right families. Aaron Devereaux was the choice catch of the season. He was rich, suave and good looking with the manners to match and a hidden mean streak.

Their wedding was the talk of New Orleans. They sailed aboard the Devereaux Clipper to Europe where they cavorted with Prince's and Princess's in the Queen's royal court. It was fashionable at the time for women to smoke. The extended honeymoon was replete with partying. Wine flowed like a river and many times sex was something that just happened not always to Laura's delight. Their lovemaking was not as passionate as their friends imagined. Laura was not a true giving partner.

Devereaux Manor was refurbished and modernized along with the Devereaux Clipper. It's sleek lines rode high in the bay outside the Manor, while the couple was away. The gardens were planted, river and bay docks rebuilt, the cooks house and servants quarters were brought up to date with electric lights. Inside toilets and small kitchens were added. Carriages, traps, wagons and coaches were restored and housed in the reconstructed press mill for sugar cane.

The old conveyances were intended to be used in old fashioned day parades.

The Gingsted clan struck fear in the people of Kalb Kove. Dirk, the father had raised his family up from poor white trash, to redneck bigots. Once he bragged, that after a raid, he'd come home to find twin boys. He chuckled, saying, "Two strong white boys, for a dead Nigger."

The Knights of the Brotherhood under the twins direction made a new start after Dirk died. The leadership passed to his sons. The torture and lynching escalated under Nathan 'Nate' and his brother Newton 'Newt' Gingsted, who held the towns people under their domination, by indirect threats of bodily harm.

There were numerous disappearances on record. A person would be here today and gone tomorrow. Church bombings, shootings and murder took place. They were stronger and more arrogant, if that's possible. Swaggering around with nothing to fear from the law nor the merchants, and especially God fearing towns people.

Inside the Gingsted saddle shop office late one night.

Nate toiled over the books. Gradually in his consciousness he heard a noise and sat straighter, looked around then heard a scraping sound. He cautiously approached the door to the shop. "Who's there?" he called, and went hesitantly into the darkened shop. "Moses is that you!?" the quiet was ominous.

As he moved further into the store he was gripped with dread. "I told you to get your black ass on home and be back here early tomorrow!"

A shadowed figure moved between Nate and the office door. In a swift movement a leather thong was looped around Nate's throat, and the assailant pulled the noose tight. Nate clawed at the garrote, trying frantically to reach his killer while charging backward. His face turned purple while he struggled to breath. He died clawing at the noose around his neck. The killer held on to make sure Nate was dead then roiled the body over and tied a special, signature knot.

That evening a crowd strained to see into the saddle shop. "Pull over John," Judge Devereaux instructed his driver.

"Yes, sir," he said, stopping abreast of the crowd.

Aaron climbed out of the automobile and pushed his way through the throng of onlookers. Inside the shop he knelt beside Dr. Crane. "What happened? Where's Newt?" he asked.

"That's easy. His usual hangout, Joe Leigh's Kit Kat

Klub," the doctor answered.

"You men take Nate's body over to the undertakers," Aaron ordered, then dusted his hands when they took the body away. Judge Aaron Devereaux, turned to Billy Ray Jeeter. "Billy Ray, find Newt, tell him what has happened, and where Nate's body is," he instructed.

"Yes sir," Billy Ray said, but stood transfixed.

"Go on, get a move on man!" Aaron said, giving him a shove. Then to the doctor, "Do they know who did this, Doc?"

"They're after Moses, the Negro who works here," he said with disgust.

"Moses would know better!" Aaron said.

"Tell these idiots that. It's because of that knot Moses makes. He's the only one ever seen use it," Doctor said, and closed his case with a snap.

CHAPTER TEN

In the dense dark woods, Sheriff Jessie Lee and deputy Jake Sykes were in pursuit of an exhausted Negro man. A few of the towns people and a bunch of drunken rabble followed the baying blood hounds.

Moses was ahead running for his life. He tripped over a tree root and fell head first into the underbrush, gasping to breathe. The man had lost his battle for mortality.

"There he is," one townsman roared, "I'll get ' im! " Then he raised his rifle to fire, but the sheriff hit the barrel as he pulled the trigger.

"Don't shoot 'im!" the sheriff yelled. "The judge will want him alive!"

"We got him dead to right sheriff!" the deputy wheedled. "He tied that knot! We all know nobody else can tie one like it but Moses."

"The Nigger did it, let's kill 'im!" the towns people shouted in agreement.

The sheriff chewed tobacco, and the juice colored the creases at the corners of his mouth. His belly bulged over his pants. He peered at the Negro man on the ground. "Nobody said you couldn't whip him a little," the sheriff volunteered.

Moses cringed away from the onslaught of the mob. They kicked and plummeted the frightened man into unconsciousness.

Jessie Lee had to stop them or explain Moses' death to Judge Devereaux. "Alright fella's you had your fun, don't kill him," he said, as a last vicious kick was delivered to Moses' body. "I said that's enough now! Get his feet Jake, we can toss him in the back of my pickup," Jessie Lee ordered.

"I ain't touching no Nigger!" Jake objected.

"You will if you want your job!" the sheriff threatened.

They carried Moses to the truck and dumped him in the rear. "Should've let us kill the no good bastard, Jessie Lee!" an onlooker yelled.

"I said go on home! You had your way for tonight, damn it!!" the sheriff swore. "Ya'll go on home the whole lot of ya!"

"We could take him off your hands. All we need is a rope, you can go fishing, Jessie Lee!" an onlooker said.

"Damn it Cal, I can't let you hang this boy. I'd lose my job!" Jessie Lee protested.

Newt stood in the viewing room of the funeral parlor. His face was red with anger and grief while looking down at his dead brother; Nate and Newt were identical twins. His crony's crowded in a circle behind him. "Who did it?" he asked, through clinched teeth.

"The sheriff caught that old colored boy Moses a while ago. He's over in the jail. I hear tell, some of the boys got a little playful with him," the undertaker answered.

Newt turned and stared at the onlookers with a cold and murderous look. "Tell Jessie Lee to go fishing," he said.

There was a gasp from the group.

"Tonight?!" the undertaker asked incredulously.

I don't give a damn what you tell him, just get the word to Jessie Lee now!" Newt roared.

The frightened man scurried out of his shop while Newt took one last look at his brother. "No Nigger's gonna do this to my kin and get away with it. On my word of honor," Newt promised. Then he gently pulled the sheet over Nate's face.

He turned and stormed out the door. His crony's followed, in anticipation of what would happen later.

Jessie Lee and his deputy left hastily by the back door of the jail, and disappeared into the darkness of the trees slightly ahead of the hooded, white sheeted figures waving torches and shouting. The Knights Of The Brotherhood converged noisily on the jail. A hubbub of vicious expletives terrorized the towns people. Those in the streets scattered and hid in fright. The Knight's chanted, "Kill the Nigger! Kill! Kill! Kill the Nigger!" they repeated.

Newt burst through the door of the jail. The riffraff crowded inside behind him, following their leader across the office. They noisily climbed the stairs to the cells where the Negro prisoners were kept separate from whites. Newt jerked his hood off, "Moses you didn't think you could get away with killing my brother! Did you believe that Nigger?! Answer me, damn it!" he bellowed.

Moses' face was battered from the beating earlier. He cringed in terror, moving as far back in the corner of the cell as possible. "I didn't kill him, Mr. Newt! You know I wouldn't do a thing like that!" Newt advanced toward the cell door, "Mr. Newt! Please!" Moses begged.

"Don't you lie to me, you black son-of-a-bitch! You did it alright. The leather was from my own shop, and it had your special knot. Nobody else ties a knot like that, but you!" During the exchange, Newt unlocked the cell door.

"Mr. Newt, please sir. I didn't do it! Here's my hand before God! I'd never do a thing like that!" Moses pleaded.

Newt charged across the cell and plummeted the man viciously with his fists, then kicked Moses into unconsciousness, he backed away, saying, "Take his black ass out the back way. We're heading for the red barn!" The Knights dragged Moses' body down the stairs. His head hit every step on the way down. The rabble dumped his body into the bed of a truck. Then drove to the barn at the end of Main street. A Knight tossed a rope over an outcropping two by four above. "Please Mr. Newt, I didn't do it. Please sir, I couldn't do a thing like that! Oh God help me! No!" Moses cried, powerlessly. Two men held him on a saw horse screaming and kicking.

"Hey! Get a hold of him there, this bastard's strong as a horse!" Billy Ray yelled, as he struggled to hold Moses.

"Kicks like a Georgia mule!" another said falling. "No! Please! I never killed Mr. Nate!" Moses cried, battling, for his life.

God fearing townspeople peeked from behind drawn curtains. Some enjoyed the spectacle, but were afraid to join in. Many stood and snickered, some were horrified.

"Get it over with!" Newt bellowed in rage, and kicked the sawhorse over. Moses' body swung kicking; his screams turned to strangling noises. The mob stood and watched the body jerk and twitch. Then it was still, as a gentle breeze caused it to turn slowly.

"Want me to cut him down Newt?" one Knight shouted.

"No! Leave the son-of-a-bitch! Let the rest of them know they can't get away with something like that. Dash some coal oil on him, and light his ass on fire!" Newt ordered.

A Knight carried out his command. They stared while Moses burned. "Did you see his face?! The bastard turned purple! I didn't know coon's could change color!" one joked.

"Get the hell outta here! Now!" Newt barked. They disappeared, leaving the smoldering body.

The next morning Judge Devereaux arrived in town to the 'Knight's' deadly reminder of the night before. "It appears the riffraff has been up to no good again," Aaron said. John, the driver stiffened, his jaws clinched. Even an Uncle Tom had feelings for his people. He skillfully maneuvered the car to the curb, in front of the courthouse. Before getting out, the judge turned to his driver, and said, "John, get Jessie Lee for me. I don't want that old excuse, of his having gone fishing. I want him in my office right away!"

"Yes sir," John replied, and drove away while the judge crossed the sidewalk and entered the court building.

Jessie Lee's cautious knock sounded on the door, then he entered the judges chamber. Aaron stopped writing and leaned back in his chair. His anger was apparent in his demeanor.

The sheriff stood on one foot then the other, twisting his hat in his hands. "You wanted to see me your honor?" he said, slightly above a whisper.

"I want that body removed immediately!" Aaron answered, and leaned forward, his elbows on the desk. Jessie Lee stood impaled on his stare. "Do you know who lynched and burned Moses' body last night?" he asked.

"Oh no! No, your honor, after I caught the Nigger, I went out for some night trawling," the sheriff mumbled.

"This story you tell about fishing, I've heard it too many times. Don't ever use the word Nigger, in my presence again! Is that clear?!" Aaron said adamantly.

The sheriff looked down sheepishly. Aaron sat silently, letting Jessie Lee sweat under his gaze. The sheriff moped his brow with a discolored handkerchief, and said, "He was accused of killing Nate."

"By whom?" Aaron asked.

"The knot was proof," the sheriff faltered.

"You and I both know Moses would never do anything like that, he knew better. His murder was the act of a bunch of out of control hotheads. The thirst for blood, anybody's blood, and Moses' was it. The kind of backward thinking, of a town full of cowardly bigots and killers!" he looked out the window and then back to the sheriff. "It was probably someone Newt and Nate had double dealings with, then you framed Moses as their scapegoat," Aaron concluded.

"But Judge, your honor I ... I "the sheriff stammered, and fidgeted. His face reddened to his hairline.

"I want you to ask around and find out who the Gingsted brothers have defrauded, " Aaron stopped him rude ly. "That should be quite a list."

"But Judge, I don't know if I can, find out ... "Jessie Lee finished lamely.

"Don't give me that song and dance! 'You will' find out, and report back to me. Is that clear?" Aaron ordered.

"I'll do the best I can, yo'r honor," was the sheriff's subdued answer.

"Your cronies will tell you. If you don't already know." "Oh no Judge! I don't know, nothing!" Jessie Lee cried. "I want that report on my desk, and soon, do you understand?" Aaron demanded.

"Yes sir, your honor," Jessie Lee answered.

"Now get the hell out of my office, and move Moses' body!" Aaron said, raising his voice.

Jessie Lee bolted from the room, taking care to close the door softly. His job depended on the Judge, and the city council. He couldn't afford to cross any of them; especially Newt. A man could wind up dead if he made Newt mad. Clearly he had his tail in a crack, and no apparent way to get it out soon.

On Main street in the light of day, a group of redneck youths. Poked fun at Negroes, as they walked along the sidewalk, outside the general store. Tom Lennox the store owner watched the meanness to the coloreds. A redneck said, "This one coming here is dark chocolate," as a black woman came into Tom's sight.

"You can be my double chocolate drop. I'll be your candy cane," one youth said, making lewd gestures. The woman walked away as quickly as possible. The rabble rousers jeered and snickered. The spectacle was heard, and observed by store owners along Main street.

"Faith, come here," Tom called.

One of the hecklers took out a rope. "Let's see how high this darky can jump?" an older Negro man came into view. The youth smacked the man on the backside. The black man jumped, and ran down the sidewalk. The group thought that was the most hilarious thing to happen that day. "Did you see how high that old fart jumped?'·· the one with the rope said, amidst gales of laughter.

"Tom, can't you do something?" Faith asked, outraged. "You know they can't fight back for fear of being lynched'.··

"Call Jessie Lee over here,' Tom said.

"Oh what good is he? He's so scared, he shakes like a leaf in the wind if he has to arrest a white man. Tom I ask you what good is he!?" Faith cried.

"None, Dut he's all we have for now. Call him before something worse happens. Those bigoted bastards, and their snot nosed kids are getting out of hand. Call Aaron while you're at it. I'll talk to him,· Torn insisted.

Another Negro man came into view. The youth with the rope popped him on his posterior. The passerby ran out of reach. This was a belly laugh for the rabble, "He jumped two feet, at least!"

Amelia Russell, an attractive black woman came in sight of Tom's window. "Here's one, this one's mine! Stay back, she's mine!" The self-glorifying young man swaggered over to her, saying, "You can definitely be my chocolate anything!" He grabbed her and whispered something in her ear, while the others snickered knowingly.

"Let me go!" she said, pushing him away.

He held her shoulders and pulled her to him again, "How about a little roll in the hay?" he said, loudly. 'Give up a little poon-tang. You can be my 'special dark meat'...

She broke free and swung her large purse, striking him on the head. The blow knocked him flat to the pavement. The silence from the others was threatening. The one on the ground shook his head, then jumped to his feet, his fist ready to strike.

The sheriff arrived as the boy was about to punch Amelia. The crowd encouraged him to hit her to teach her a lesson. Law abiding citizens distanced themselves from the conflict. Some giggled nervously, as the young redneck with his fist drawn, said, "I'll teach you to hit a white man!

"Hey! Hey! Hey! Hold on there!" Jessie Lee shouted.

"She hit me! Knocked me down like a dog! No nigger hits a white man in this town, and lives!" the youth argued.

"Arrest her Jessie Lee! Then go fishing!" another youth suggested.

"She'll hang just like Old Moses did!" the first one yelled.

Amelia shook with fear as the ruffians gathered around her again to strike her. Tom Lennox came out of his store.

"Hey! None of that now. She's in my custody," Jessie Lee repeated.

"We know, about your custody!" one shouted.

"Yeah Jessie Lee, you go fishing and we'll take care of her, whilst you're gone!" a red faced stripling responded.

"The black bitch is dead meat! Dead meat! Do you hear me!?" another yelled..

Tom interceded, saying, "Sheriff, Judge Devereaux wants you to bring Amelia to his courtroom. I've already talked to him. If he needs me further, tell him to call me."

"I'll do just that Mr. Lennox, Jessie Lee groveled. "The Judge said, no harm should come to her en the way there, Tom cautioned.

"You know me, Mr. Lennox."

"Yes Jessie Lee, I'm afraid I do know you," Tom said, then to the kids, "You boys go on over to the courthouse, all of you. The judge wants to see too." Amelia was shoved roughly into the back seat of the sheriff's car, and her purse was tossed in behind her.

"Just another dead, nigger!" the first youth said, as he rubbed his aching jaw. There was a hubbub of jeering when the sheriff's car drove toward the court building.

"You boys go on now, the judge is waiting. He wants to see you, now!" Tom said.

"Yes sir," they said, going noisily across the street, toward the courthouse. The young whites, took comfort that they lived in the South, especially, at a time when Negroes were at the mercy of the white man's whims.

In the courtroom, Judge Devereaux looked down on the brawlers. Jessie Lee held Amelia in the back of the court room. "I'm told you boys were harassing people on the street today." The judge said. And looked at them with a stern gaze, "Did you do that?" Aaron asked.

"We was just having a little fun, your honor," one said. "There will be no more fun like that in the future. Is that clear?" he stared at them individually, allowing them to squirm in discomfort. If I hear of you bothering anyone again, or this woman anymore. I'll have a talk with your parents. I know who you are, your names are here on this list," he said holding up the paper with the names. "Now go home, and behave yourself." On the way out, the first youth shook his fist at Amelia.

"I saw that gesture," the judge warned.

The boy looked around surprised, "It didn't mean nothing your honor."

"If anything happens to her, I'll see you first, understood?" The ragtag brats frowned at Amelia, then walked with ill-temper out the door.

Jessie Lee stood to attention in back of the room.

Judge Devereaux turned his attention to them, while the door closed behind the boys. "Bring her forward," Aaron ordered.

Then sheriff brought her forward, "Her name is Amelia Russell your honor." She stood straight, her head was held high, with her eyes downcast.

The judge saw the young black woman with a neat figure. A product of a century of the white man's inbreeding. "I know who she is Jessie Lee. Her mother worked for my mother before she died. Amelia had spunk as a child too," he said, pausing. "Look at me, Amelia."

She reluctantly brought her eyes to meet his. As they faced each other, he found himself staring into intelligent clear hazel eyes.

"Did anyone ever tell you, you look like Josephine Baker?" he asked. She shook her head. "I had the pleasure of meeting her while I was in Europe. I respected her zest for life, too." Aaron stopped talking several moments remembering, then said to Amelia, "That was brave of you taking on those boys. You could have been killed by that riffraff? You can't hit a white man, and go free in Georgia. "You know that, don't you?" Aaron asked.

"Yes sir," Amelia answered.

"I can't let you get away with that scot-free. So I'm sentencing you to ninety days," he said.

Panic gripped her, as tears formed and spilled down her cheeks. "Your honor," she said, hesitantly. "Sir, I have two children to care for," and wept into her handkerchief.

"Where is your husband?" Aaron asked.

"In service, your honor," she replied.

"Overseas?" he quizzed.

"Yes sir," she said, drying her eyes.

"Do you work?" the judge continued.

"Yes sir, the Kalb Kove Country Club, sir."

"Who takes care of your children while you work?"

"Mother Russell, sir," Amelia answered.

"I'm going to rescind your sentence in jail. No confinement, you can work it off for my wife. I'll let your employer know, the judge said.

"Yes sir, thank you, sir," she said gratefully.

"Jessie Lee, see to it that Amelia gets to the manor every morning." the judge instructed.

"Yes sir! I'll see to it myself," Jessie Lee answered eagerly.

"You're dismissed," Aaron said, slamming the gavel down.

The sheriff took her arm and started out.

"Amelia, I heard about Lyla, I'm sorry," Aaron said quietly.

"Thank you, Judge Devereaux."

"Do you have boys or girls?" the judge asked.

"Boys, sir," she answered.

Aaron smiled and waved them out, in dismissal. He leaned back in his chair while they walked out of the courtroom.

In the vast living room of Devereaux Manor, Aaron and Laura were having after supper wine. Their marriage had become comfortably, convenient and not always convivial. "Lyla's daughter, came before me in court," Aaron said.

"I don't know Lyla," Laura replied.

"She was my mother's personal Negro maid, when I was a boy. Amelia, was a sassy little girl, who bit my finger once," Aaron chuckled.

"What did she do?" Laura asked, sipping her drink.

"Some redneck kids harassed her, and other Negroes on the street today. She knocked the hell out of one," Aaron laughed.

"That bunch of trash, they have 'no' fear of reprisal. It's just awful!" Laura said in a strong Southern accent.

Aaron drank from his glass, saying, "The Negroes live in the South, Laura. That's the way it is here. Tom called and told me how it started."

"What did you do about her?" Laura asked.

"I gave her ninety days," Aaron answered, offhandedly.

"Aaron! Why?! It wasn't her fault!"

"I might have saved her life. The Knights of the Brotherhood would kill her, and her whole family in the middle of the night. They've been known to do worse, in the past," he said.

"They're so coarse. How awful!" she cried.

"Besides, it couldn't appear she had gotten away with hitting a white man, even if he was an ass. And, it could give other Negroes the idea. Then, there could be a blood bath," Aaron explained.

"What do you mean, a blood bath?" she asked.

"A race riot can be quite bloody. Negroes are pushed past the breaking point after being lynched, improper imprisonment and forced labor. The riots in the South have been devastating." He drank from his glass, then rolled it between his palms. "America still can't hold it's head high because of the injustice. Long after the Civil War, there's endemic poverty." He stopped with a grimace of distaste. "Downward mobility is a reality for Negroes and poor whites. A type of class and cast system. And I find myself a part of it!" he said, vehemently.

Laura finished her drink, and reached for the decanter. She had been hitting the bottle heavily, and was getting a little drunk. Her drinking had changed their sex life. She was too intoxicated most evenings. The excitement was gone, their life had become hum-drum.

"Laura aren't you having too much, to drink?" he asked, staring at her, as quiet fell over the room.

"It makes me feel warm inside. I like feeling warm inside. You should try it sometime," she slurred.

"It's been a long time since the loss of our son. You should get out, go to the Country Club," he encouraged.

"I've never belonged there and that goes for the whole damn town.

'I just, don't belong!'" she declared.

"Kalb Kove, is our home," he said.

"Aaron, let's go back to Europe. We were so happy there, the gaiety!" she said, dancing around unsteadily. "The fashions, good times, everything was alive! Different people!" she pleaded, with her palms together.

"Playtime was over, it was time to start a family and manage Devereaux Enterprises," he said.

"Aaron, the business takes care of itself. It has for years. Nobody would dare steal, or misappropriate anything."

"And the sons I'd hoped for, but that will never be, will it Laura?" he fired back, ,and swallowed the last of his drink, then stared into the empty glass with ill-temper.

"We tried! I tried! Three times! I'm sorry, I failed you! Can't our love be enough?" she asked.

"Our love, such as it is, will have to do, won't it my sweet?" he said, looking at her evilly. "You can't have a child." A nasty smile twisted his mouth. "That makes you my, barren-ess." He crossed the room to the bar, "Let's have another drink, a real drink this time," he said, with brusqueness.

Aaron poured three fingers of scotch, then raised his glass in a mock salute. "To you Laura, my 'barren-ess'," he declared.

"Aaron, you're a miserable human being. You can be so cruel," she replied, as tears formed in her eyes.

"Does that include, coarse and uncompromising?" he asked, draining his glass.

She burst into tears, and ran sobbing from the room. His laughter rang out and surrounded her. Laura held her ears to shut out the grating sound. As she stumbled upstairs, it followed her into the bedroom, where she threw herself on the canopied bed.

The next morning at breakfast, Aaron folded the news-paper when Laura came into he room. Her eyes were red and swollen. "Good morning Aaron," she spoke, softly.

He nodded, and said, "I want you to plan a dinner party, for the thirtieth of the month. Invite all the young and old cronies of Kalb Kove. We need some laughter in this house."

"No one will come!" Laura exclaimed.

"No one would dare risk staying away. You plan the party, they'll be here." he spoke with confidence.

"Aaron, they hate me!" she said.

"There's one difference, they don't dare show it. I won't tolerate their disrespect and everyone knows that. This is my town, you should know that," Aaron said, without conceit.

"Aaron! Really!" Laura was taken aback.

"What can I say. That happens to be another fact of life in Kalb Kove. Oh, and by the way, I didn't tell you. I rescinded Amelia's ninety day jail sentence. She'll be working her time off for you. Jessie Lee will bring her every day, starting today. He'll pick her up," Aaron said. Laying the paper beside his coffee cup, he started out the door.

"What will she do here?" Laura asked.

"Have her do whatever servants do, and don't coddle her. She's a county prisoner, in a sense," he said.

"Why did you do this, Aaron?"

"Mostly in memory of Lyla. And then again, it might be because Amelia had nerve enough to bite my finger when she was a little girl," Aaron chuckled. "She always had a sassy answer for everything," he said, and kissed Laura lightly on the lips, patted her shoulder, and walked out of the room.

CHAPTER   ELEVEN

On the sidewalk outside the court building, Aaron was about to go inside, as Jessie Lee was leaving. The sheriff stepped to one side with a servile demeanor. He stood, nervously on first one foot then the other. "Good morning Judge Devereaux sir, nice day," he said, in a conciliatory tone.

"Good morning, Jessie Lee I want to see Newt and Billy Ray right after lunch," the judge commanded.

"I'll tell 'em yo' honor."

"Did you take Amelia? My wife is expecting her."

"I was just on my way, yo' honor," the sheriff answered.

"The matter is important, tell them don't be late, one o'clock sharp. Don't forget," the judge cautioned.

"I'll have 'em there your honor, one sharp," the sheriff said, holding the door open for the judge.

The men arrived at one. 'Newt, you both know these boys I believe," Aaron said. Looking at them while passing the list across the desk to Newt.

"Yes sir, what did they do?" Newt asked, with a pronounced Southern accent. He chewed on a lighted cigar in the corner of his mouth, and read the list with a squint.

"They caused trouble outside Tom Lennox's dry goods store yesterday, and ran some of his customers away," Aaron said, stopping to look at both men. "You'll agree, that isn't good for his trade, nor is it good for anyone's business on Main Street."

"You're right there, your honor," Newt agreed.

"You seem to have a finger on the pulse of Kalb Kove," Aaron said, smiling. "I want you to keep them in check. I'm sure I can leave this little problem in your capable hands, and Billy Ray's too."

"You sure can, your honor," Newt replied. "Tell Mr. Lennox he won't have to worry about them again, Judge Devereaux."

"Thanks for coming," Aaron said, as he stood and shook Billy Ray's hand. Then extended his hand to Newt. Their eyes clashed in knowing stares, like two silent warriors, sizing each other up. "Newt thanks. I knew I could depend on you."

"It's as good as done Judge," Newt said, before he closed the door.

Aaron wiped his hands with a clean handkerchief in distaste, then threw it in the waste basket.

Newt and Billy Ray walked in close conversation. "Take this list, we got to put a stop to this mess. We don't want to show our hand too soon, Billy Ray," Newt instructed.

"I'll get it done Newt, don't you worry!"

"Get on to their folks, tell them, to see to their kids. The time will come when we'll run this whole county. Now get a move on," Newt ordered.

Aaron stood in his window, and watched the men talk. Finally, Billy Ray went in one direction with the sheet of paper. Newt entered his saddle shop. Aaron went to his desk and dialed a number, waited, then said, "We have to meet? I have instructions."

"Same place and time," a whispered voice said, then the connection was broken. Aaron leaned back in his seat. A dispassionate smile creased his lips.

John drove Aaron along the oak lined drive to the front door of the manor. They arrived just as Jessie Lee shoved Amelia into the back seat of the police car. The sheriff became conciliatory at the sight of the judge. "Good evening, your honor. Did the boys get there?" he asked.

"Yes they were there, thanks sheriff," Aaron said, going through the door before Jessie Lee could reply. Aaron stopped at the hall table and shuffled through the mail. He looked up as Laura started downstairs. Laura and Cora had taken great care for her to look her best for supper. "Laura," he smiled, saying, "You grow more lovely with each passing day, breathtaking, is this a special occasion?"

"No nothing special except you and me, together," she said, her speech slightly slurred. "Oh by the way, Amelia is a pretty Negro woman."

"I fail to see the distinction, of a special evening at home, just you and I, and Amelia's looks, the correlation escapes me," his answer was short and cynical, as he tossed the mail on the table.

She stumbled off the last step, and fell against the wall. He hurried to steady her, then smelled the whiskey on her breath. 'It seems you've already drunk your supper," he said angrily.

"I've had a couple, and I'll have you know I'm not drunk!" she said, shoving his arm away. "I don't need your assistance."

"I'll have my supper at the Country Club!" He said, heatedly, walking away in distaste to the front door.

"Oh Aaron, come back! Please don't go! I didn't mean that!" she pleaded, as he slammed out the door.

Cora the maid came into the hall at that time. "Miz. Devereaux, come on with me. I'll help you upstairs so you can rest. Later, I'll fix you a nice supper tray, and bring it to you, when you feel better." Cora guided Laura to the stairs, steadying her as they climbed the steps.

"Yes! Yes that's it," Laura said, giggling. "I need rest," hugging the maid's arm. "Cora you take such good care of me. I don't know what I'd do without you," she said.

"Yes Miz. Devereaux, I'll help you all I can."

"The judge, wants me to have a dinner party at the end of this month. Will you help me then?" Laura asked.

"Yes ma'am Miz. Devereaux, I sure will."

"You know, the women in this town hate me!?" Laura said, in a drunken whisper with a wink.

"I'm sure they don't hate you. They don't know you like I do," Cora reassured.

"Oh yes, they hate all outsiders and I'm the 'outsider' who married one of their own. A 'Mata Hari' that's me!" she said, stumbling over the top step.

"Careful Miz. Devereaux," Cora said, helping her to stand.

"Yep, I just took him, stole him right away from some, simpering, little Georgia grown, Southern belle," Laura said, and giggled, flinging her arms wide. It struck her as hilariously funny, and she laughed uproariously. Cora went ahead and opened the bedroom door. She helped Laura to bed, still giggling.

In Joe Leigh's Kit Kat Klub on a Saturday night, the meeting place was noisy as a jukebox played a popular country western song, over loud laughter. Waitresses served bottled beer. Couples danced, they hooted and yelled. Newt sat at a table lighting a cigar. Newt and Billy Ray were joined by J.D. Carter, who poured his drink from a bottle of moonshine hidden in his coat pocket. "Ya'll better come with me tonight, we'll have a good time," he invited.

"Nope, and you'd better leave that colored stuff alone. Your pecker's gonna fall off one of these days," Newt answered. "If that rot gut don't kill you first, she will."

"After tonight, I'll die happy," J.D. cackled.

"Hard head makes a soft ass, 'pecker' in your case."

"You don't know what you're missing," J.D. said. "But if you won't have none of my moonshine, it's just that much more for me," he said draining his drink. Then he strutted away, adjusting his cowboy hat at an angle when he left the road house.

"Since he got some colored stuff in high school, he just gotta have it," Billy Ray chuckled.

Newt had a peculiar look on his face while he watched J.D. leave. He seemed momentarily disconnected from reality before turning his attention to Billy Ray and his drinking.

"Damn fool's gonna get himself killed below the tracks some night," he said drily. Then he stood abruptly and finished his beer. "Come on I'll drop you off. I have something to do," Newt said, slamming the bottle on the table.

"I can sure use a ride tonight, thanks Newt," Billy Ray answered, and hurriedly gulped his draft.

They threaded their way through the crowd of dancers and waitresses. The noise from the music was deafening. Nobody talked below a shout. When they closed the door, the noise inside seemed to come from somewhere in the distance.

Aaron entered the Kalb Kove Country club's Tack Room Bar and walked to a table where Torn and Dr. Crane were sitting. "Aaron! Join us!" Torn called, then turned and signaled the waiter, saying, "Josh!"

"Will you have Cognac tonight Judge?" Josh asked, and waited for his order.

"Not tonight. I need something stronger, make it a double scotch on the rocks and keep them coming," Aaron answered.

"Better go easy on that stuff Aaron, your head will tell the tale in the morning," Dr. crane cautioned.

"I need it tonight old friend. Besides John is here to drive me home," Aaron replied.

"Does this bout of drinking involve what's going on in the county these days, white purity and all that?" Tom asked.

'That and other more personal things," Aaron said. "This Brotherhood for the purity of the white race is rubbish. There has been bastardization at the races since slavery began and they've probably caused most of it."

"You're right. There was a time when we wouldn't allow that type in town. The coloreds are leaving the South for other parts of the country. 'They think' for a better life," Dr. Crane said.

"We know Newt is the instigator of all the troubles," Tom said.

"Yep, he has a strangle hold over the Brotherhood, and that goes for the towns people too," Dr. Crane interjected. "It's going to be difficult, breaking his control."

Aaron's drink arrived. He gulped down half, before putting the glass down. Then he pointed to Josh for a refill. "The Brotherhood was dormant for a long time. Newt's father revived it. We can't allow the carnage to continue," he said.

"I'm afraid there'll be a riot. The harassment of the coloreds in front on my store didn't help matters," Torn said, as a worried frown creased his brow.

"I'd say that would be a nasty turn of events," Aaron acknowledged.

"Let's change the subject," Dr. Crane suggested.

Tom breathed a sigh of relief. "Alright by me," he said and drank from his glass.

Aaron drained his glass, and held it up for a refill. "I just delivered the seventh son for the Sanders."

"The bank teller, doc?" Torn asked.

"We have to figure a way to get Sanders out of the house somehow," the doctor joked.

"Here! Here!" Aaron felt good. "Josh, do this again," he called, then turned to his friends. "Better still, how to get him out of bed. Let's drink to all seven," he said, laughing.

Josh was kept busy refilling their glasses while they got deliciously drunk. It turned into a good night for the waiter, because the tips were generous.

At another place in Kalb Kove, Jessie Lee left the Depot Cafe after supper picking his teeth while he walked toward his pickup truck. Newt stood in the shadows, chewing on an unlighted cigar. His eyes were slits, as he watched the sheriff several moments, "Hello Jessie Lee," he spoke softly.

"Ah, Newt! I didn't see you there in the dark," the sheriff said. He panicked, as his heart thumped wildly.

"I hear you've been asking questions around town about the death of my brother?" Newt's voice was forbidding.

"I ... um, well, I ... ah," Jessie Lee said nervously as he stumbled over the words.

"I want to know what you've found out, and where you heard it. Now?" Newt demanded.

"Nothing so far, Newt." the sheriff's voice cracked.

"Who told you to ask around?" Newt asked.

"The t-t-t-town counsel," Jessie Lee stammered.

"Meaning Judge Devereaux?" Newt said. The air around them seemed still, suffocating, while time dragged.

Jessie Lee could taste the bitterness of his fear. The evil expression on Newt's face was depraved. It sent shivers down the sheriff's spine, and his bladder felt weak. He knew if he made a move to get away he would be killed. "He was there, but the whole counsel agreed. Newt, it's my job."

Newt moved his cigar around in his mouth and gathered Jessie Lee's shirt front in his hands, then pulled the sheriff close, face to face, saying, "I want to be the first to know if you find anything. I want it, get my drift?"

"I ... I ... get you, Newt. You'll be the very first to know, about anything I hear!" Jessie Lee groveled.

Newt released his hold on the sheriff's shirt. And in a matter of fact manner smoothed the material over the frightened man's chest, saying softly, "If you don't tell me, maybe the Brotherhood will have to pay you a visit some dark night. You never know," he said, brushing an imaginary speck of lint off the sheriff's shirt.

"No cause to talk like that, Newt. You know me, always willing to help out," he said, as sweat oozed from his pores.

"Yeah, I know you Jessie Lee. Always a mile away when something happens. Of course it's always best not to know too much," Newt said, grinning. He put the cigar in the corner of his mouth, chuckling as he walked away lighting it, disappearing in the darkness.

Jessie Lee couldn't breath normally until he had driven away, sweating profusely. He swallowed repeatedly because his breathing was labored. It was clear to him that tonight he was close to dying. "This job ain't worth the aggravation. I almost lost my supper," he muttered after a long sigh.

In the darkness of the trees, Newt watched the truck until it disappeared from sight.

The next morning Amelia hugged her sons Eddie Jr. and Curt and walked out to the dirt road in front of the small shack. Mother Russell sat on the porch and watched Amelia as she stood waiting.

Newt swerved his pickup truck, and stopped in front of her, sending gravel and dust flying. Mother Russell sat stiff and straight. Fearful, she held the boys and watched this mean spirited man lean out the truck window saying, "Hey gal, you gotta live in Kalb Kove after you're out from under the Judge's sight," he barked. She looked down and turned away.

His rage and hatred for the Negro simmered to the surface as always. He cocked and pointed his rifle even with her head. Mother Russell and the neighbors looked on in terror and helplessness. She tried to cover her grandsons eyes from the spectacle out front.

"Nigger, don' t you turn away from me!" Newt exploded. "I'll blow your uppity head clean off, Judge or no Judge! You better face me when I talk to you!" Amelia turned slowly and raised her eyes to his. Her lips were pressed together, and her face blanched with fear. "Look at me, you black bitch! You got two pickaninnies. Any more trouble outta you, and you'll get you a night visit. If you're not too dumb to understand, I'll make it clear, all of you can be wiped out," he snapped his fingers, "Like that, think about it," he threatened.

Tears welled up in her eyes, then spilled down her cheeks. He uncocked the gun, saying, "We don't need no more coons in this town!" His tires kicked up gravel as he sped away.

Amelia stood stunned, unable to move after the encounter.

"Amelia, chile?" Mother Russell called timidly. The neighbors started toward her.

Amelia held up her hand to stop them. "I'm alright, take care of the boys. I'll be fine Mother Russell, all of you.

I'm alright, just take care of my boys," Amelia repeated. Her voice was shaking.

CHAPTER TWELVE

John, the Devereaux driver, arrived to pick Amelia up as she dried her tears. He came to a slow stop, and waved to Mother Russell, who sat frozen on the porch. Amelia leaned into the automobile, "I thought the sheriff was coming?" she asked, with a quiver in her voice.

He could see the terror in her eyes, "The Judge told me to come today. Get in, up here with me." She climbed into the front seat, and he drove smoothly away. They didn't speak while she made a visible effort to calm herself. Finally, "What did he say to you?" John asked.

"Who?" she responded.

"Who else?" John replied. "That ole Newt Gingsted."

"He just threatened me and my family, is all. He said they didn't need anymore coons in this town," she said, her voice filled with loathing.

"Tell the Judge." John said.

"What good, would that do?! He's one of them! Can't you see that?!" she exclaimed.

"Want me to tell 'im?" John asked.

"He won't do anything about it," Amelia said. "If I had been a white woman, I wouldn't be working off this sentence."

"He might have saved your life. Thank God, you're alive and can work," he said. John was, what was known as an uncle Tom. He kept the white man apprised of what happened in the black community.

"Mr. Johnson, you sound just like him!" she accused.

"I've seen colored people lynched for less," he said.

"Look at ole Moses, he never did nothing, and he's dead."

"I need to get away from here! Go back to Philadelphia! Never should have come back here!" she said desperately looking around like a caged animal.

"Don't run off! You'll be in a whole lotta trouble if you do. Amelia you stay and work it out, then leave.

"I'll try, but it'll be hard," she said.

"These are trying times, your children need you. Specially since their daddy is over seas," he said, driving on. The big car was the ultimate in comfort; something most Negro men of that day could only dream of. John changed the subject, "How is Eddie?" she smiled for the first time since she had left home. The smile transformed her face into a radiant and delightful image. "Now that's better, a smile on your pretty face," John said, laughing.

"He can't tell me much," Amelia answered, "But he's been in the thick of the fighting for some time now."

"When things get rough, think of your husband Eddie. And you can always talk to a' old man like me. I'm good company." She laughed out loud. John continued, "This will be over someday and you and your family can live like human beings."

"Thank you, Mr. Johnson. I needed that little pick me up, this morning," she answered, looking over the land, pondering while they rode along.

John turned into the tree lined drive to Devereaux Manor. Affluence and abundance were all around, and she couldn't lead a quiet, peaceful life until Eddie came home.

"Amelia I'm a' old man, so take it from one who knows," John said. "The South is no place to raise a colored family in this day and age."

"Yes I know, but I needed help when Eddie went into the Army. We discussed it, and Mother Russell said she would be glad to help out. So here I am," she replied.

"You'll get out as soon as you can when Eddie get's back. And don't come down here no more 'til things get better. The 1950's is not the time for a colored man," John stated. They arrived at the Manor. John drove around to the back and stopped a moment to chat.

"Things will never change down here, these people have it made. The law is on their side, and we don't stand a chance," she said.

"Chile my grandmother always said, the bottom rail would rise to the top someday," he said, prophetically.

"We're definitely, the bottom rail," Amelia agreed. "You have to trust in God's word."

"Yeah 'in God we trust' and they get the cash, right?" she said, laughing, and squeezed John's hand. Amelia climbed out of the limousine and entered the house by the back door.

Inside the sun porch breakfast room, the panoramic view stretched past the gardens of flowering plants. Neat rows of servant quarters nestled among the trees. The view reached the river and parts of the bay. Negro workmen were already in the fields. Others were en the way to their assigned jobs.

Those in the fields were hard at work, and bent their jacks to the drudgery. Black muscles coiled, rippled and gleamed in the sunlight, while sweat dripped from their pores.

Aaron sipped his coffee and watched the conversational exchange between John and Amelia. From his vantage point, Amelia climbed out cf the car revealing shapely legs above the knees. She wore a simple, starched and ironed, cotton dress.

Her resemblance to Josephine Baker was more evident in the

sunlight. She walked with the same spring in her step, a vitality for life. He smiled and left the window. While he remembered his visits to the Paris theaters, Aaron walked to his seat, to read the paper.

Laura stood in the door and watched him sip from his cup. He had a good face and smile, if he smiled. A strong chin. His dark hair accentuated his green eyes. Aaron set his cup down, then stood to leave. Laura came the rest of the way into the breakfast room. "I'll be home for lunch," he said, as he went toward the door.

"Do you want something special?"

"Tell Cora, she knows what I like," he said, and kissed her on the cheek then left the room.

Cora brought orange juice and coffee, asking, "What can I get you to eat this morning Miz Devereaux?"

"This will do just fine Cora," Laura answered. The maid turned to leave. "Oh Cora, the judge will be home for lunch."

"Yes ma'am. Miz. Devereaux you can't nourish the body on what you eat," Cora said, concerned.

"I don't want anything," she said.

"I have just the thing. It's been known to whet your appetite, Cora coaxed.

Laura's laughter transformed her beautiful face into a vision seldom seen in the past weeks. Her drinking and smoking was excessive, more than Aaron had imagined.

"If it's that powerful, bring it on Cora," Laura said. Cora left the room. Laura's smile vanished, and her face closed into it's usual depressed lines. She went to the window and stared out at the bay, just as another troubled Devereaux wife had in the past. Negro children from surrounding plantations played along the hillside, near the bay. The workers in the fields raised their voices in a rhythmical song, as their ancestors had over hundreds of years. The cadence was repeated over and over again, in different, throbbing beats.

The Devereaux estate had always been a happier place than most plantations. Henri Devereaux treated the slaves like human beings; moreover he freed them. They were given the option to leave, or stay with him, for pay. This was unheard of in those days. All children were educated on the grounds. The school bell rang, and they had to go inside.

Most were smart, bright eyed and some were exceptional. Colleen had started the school in her lifetime, her one burning desire before her death.

Laura watched the children, a cruel reminder of her failure to bare an heir for Aaron. She poured a stiff drink and took that first scalding swallow of the day, then turned back to the window with a cigarette. Laura drank and smoked in the beginning at parties, but now liquor had become a soft, soothing, calming and somnolent crutch. Her means of escape from the realities of her life.

Her physicians had told her she would never have children. She was resigned to that. Laura had heard them say that drinking was a detriment, and smoking added to the problem. Perhaps, she had tried to escape from the harsh reality of being matron of Devereaux Manor, a considerable responsibility.

Laura never had to deal with the power that the Devereaux name had placed on her delicate shoulders, a heavy load for her to bare. Her father, had been her shield and benefactor, the purpose of her life before her marriage.

Actually was what to wear to a ball, the latest hair style, and who would be there to see them, handsome eligible bachelors, and who was the best looking. Women were not heard in her time. They were pretty fluffs of fragile humanity, to be placed on a pedestal to see, never to discuss anything of substance.

A true Southern belle was not the weak stripling of a girl. Instead, she was a tower cf strength who could and would fight like a tiger for her family, and proper Southern values. Acceptance was difficult to attain for outsiders.

Sisterhood, among women of all races, was not a visible sight to see. Some Southern women treated Negro servants as chattel. Perhaps because they were in a certain kind of bondage hemselves,   they would strike cut at the people who could not fight back. When there were those, who in their own quiet, God fearing way, gave comfort to the least powerful.

Laura mused about how alcohol had caused her declined sexual gratification, that along with tobacco abuse. The ways some human beings follow for relief from the tensions and anxiety in their lives. Most probably, it was not the peer group, but a significant family member who served as an alcoholic model in the formative years.

Laura's depression had manifested itself over several years. There was no consolation, and she always felt tired. Her mood swings went from great highs, to abominable lows. She didn't feel physically ill, but she was not comfortable either, and couldn't meet her obligations. She appeared beautiful and normal between drunken binges.

In her youth, there was talk that her daddy had another family in the French Quarter, a brood of halfsisters and brothers 3he had never met. Her father would be gone for long periods. During those days or weeks her mother stayed in her room. The servants would say with knowing looks that the mistress had the vapors. Laura giggled, "I always wanted to know what the vapors meant, now I know," she said, and swallowed the last of her drink, then poured another before going back to the window.

The Georgia Belle had been restored, it was a lovely sight as it cruised down the Savannah. The side wheels turned smoothly forward, a steady beat as the water boiled like a cauldron underneath the paddles.

The children came out for recess, and were thrilled as they ran along the bank. They waved and called to the workmen on board the riverboat. The Captain signaled to the second officer to pull the cord twice. The bell jangled, as great white clouds of smoke belched from the smokestacks.

Cora came back with her breakfast, saying, "Come on chile, have some breakfast. I made it special."

Laura went reluctantly to the table, and was pleasantly surprised to find foods she had enjoyed in New Orleans.

"Oh Cora! Who told you what I liked for breakfast?!"

"I have my ways Miz. Devereaux," Cora answered.

"You take such good care of me Cora, thank you," Laura said, hugging the maid's arm. She ate more than toast for the first time in a week. Later she went outside. While in an expansive mood, Laura walked in the gardens. The Oleander plants were in bloom, lavenders, crepe myrtles mixed with acacia and fragrant magnolia trees. Her view from this particular garden faced the river, lined with weeping willow trees. Wind blew the drooping limbs gently; there was a wealth of wild flowers bursting with color. Then she looked up at the balcony in the rear of the manor where the iron work was as delicate as fine lace. The master bedroom had a view on three sides of the creek, and the land beyond, the river, to parts of the bay, and the cozy little cabin with the breezeway.

Laura walked past the kitchen house, and down to the river through the grove of weeping willow trees. She sat in the shade on the cool grass. She had everything to live for; nevertheless, she was in despair.

"Why, am I here?" she murmured, staring at the gentle flow of the river. "God, I need a drink!" then started back to the manor. The sun was uncomfortably hot, and beat down on her as she walked to the mansion which appeared so far away.

CHAPTER THIRTEEN

In the living room after lunch, Amelia washed the bay windows that overlooked the oak-lined drive to the manor, and a large part of the bay.

Aaron entered and sipped his coffee, put the cup on the mantle, then walked toward her. Amelia cleaned the glass vigorously; intent on her task. A film of perspiration formed on her forehead. Her face glowed from the exertion.

"Amelia?" he said, softly, when he stood beside her. Startled, she turned and stumbled over the bucket.

He laughed and held her shoulders to steady her, saying, "I didn't mean to scare you." She looked into his steady gaze momentarily, then quickly away. "I want you to work the night of the dinner party. Will mother Russell be able to keep your children?" Aaron asked. He could smell the warm must of her. His hands lingered on her shoulders longer than necessary.

Amelia nodded.

"John will pick you up, and the hours will be deducted from your sentence," he said.

"Yes, sir."

He left the room while she turned to the windows angrily. She threw the wet rags into the bucket, causing the water to splash on the floor. A look of dismay crossed her face, as she attacked the problem of cleaning it up.

She frowned as her anger boiled to the surface. "Bastard! It's not enough I have to work in this damned house," she said, vehemently. "Now, I have to work for his miserable entertainment!" Tears formed in the corners of her eyes and spilled down her cheeks. She wiped them angrily on her sleeves, then finished the windows. "Life for some is not fair! I should have stayed in Philadelphia!" she muttered, angrily.

Aaron's view from the limousine was her as she stretched to reach the top panes to clean. A wry, smile appeared momentarily. John watched him knowingly in the rear view mirror. His jaws clinched in an antipathy he could not show in the South because of his fear of death.

Supper was over, and the guests were in the grand ballroom. The chandeliers shone like stars against the high ceiling. The ballroom floor was crowded with dancing couples. While guests moved in and out of the French doors to the Veranda's in the moonlight, waiters weaved their way through chatting groups of couples with platters of food and drinks.

The orchestra was flown in from New Orleans, and played a Nocturne. Amelia served hot hors d'oeuvres to three women, the biggest known gossips in Kalb Kove. They kept her there as they picked over the platter of food. "Everything looks so good. I don't know what to eat!" Joan said, then tasted a morsel.

"We could keep the whole thing here, just for us," Elsie snickered.

"Take something, you can always go back," Lyza urged.

"The girl can bring the tray back too," Elsie said, and waved Amelia away.

Joan elbowed Lyza in the ribs. "Ouch! Why did you do that?!" Lyza asked, rubbing her side.

"Look!" Joan whispered loudly. "Look! Look at our hostess, she's getting as drunk as a skunk!"

"She smokes like a chimney, and she's so pretty too. What a shame, it's such a waste," Elsie added.

Laura was having another of many drinks, a cigarette constantly in her hand. She was beginning to teeter as she made her way to the bar. "That's at least, five drinks since I've been here," Lyza pointed out, self-righteously.

"She's from some family in New Orleans, probably drank all the time," Elsie said. "She's not a true Southern belle, she doesn't belong here in Kalb Kove."

"The first family in New Orleans I heard," Lyza whispered behind her hand. "You know, she can't have children."

"It's a shame too. All that money and no heir to leave it to," Joan sniffed.

"I hear she lost three babies already," Elsie paused.

"Well, don't worry about the money," she moved closer, to impart some of her knowledge. "I know for a fact, the Devereaux's have a whole bunch of half-breed kids in France. They educated 'em all, and some of 'um are whiter than some of us," she finished, in a loud whisper and winked an eye at her friends.

"She's catholic you know. They can't get divorced," Joan added.

Lyza sat up straight and whispered, "Oh, oh there she goes again." Laura came into view and moved toward the bar. "My maid told me, she smokes and drinks like a man."

"We know how the coloreds talk amongst themselves," Elsie said.

"Well, she shouldn't talk about a white woman that way, even if Laura doesn't belong," Lyza said, self-righteously.

"Oh, I ask her things and she tells me. It's not like Laura is one of us you know," Joan said. Aaron came around the corner at that time.

Elsie placed her hand nervously on Joan's arm. "Oh Judge Devereaux, it's you! This is such a nice party and the 'food' is wonderful!" she said sweetly.

"I'm glad you ladies could come. True Southern ladies always brighten my day," Aaron said, then bowed politely. He took a drink from a passing waiter, and continued out to the veranda.

The women whispered behind their hands when he was out of hearing range. "That poor man," Lyza said pityingly.

"No better for him, he could have married a nice girl from his home town," Joan sniffed indignantly.

Outside a small church, 'The Knights of the Brotherhood' circled, yelling in the light of the fire. The church burned while they clamored. 'White purity! Our white purity! No educated Negras belong in Kalb Kove! We'll tell you what you ought to know! You can't think without a white man!" raucous laughter ensued. Newt bellowed above the brouhaha, "You people don't need to read! Pretty soon you darkies will want to marry our women, and run things," he said, over a hubbub of agreement from the crowd.

The party went on at Devereaux Manor while sounds of gaiety filled the air. Aaron stared into the darkness brooding as he sipped his drink.

"Amelia is a good looking wench," Tom said, and stood beside him.

"Exactly what Laura said. It comes from a lot of sleeping around through the years," Aaron chuckled. "She could sure take care of herself, when her mother worked for us, even as a little girl."

"She held her own with those yahoos, too," Tom replied. Aaron changed the subject. "There's another problem," he said after a long moment of silence.

"Yes I know. The respectable people of Kalb Kove want to clamp down on the 'Knights' rampages. It's certainly for our collective survival," Tom answered.

"I had two of them in my office. I'm positive Newt is behind all of it. He's a closed-minded man," Aaron answered.

"His brother's death put the pressure on, and that nitwit Billy Ray follows him around like a puppy," Tom said.

"Yep, maybe something should have happened to Newt and Billy Ray," Aaron suggested.

Tom straightened his shoulders, laughed and raised his glass in a salute, saying, "This my friend is a party! We can talk about that tomorrow. Now we eat, drink and make Mary."

They walked across the veranda and through the doors. Aaron went to the bandstand raising his hands for quiet, saying, "I would like to drink a toast to my lovely wife! Laura come up here sweetheart." She walked across the dance floor. Not quite drunk enough   stagger, she teetered on the edge. He took her hand and helped her to the platform. Aaron continued, "I want my neighbors to meet my beautiful wife." Then he hugged her affectionately. Laura's breath was whiskey ladened. Aaron frowned and kissed her cheek. Holding her tightly around the waist, he whispered angrily, "Stay away from the bar!" Then to the crowd, he continued, "Everybody, my wife, Laura Devereaux, my barren-ess." Laura stiffened and gasped, he held her steady. Aaron cupped her face gently with one hand, and said fiercely into her ear, "Wipe that look off your face and stay away from the damn bar!" The gathering applauded. "Everybody, the night is young! I'm going to dance with my wife! Enjoy yourself." Aaron lifted Laura down and they danced through the musical arrangement, her head nestled on his shoulder. To the guests they appeared just like any other happy couple. When the dance was over, he led Laura to a corner where Faith Lennox and a group of women chatted. Aaron went to the bar with his friends and proceeded to get drunk.

The next morning Laura stood gazing dispiritedly out the bedroom window. Aaron groaned and rolled over, then sat on the edge of the bed, holding his head in both hands.

Laura turned and leaned against the window frame, saying, "Aaron, you went to great lengths to be mean to me last night. Why?"

"Did I really? Then why do I feel so damn lousy?" he replied.

"Why can't we go back to the continent? We were good for each other. You never hurt me in Europe," Laura said.

"Did it ever occur to you that it might hurt me to see you drink yourself into a stupor every night?" he retorted. Shrugging into his robe, he started to the bathroom.

"And if I stopped?" she asked softly.

"Try it and see," he said, slamming the door.

After breakfast, he took Laura's hand and said, "Faith has invited you to the Country Club for the 'Women's Annual Luncheon' next Friday."

"Aaron! Must I go!" she exclaimed.

"You have to get out more, meet people. They're just like any other group of human beings; they live and gossip. You might like them," he said.

Laura mulled it over. "It's true, Faith isn't like the others. She's friendly. I think she likes me," Laura said.

"She can introduce you to the rest of Kalb Kove." He laid the paper down, saying, "I'll see you at supper." On his way out he looked into her eyes and kissed her on the lips.

Aaron walked through the wide hall and out the front door, into the cool morning breeze. "Good morning, John," he said.

"Good morning, Judge Devereaux." John closed the car door. Then went around to the driver's side and maneuvered the automobile to the road to town.

"John, what do you know about Amelia?" Aaron asked.

"Nothing much, yo'r honor."

"Do you know her husband, Eddie?" Aaron inquired.

"Yes sir, he's in Korea somewhere, and Amelia lives with his mother, until he gets home," John said eagerly.

"Does she expect him soon?" Aaron asked.

"I don't know Judge Devereaux, she didn't say."

"Find out when he's expected," Aaron instructed.

"I sure will, yo'r honor," John said, and was quiet for several seconds. "Judge?" he said, cautiously.

"Yes John?"

"Sir, I don't mean no harm, but ... yo'r honor ..."

"Go on, tell me what's on your mind, you can speak freely, you know that, John."

"Ah ... ah ... Mr. Newt made a threat against Amelia and her family," John said, keeping his eyes on the rear view mirror to make sure he was not in trouble for talking against a white man.

"When?" Aaron asked.

"The first day I picked her up, yo'r honor."

"You saw him there?"

"Yes, Judge."

"I want you to keep me informed. If anything like that happens again, tell me right away," Aaron instructed.

"She's scared, yo'r honor. So scared she talked about running. I told her not to get herself in no more trouble."

"That was good advice, John." Aaron sat silently staring out the car window; although he didn't really see the wild flowers along the roadside. The lush green trees did not exist in his contemplation. When he returned from his reflection, "Stop at Dr. Crane's office, John," he ordered.

"Yes sir, Judge."

"Leave the car for me. I'll drive myself home tonight. Jessie Lee can take you back this morning," Aaron replied.

Across town in the Depot Cafe, Newt and Billy Ray had finished breakfast. A country western song blared from the jukebox. Newt held a warm coffee mug between both hands. Then with more sensitivity than usual, said, "Billy Ray, Nate was my only good friend after my daddy died, besides you," Newt's voice was gentle.

"Well thank you, Newt," Billy Ray said, grinning like a big fuzzy dog being petted by his master.

"I remember my daddy saying when Nate and me was born, the Brotherhood had strung up a black buck that night, and when he got home, he had two boys of his own," Newt chuckled. "You get it? Two for one," then he paused. "I miss my brother," he said sighing.

"The brotherhood goes back that far, Newt?" Billy Ray asked.

"Yep, my daddy run it, and turned it over to Nate and me before he passed on," Newt said.

"You was twins. You was just like each other," Billy Ray said extraneously.

"I swear at times 'we thought alike'," Newt chuckled.

"You was the spit and image of each other, Newt."

Newt sat up straight suddenly in his seat, staring out the window frowning. "Did you see that?! Did you see what that nigger did?" he said.

"What?! Who? What happened?" Billy Ray asked, looking around baffled.

Newt shoved his chair over violently, and ran out of the cafe. Billy Ray followed as Newt took long galloping strides. Outside, Newt grabbed a black boy by the arm, spinning him around. The patrons of the cafe stared from the window.

"Nigger! Who do you think you are? Walking on the sidewalk, next to a white woman?!" Newt barked.

"What?" the boy asked, surprised.

"Don't you say 'what' to me, black boy!" the youngster was dumbfounded. "You step off the sidewalk when you meet a white woman! Get that through your thick, nappy head! Do you understand me!?" Newt yelled.

"Yes," the boy replied.

"Yes, sir!" Newt shouted. He squinted, his eyes, "You one of them uppity black boys! Where you from, boy?"

"Yes, sir! New York, sir!" the Negro said.

"You gonna learn some manners while you're here, boy!" The youngster didn't show the fear Newt expected. "Don't you look at me like that! I'll blow your nappy head right off," Newt said, taking his gun from his belt, aiming it at the boy's head. The teenager sweated profusely, turning he ran in terror. Newt shot him in the back and continued to fire until the gun was empty; the townspeople scattered. The gauntlet had been tossed. A killing in the street in broad daylight. The challenge to be taken up by anyone who had the courage.

Jessie Lee, and his deputy witnessed the murder. "We gotta get outta here!," the sheriff said.

"You got it right, let's go! I don't want to know about this!" Jake said. Grabbing his hat. They scrambled out the back door.

The scene, unfolded outside the cafe as Billy Ray turned the boy over. He shoved an open knife into his limp hand. 'Nothing else for me to do but kill him Newt" Billy Ray said. Then he took the gun from Newt's hand; hatred still distorted Newt's features.

"Billy Ray, get somebody to clean up this mess," Newt sneered, then spun around and stalked into the cafe. A few Negro townspeople at Billy Ray's order, moved the body to the colored undertaker.

CHAPTER FOURTEEN

Jessie Lee stood across from Judge Devereaux, "You say it was self-defense?" the Judge asked.

"All the witnesses say so, your honor," the sheriff said, but could never quite bring his eyes to meet Aaron's.

"Jessie Lee, that boy was shot in the back 'six times'," Judge Devereaux said, in perplexity.

"Billy Ray was protecting Newt, from that uppity nigger from New York, judge."

Aaron clinched his teeth momentarily. "That word, is never to be used in my presence again. I told you about that before," he said, in a deadly tone.

"I'm sorry your honor, I forgot," the sheriff answered, sheepishly.

"Don't let it happen again, or you'll suffer the consequences!" Judge Devereaux warned.

"It won't happen again your honor," Jessie Lee said, and swallowed nervously.

"Bring Newt and Billy Ray in," the judge said. The sheriff sprang for the door and returned with the men. Newt swaggered in. Billy Ray followed with more confidence than ever before. Judge Devereaux's anger was apparent when he asked, "Now, tell me exactly what happened?"

Billy Ray spoke first, "This black boy from up North was giving Newt some back talk." Newt nodded in agreement. The sheriff nervously twisted his hat in his hands. "One thing led to another," Billy Ray continued. "Then this black fella pulled out a knife. Your honor, I couldn't let him cut Newt. You know how they are, I had to back shoot him!"

"It happened just like that, your honor," Newt said, with thinly veiled seriousness.

"Go on, Newt," Judge Devereaux prompted. The story left a bitter taste in Aaron's mouth. The Judge knew it was a lie, but he had no proof.

"I was telling that colored boy, when he meets a white woman on the street, the law says he steps off the sidewalk to let her go by."

"Newt, I make the law in this town, and that's not one. My grandfather adapted the city charter for Kalb Kove, and it's not there!" Aaron's voice was fierce.

"He walked right next to one of our white women in broad daylight!" Newt replied. "Then he looked back at her. T couldn't let him get away with that!" his answer, was bad-tempered and just as fervently stated.

"Any more witnesses?" Aaron asked.

"Yes, your honor, the people on the street and the cafe, they all said the same thing," the sheriff answered.

Judge Devereaux glared sternly at them, his voice barely above a whisper, "You will understand this clearly! I won't tolerate anymore killing in Kalb Kove. This town has been a safe place to live and work, it will be again! Do you understand!" His voice had risen while he spoke, and rang out as he talked.

"Yes sir, we understand, yo' honor, sir," Newt said, impudently.

"Yes sir, Billy Ray echoed, but had lost some of his bravado.

"Now get the hell out of my office. I don't want to see you here for anything like this again!" the judge ordered.

Billy Ray and the sheriff scurried out. Newt followed with deliberate arrogance. The law was friends of the white man, and they felt free to do as they pleased.

Outside Aaron's office there was a heater vent. Through which voices carried into his office. The three men stood momentarily near the outlet. Judge Devereaux turned in his chair when their voices filtered through. "Newt, I told you the judge would be mad!" Jessie Lee said.

"To hell with Judge Devereaux! He'll have to reckon with me soon." Their voices were cut off when they closed the outside door. Jessie Lee's response wasn't heard.

Aaron's manner had changed stoically as he picked up the telephone receiver, dialed and waited. "Tom, we have to talk." He listened. "After supper, in the Tack Room."

The judge was nursing a drink when Tom arrived. "Aaron, I thought I would be here ahead of you. You should be home with your pretty wife," Tom joked.

"I had some serious thinking to do, Tom," Aaron replied.

"I know the problem," Tom said.

"Yes. I'm glad you came early. I needed to talk with you about the shooting," Aaron said, taking the last drink from his glass.

"Just name it," Tom sampled his drink.

"You're right about the Knights. I have an idea how to get them under control, but it'll take time."

"Newt's hatred of the Negro was more fierce than normal. It's more like a preoccupation with him," Torn said, turning to the waiter, signalng for a refill, "Another bourbon and branch, Josh." Then to Aaron, "I've checked and it seems, Newt's wife ran off   with a Negro soldier from Clay County. He's been even meaner after that. And poor Billy Ray has followed him around like a lackey recruit, agreeing with everything that degenerate does."

"I have a few calls to make tonight," Aaron said, slapping his palms down on the table. "Thanks for coming, Tom. It's clear what needs to be done. I think I'll get home to the little woman," Aaron said, tipping Josh.

On a back road late in the night. Newt followed an old pickup truck, with a hound dog that rode in the back. The animals head hung over the side of the truck bed. Newt watched the truck weave back and forth over the narrow rutted road. The dog swayed in the moonlight, with the motion of the pickup. When the drivers came to a wide spot in the road, Newt pulled up beside J.D.'s vehicle and tapped the horn. "Hey partner!" Newt shouted.

"Hold on Newt!" J.D. yelled back, then maneuvered the truck to the edge of the lake. He climbed unsteadily from the cab of the pickup. Newt stopped in back of the vehicle. "Newt ole buddy!" J.D. said, taking out a pint of moonshine and drinking from the jar. "Want some?" he asked, offering the container to Newt.

Newt took the jar and looked at the liquor with a smirk, then handed it back, saying, "No, you go ahead. I don't like that kind."

"Don't mind if I do," J. D. chuckled, then took another drink from the jar. "That's smoooth, the best I ever made. Newt, what brings you out this way?" J.D. asked, not seeing the look of hatred burning in Newt's eyes. All he saw was his friend's fake smile.

"J.D., you're not scared to drive this back road by the swamp all by yourself?" Newt asked, pointedly.

"Nope, ole Dodger is with me, and my pickup truck is trained to go home on the darkest night," he said, and patted his truck.

"You ought to be careful, something could happen to you out here all alone. These are treacherous times," Newt warned.

"I been coming this way since I was knee high to a duck's ass. Ain't nothing happen yet, Newt," J.D. laughed.

"One of these night's, your luck's gonna run out," Newt said.

J.D., still didn't get the import of Newt's remarks. He was involved with the jar of moonshine. "You sure you don't want some of this? Best I ever made. It'll grow hair on naked balls," J.D. said, laughing at his own joke.

"You been over to Big Sadie's?" Newt asked.

"Yep," J.D. said, sipping the liquor.

"I told you, your pecker's gonna fall off if you don't stop screwing that Colored broad," Newt said.

"Newt, I got something to tell you I never told nobody before," J.D. chuckled, screwing the top on the jar. "Me and Sadie got a son in 'Deeetroit'. Cutest little fella, looks like me. Newt think about it, somebody who looks just like me!" Newt's face hardened, his eyes cold with hatred. He slowly took the Bowie knife from the sheath on his belt.

The little man still hadn't noticed until now, too late, the change in his so-called friend. He saw the knife as Newt advanced threateningly toward him. His eyes widened and he dropped the jar, saying. "Newt we've been friend's all our life!"

"No nigger lover is a friend of mine!" was Newt's deadly reply. He moved slowly and deliberately toward the frightened little man.

"We'll leave town! Yes, that's what we'll do, leave town!" J.D. said, stumbling over the rut as he backed away. "Newt please, don't do this! You won't never see us again!"

"Too late for that now. You brought another nigger into the world," Newt said. He grabbed J.D., drew his hand back and viciously, delivering the first deadly thrust.

"Newt! No! No! Please! No!" J.D. pleaded. "Aaaaahhhhh."

Newt maliciously stabbed J.D., quickly looking around stealthily, and lowered the body to the ground.

A Negro man on his way home heard J.D.'s cries, and looked through the brush in time to see Newt stab J.D. repeatedly. The dog jumped out of the bed of the truck. He whined and ran back and forth barking.

The Black man moved back into the darkness of the trees. Newt looked quickly around again, kicking at the circling, barking dog, "Get away from here, you damn mutt!" The black man watched Newt drag the body to the driver's side, then shove it behind the wheel of the pickup. J.D.'s killer released the hand brake and waited while the truck rolled down the incline into the swamp. Newt stooped and washed his hands and knife in a pool of water, then kicked dirt over the blood in the road.

The dog continued to bark from a distance. Newt lit a cigar and stayed until the slime covered the letters of the make of the truck. "I told you your pecker would fall off! That black bitch is next!" Newt shouted, and climbed in his truck and drove away. His deranged laughter could be heard across the lake, if anybody had been listening. The dog howled in the wake of the truck.

At a shack deep in the woods, the Negro man who had witnessed the killing, knocked loudly on the door. He yelled repeatedly, "Sadie! Wake up! Sadie! Wake up!" A dim light was turned on, inside the front room of the shack.

A large Creole woman flung the door open. "What do you want?" she said. Then less savagely, "Mr. Sams, what's wrong?"

"I just saw Newt kill J.D.! They're on the way here now! You best to get outta here directly!" She stood frozen with fright. Mr. Sams had to shake her to get her to move. "Sadie! You gotta hurry! I'll take you, but you gotta come on, now!" he said urgently.

She sprang into action as precious time passed. Finally she came out buttoning her dress. They jumped in Mr. Sam's old car. He tried numerous times to start the engine, as Sadie watched anxiously. "Take me to the Clark County Depot," she said.

"I have a little money, we kin probably get some more on the way to the depot," he answered, and worked desperately to start the automobile.

"That's alright Mr. Sams, I have some. J.D. took care of me tonight," she said. The battery weakened, then died completely.

Farther away down the road, three pickup trucks filled with the sheeted figures of 'The Knights of The Brotherhood' were on the way to her house. The hooded rabble shouted as the trucks rumbled along the dirt road.

Mr. Sams and Sadie tried repeatedly to start old cars motor, "Come on, we'll have to push! Hurry!" he shouted, scrambling out of the car. She didn't move quickly enough,

"Come on, woman! You gotta help me push!" Mr. Sams yelled.

"I'm going as fast as I can," she replied. Then they saw the headlights of the trucks through the trees as they came closer. The shouts grew louder and more raucous with every passing second.

Sadie and Mr. Sams, struggled frantically as they pushed the car every agonizing inch to the edge of the downgrade. "We just have to get it to the top of the hill. It'll roll down from there. We kin get it started on the slope," Mr Sams said. They strained to roll the car the last few yards. The shouts from the Brotherhood were heard near the bend in the road, just a short distance away. The trucks came around the curve as the old car rolled down the hill. It was swallowed up in the darkness and out of sight when the motor caught.

The trucks rolled to a stop in front of the shack. A lone light burned inside the shack. "Kill the nigger bitch!" One Knight shouted. The cross was raised, and someone set it on fire. Torches burned, lighting the darkness.

"Sadie! Come on outta there gal!" Newt bellowed among a hubbub of shouts.

"Let's go on in there, and get her out." Billy Ray said.

"No use hiding! Come on out, or we'll come in and get you!" Newt called.

"Drag her on out here!" the mob hailed.

"Hang the nigger bitch!" they yelled.

"Go in and get the black slut!" Newt ordered.

They rushed the shack and kicked in the door, broke windows, and tossed over the sparse furniture. Billy Ray came out, "Nobody in there Newt, he said.

"Search the bushes, that shed and the crib out back!" Newt's commanded.

They searched everywhere. Billy Ray came back, "Sadie ain't no where to be found, Newt."

"Burn the son-of-a-bitch down to the ground! And let's get the hell outta here!" Newt ordered. He was furious, and it showed. The Brotherhood tossed torches on the roof, and through the broken windows. The shack burned like a tinder box of matches.

Inside the sheriff's office two weeks later. Deputy Sykes poured a cup of coffee. "J.D., that ole moonshiner disappeared over two weeks ago," Jessie Lee pointed out.

"Along about the time Big Sadie's shack burned down and they ain't been seen since," Sykes answered.

"What you think happened?" Jessie Lee asked.

Sykes shrugged his shoulders. "I ain't paid to think, that's your job sheriff," he said, then made a face when he tasted his coffee.

"I'm gonna nose around Kalb Kove. You go on out to Joe Leigh's Kit Kat Klub, see what you can find out, Sykes."

"That ale hound dog of J.D.'s has howled out by Swamp Glen all the time. Everybody living up hill from the swamp's, been complaining," the deputy answered.

"Judge Devereaux ain't gonna like this, one bit!" the sheriff said, shaking his head. "Coming so close to the killing of that colored boy from New York. Then the shack burning down and all."

Deputy Sykes set his cup on the shelf, and adjusted his cowboy hat, then left the office. Jessie Lee lingered a while longer, as deep lines of worry creased his brow.

Aaron sat in Torn Lennox's office. His back was to the window that overlooked the floor of the store. "We've had a Negro church, with all the books donated to the children burned, and now two more disappearances," he said.

"Aaron, we have no proof of any foul play. It's frustrating, our hands are tied. We need facts," Torn said.

"We know who's behind all of it. Tom, it's long past time for action. Who knows what'll happen next?" Aaron said.

"You're right, they've gotten too big for their breeches. I agree, we need to do something, but what?" Torn asked.

"Nobody will talk? Townspeople are afraid to move," Aaron paused. "I know of men who might help. I'll call again tonight. It's not easy to set up. I want you to talk to the other merchants," Aaron said, pacing the floor.

Actually, Aaron was tall for a Devereaux, over six feet. At another time in his life, he would be considered urbane. However, this was not the time for sophistication.

"Good idea. We could use some assistance. Let me know what I can do from this end," Tom offered.

"Newt went so far as to threaten Mother Russell, and her family," Aaron said. "Before their neighbors."

"Yeah. He's that kind of son-of-a-bitch," Tom said, leaning on his desk. "I'm worried about a race riot. The same as in Mississippi and Birmingham last year," Tom asked.

"Yes, and God help us if that happens here. There are Negro soldiers coming home from Korea. Most of them bring weapons home."

"They've been to war for this country, and have to come home to find the same old, Jim Crow laws," Tom pointed out.

"They won't take it Tom, and shouldn't have to."

"It scares the hell outta me," Tom admitted.

"I'll call you later," Aaron said, turning to go. He waved as he closed the door softly.

Tom had a view through the window of Aaron when he walked across the aisles of the store. Drumming his fingers on the desk as he gazed over the store. He thought, Faith's and my years of hard work could go up in flames. Their accomplishments gone in a matter of minutes.

In the Lincoln Town car, Aaron drove slowly past Mother Russell's shack. The two women laughed and talked in pantomime, while two small boys played nearby. A neighbor strummed a guitar, and sang a popular blues song. In a dark lane in the shadows, a distinctive pickup truck was parked at an angle for Newt to see everything that happened. He watched Judge Devereaux when the big car drove in front of his vantage point. Newt chuckled quietly, "Well, well, well, could this be a taste for dark meat, maybe? Or just looking over the situation, yo' honor?" he said softly, and chewed on the unlighted cigar. As the luxury car passed within a few yards of his truck, his cold blue eyes followed the annoyance of his life from beneath heavy lids. The look was sly, calculating and reflective. "Well now, Judge Aaron Devereaux, I'll see you later," Newt said, vehemently. His laughter was a crazed cackle. He slapped his hand on the steering wheel.

The hilarity never reached his frigid stare. "Dark meat, I got you now, Mr. high and mighty judge. I'll be watchin' and waitin'," and drove off as his deranged laughter reverberated in the cab of the truck.

At Devereaux Manor the next day, Amelia was cleaning the hearth. Aaron sat close enough to see the thin film of perspiration on her forehead while she attacked her chores vigorously.

Laura bustled in like a dainty Barbie Doll. "Aaron the Country Club luncheon is in two days, and I don't have a thing to wear," she said, her Southern accent clearly evident.

He stopped reading and encircled her slender waist with one arm. "We can remedy that, John will drive you to Savannah tomorrow. You can shop the day away. I'll drive myself to the office," Aaron said.

"I want to knock this town on it's ear!" Laura said, looking at herself in the picture window, she pirouetted to gaze at her figure.

"I'm sure you will, dear," Aaron said, folding the paper to leave the room after kissing Laura lightly on the lips.

Laura turned and stared at Amelia who was putting her cleaning equipment away. "Amelia? That is your name isn't it?" she asked.

"Yes ma'am." Amelia replied.

"Aaron told me your mother worked for the Devereaux family," Laura said.

"Yes ma'am, she was Mrs. Devereaux's personal maid."

"Where is your mother now?" Laura asked.

"Mother died, soon after we moved to Philadelphia," Amelia answered.

"I'm so sorry!" Laura responded, sorrowfully.

"She died some time ago. I'm grateful she didn't have to suffer," Amelia said, turning to the cleaning materials.

"I see you're finished there," Laura said. " I have a dress to be ironed. It's on the ironing board in the pantry."

"Yes ma'am," Amelia answered.

"Be careful of the lace, it takes a warm iron, understand?" Laura cautioned.

"Yes ma'am, I understand," Amelia said.

"Do you think you could address me as Mrs. Devereaux?" Laura asked. "Ma'am makes me feel old."

"Yes, Mrs. Devereaux," Amelia replied.

"That's better," Laura said, with delight. She was like a butterfly, and danced happily out of the room. The changes in her moods had been a mystery to the servants.

"Whoop tee do! I get to iron the mistress' dress now," Amelia said sarcastically, and followed at a slower pace.

John drove Laura to Savannah. He would glance in the rear view mirror and smile at the flights of her thoughts. She changed her mind many times on the drive to Kalb Kove.

In town she saw Faith Lennox in front of Lennox Dry Goods Store. "John stop! I want to talk to Faith," she ordered. Then eagerly opened her window when he glided smoothly to a stop. "Good morning Faith! I'm on my way to Savannah, can you come shopping with me?" Laura asked.

"I wish I could Laura, but we have some merchandize that has to be uncrated. I need to be here to supervise the unpacking," Faith replied.

"Tom works you too hard," Laura pouted.

"I want to do it, keeps me involved. Laura, you look so lovely today!" Faith said.

"Thanks, Faith, you're delightful. I'd better go if I want to be back by suppertime."

"Have a good day," Faith said, and stepped up on the curb. The automobile drove away. Faith lingered a moment, then went inside.

"John, It's a glorious day!" Laura said expansively.

"Yes, ma'am, Miz Devereaux," he said.

She looked out the window happily as the automobile moved smoothly along.

Newt did not miss Laura's chat with Faith. He stood in the window of his shop and watched with squinted evil eyes. When the big car drove from sight, he turned back to his task, a beautifully handcrafted saddle. His great love for leather was evident in his work. He rubbed his hand lovingly over the smooth, shiny surface of the saddle, then looked closely at the contours in search of any flaw that might be there. Newt used a soft, clean cloth to polish the satiny, pliable leather. His father had taught him and his brother the craft. Now he was alone, to continue the art. He stopped polishing to gaze out the window, and his stair softened as he remembered his father and brother.

Aaron worked at his desk in his study, ledgers stacked before him.

Laura came in with a flourish. "I should go shopping more often! Everything was so wonderful! The gowns, The hats! Just everything!" she said, kissing him happily on the lips.

He leaned back in his chair, and smiled as she floated around the room. "It's good to see you laugh again," he said, quietly. Laura hugged him from behind and he gently touched her arm.

"You were right. I should get out more often, and I will," she said, going to the liquor cabinet, pouring a stiff drink. He frowned, but didn't comment. Laura walked to the door, and looked over her shoulder seductively. "I'm going to have this drink and a shower, then to bed. Won't you join me?" she asked.

"The books need quite a bit of work, it could take some time," he replied.

"Don't be long. I'll make it worth your while, and maybe even better," Laura said, giggling.

"I'll hurry," he said, and turned to the stack of work.

After several minutes, he tossed his pen on the desk. "To hell with this. I'm for that shower. The best offer I've had for a long time," he said, slamming the door. Moments later he went into the bathroom nude, and walked into the shower, saying, "Madam I'm here to soap your body."

"Aaron!" Laura said, giggling.

"I decided to take 'something better' and put a label on it later, he said, as their bodies fused in the spray.

CHAPTER FIFTEEN

Aaron walked to the car with Laura that Friday. His arm encircled her waist, when he kissed her good-bye. John held the door for her then went to the driver's side.

Aaron leaned in the open window, "Have a good day sweetheart," he said, then watched the car drive out of the spacious driveway.

Upstairs Amelia was cleaning the banister when Aaron came to the bedroom door, and said, "Amelia, the mirror in here need, polishing."

"Yes, sir," she replied.

He waited while she gathered her cleaning materials, then followed her into the bedroom, locking the door quietly. She polished the mirror to the dressing table. Aaron stood close behind her. Surprised, she tried to move away. "When will your husband come back from Korea?" he asked, touching her shoulder.

"Soon, Judge Devereaux," she said, trying to edge past him, but he grasped her around the waist. Amelia struggled against his clutches. She broke free and ran to the door. Aaron followed and hurled her across the room to the four poster bed. He grinned and pulled the zipper down in her dress, and shoved the top off her shoulders. She fought bravely, but he pinned her arms to her sides.

"You have a lot of fight," he said.

"Judge, please don't do this! The servants will hear!" she reasoned, grabbing at straws.

"Who? John is at the Country Club, and Cora, I sent to town for supplies. The others have chores elsewhere," Aaron said, pushing her down to the bed and dropping his robe to the floor, quickly undressing her. She resisted valiantly as she breathed in labored gasps. "What difference would it make if they were here? They can't help themselves, and no one would come to help you, sides again." he said, pinning her arms to her

"But judge, you're married! My husband is in Korea! Doesn't that mean anything? You can have anybody you want! Why me?!" she asked. He held her wrist when she tried to scratch his face, then ground his mouth down on hers. She resisted by turning her face from one side to the other. He moved his mouth down to her neck and shoulders, then tasted one breast and the other.

"Your husband can't help you here, in Georgia," Aaron whispered, brusquely. "He's far away, and your body was made for love. I've watched you and wanted you, and today I'll have you."

"No!" she cried angrily. Her desperate battle was no match for his.

At the Country Club the luncheon was over. Faith and Laura left the dining room. "This has been so much fun!" Laura bubbled.

"For me too. We'll have to do this again, soon," Faith answered.

"Oh I'm so late! I must go, Aaron is waiting!" Laura exclaimed.

"I'll walk you to your car," Faith said. In the parking lot they waved to ladies from the luncheon.

"John, take me home!" Laura said, expansively.

"Yes, Miz. Devereaux," John answered.

In the Devereaux bedroom, Aaron ground bruising kisses on Amelia's throat, her face and her lips. He could smell the perfume of her body, pushing him beyond reason. Their sweaty bodies molded together. Her desperation turned to pain when he entered her. His thrusts were rough and jarring. Aaron forced his kind of Southern carnality on Amelia, his envisioned omnipotence, and the taking of anything he wanted.

Sexual assault on a woman, black or white without her consent. Any charge of rape was not an option for Amelia. Aaron had unlimited mastery over her, and exercised his man given authority.

As John chauffeured the car through the streets of Kalb Kove. Laura enjoyed the ride. A breeze swayed the trees as they passed. The wild flowers were a kaleidoscope of colors. Laura chattered about everything from the luncheon to the flowering plants.

In the bedroom, Aaron lay spent when he rolled away from Amelia, breathing heavily. She sobbed as he turned back to her with one hand on her abdomen, and touched her breasts. "You were excellent. We'll have to do it again when there's more time," he said. His gaze, roamed over her body. "You'd better get dressed, my wife will be home soon, and don't forget to change the linen," he said. Before going to the bathroom, he turned to look at Amelia sitting in the middle of the bed, clutching the sheet to her bosom. Her shoulders and face were golden in the afternoon sunlight that filtered through the curtains. Aaron was taken aback by her attractiveness and vulnerability. In that instance, he had a moment of ambivalence. "You're a lovely woman. I would keep you close to me if you were mine," he quipped. Turning to touch her face, she cringed away. He went into the bathroom chuckling.

Amelia crawled slowly out of bed to get dressed, then jerked the sheets off the bed savagely.

He came through the bedroom, freshly showered and dressed. Aaron touched her shoulder, Amelia drew away. "I'll see you again soon, very soon," he said softly, his stare lascivious.

John drove through the tree lined drive to the Manor. Laura opened the car door on her own. She ran swiftly and daintily up the steps and opened the door into the entry hall. Aaron was halfway down the stairs when his wife whirled through the door. She was vivacious, delighted and bubbly. Laura laughed, and tossed her hat on the hall table with abandon. "Darling! I had a wonderful day! Faith and her friends are marvelous!" she declared.

He stepped off the bottom step as she threw herself into his arms. "I knew you would like it," he said, softly holding her. He watched over his wife's head when Amelia left the bedroom clutching the soiled linen and cleaning equipment, hurrying to the backstairs. "Come, tell me about it over a cool drink," Aaron continued, guiding Laura to the study.

That night while Aaron worked in his study the telephone rang. "Hello? Judge Devereaux here."

A man's voice with a rasp grated in his ear. "Be careful, your movements are watched. One of the watchers is in the yard of the woman given ninety days," he said.

"Is there a problem taking care of him?" Aaron asked.

"No," the voice answered.

"Do it," Aaron ordered. "Is the other matter resolved?"

"Done. The other situation will be completed soon," the voice replied. The connection was broken. Aaron turned his chair and gazed in meditation into the night. From Aaron's vantage point, there were areas of light in the servants' quarter.

Near a shed in the back of Amelia's house. Billy Ray, crept from one shadow to another. He looked around surreptitiously, then hastened across the yard to the house. He skirted the edge of the back porch, passing through a pool of moonlight to the bedroom window. In a dark wooded area, nearest the bedroom side of the house, two men watched his movements.

"Let's take him," said a harsh whisper. They used the shadows of the trees, as they crept closer. Billy Ray was about to pry the screen off the window, when one man slipped a leather noose around his throat. The other muffled his attempt to cry out. The victim struggled to breath, clawing at the garrote choking the life out of him. The men propelled him backward into the trees, and lowered his dead body to the ground. One tied a special and unique knot. "That does it for him, he's dead. Where do we put the body?" one asked.

"I know just the place," was the rasped answer, as they carried the body away.

Inside Amelia's bedroom, as she looked out the window when Mother Russell came in, "What's wrong chile?" she asked.

"It's nothing, Mother Russell. I thought I heard a noise, but I don't see anything."

"I'm not just talking about now. You had something on your mind when you got home today," Mother Russell said.

"I miss being home," Amelia said, smiling. She hugged the older woman. "Do you think you could get train tickets for the boys and me?" she asked.

"Will the judge let you go!? I don't want to cause you no more trouble." Worry creased Mother Russell's brow.

"I'll ask tomorrow. It's only for a few days," Amelia said.

"You know I'll help you anytime I can chile, if it's alright," she said, touching her daughter-in-law's face.

"You get some rest. I'll ask," she said. Mother Russell started out the door. "Mother, maybe you should get the tickets in your name, because I don't want any trouble with Newt Gingsted," Amelia added.

"You right. I'll do just that chile. I sure will." Mother Russell said, leaving the room.

Amelia stood at the window as tears spilled down her cheeks. She turned and fell into bed burying her face in the pillow. Her sobs shook her whole body. She was here, separated from her husband. Now, she was being emotionally drained, because of the life she was forced to lead. The trap was sprung, and she had spiraled down into the depth of despair. It was certain she had to get away, or at least try.

In front of Newt's neat white house, Billy Ray's body, was propped up behind the wheel of Newt's truck. The leather thong around his neck, squeezed a furrow in the soft tissue. His killers disappeared into the night before the body slumped over on the horn of the steering wheel. It blared loudly, shattering the quiet. Newt burst out of the front door with his gun drawn. When he saw Billy Ray in the dim light from the house, he lowered his weapon. "Billy Ray?" Newt yelled. There was no response as he crept nearer. "Billy Ray, what you doing in my pickup?! You better get your drunk ass, outta my truck!" still no response. He went to the driver's side and jerked the door open. "You damn fool!" The lifeless body of Billy Ray fell out of the truck at Newt's feet. The dim light from the truck revealed the leather thong around the dead man's throat. His eyes bulged, staring blankly in the night. Newt, alert, crouched, his gun ready.

He looked anxiously around, his eyes darting everywhere. The quiet was ominously threatening as Newt ran into the house, grabbed the telephone, dialed, and waited impatiently. "Come on, Come ooooon," he coaxed. "Bubba, get some of the Brothers and get over to my house! Somebody just killed Billy Ray!" Newt listened, then yelled, "Yes, God damn it! I said they got Billy Ray and propped his dead body up in my pickup truck!" There was squawking from the other end of the line. "Yeah, bring the sheriff too. I don't know what good he'll be. Just get over here fast!" he barked.

Amelia worked the next day, and took great care not to come in contact with the judge. Her concern was not necessary, he had gone to his office early, for a more pressing problem, 'The Brotherhood' topped his list. John had heard through the grapevine of Billy Ray's murder.

Older Negroes in the county were anxious. They feared retaliation against them; and stayed inside. Younger black men were more forward and gathered in churches, schools and basements to plan for any attempted counteraction from the Brotherhood.

In the darkness, Amelia stood near the end of the depot platform. As she prepared to climb aboard the train, two men materialized out of the shadows. "You don't want to get on the train, Amelia," a harsh voice cautioned. He motioned the second man, who took the one suitcase, and the little boys to a truck. The other shoved Amelia into the back seat of a car.

She was petrified for her children and herself. "Where are you taking my boys!? Please don't hurt my boys!" she cried. He turned the automobile and drove away in silence. "Please sir, don't hurt my children! It's not their fault, they're just babies! You wouldn't hurt innocent children!"

They drove for several minutes before he stopped in front of her house. The boys and her suitcase were on the steps. The driver walked her to the porch where she held the boys as tears flowed down her face.

"Try this again," he said, pointing his fingers like a pistol at one boy's heads and made a pop with his lips. "Off with their heads," he warned. Laughing, he turned abruptly and went to the car and drove away.

"What happened chile?" Mrs. Russell said from the door. "We missed the train," Amelia dried her eyes. "I'm being watched, we couldn't leave!" she wept.

"Go on to your room. I'll put the boys to bed," the older woman said, helping them inside.

Mother Russell sat on the edge of Amelia's bed. She held the younger woman's face gently, "The judge is after you?" she stated simply.

"Oh mother, he forced me!" Amelia said, bursting into tears sobbing against her mother-in-law's bosom.

"Honey you're not the only one. He did this with other servant girls when he was young and wild. He never asks. He takes what he wants from people that can't help themselves," she said, hugging Amelia, rocking her back and forth. "He used all kinds of women. His daddy was always getting him outta scrapes. One time he kept a girl locked in his room. Jealous of anybody that went close to her. Old man Devereaux had to send him to France that time," she said, turning up her daughter-in-law's face to dry her tears. "You're pretty, colored and can't help yourself, honey. Just try to stay out of his way. I can only bind your wounds if you're hurt."

"Mother what can I do? They scared me tonight! We could disappear and no one would know what happened!" Amelia said.

"Do the best you can until the sentence is over, chile."

"I don't want them to hurt my family. My children could have been hurt or killed!" Amelia cried, drying her eyes. "You only have a little more time to work off. In Georgia, I can't help you with the law and when a white man lusts for you," Mother Russell said.

"Maybe I should have let those animals humiliate me on the street that day! I wouldn't be in this mess now."

Mother Russell held her by the shoulders. "No, the Bible says above all else, stand. You stood up for something, and you have to know, you made the right move that day," Mother Russell pointed out.

"But Eddie won't love me anymore!" Amelia cried.

"We can't do nothing about the way it is in the South. This has happened for well over two hundred years. I don't think it's gonna stop, no ways soon," Mother Russell said, then repeated, "I can help you if you're hurt, but I can't do nothing when a white man wants you. You get some rest. We'll figure something out tomorrow."

In Aaron's study he said into the telephone that day, "Thanks for the information Dave, kiss Janet for me," he listened, "Tell me, how did you get the job of a bureau chief?" Aaron listened and laughed. "We have to get together sometime." He listened again then placed the receiver down. Chuckling, he swiveled his chair to look out the window.

The next morning he watched Amelia from his office window, while she laughed and talked to a Negro man. Aaron's eyes narrowed as he gripped the pencil in his hand until it snapped. The verbal exchange lasted for several minutes, then she moved on, turning to wave to the man who said something in return.

The Knights Of The Brotherhood marched into the town square of Kalb Kove in full apparel. They brandished their torches and shouted in solidarity. The masked and sheeted figures posed an obvious threat to the townspeople.

Those with courage peaked out from behind curtains. Newt uncovered his face and shouted, "The Brotherhood, is here tonight to let the people of this town know; one of our brothers was killed!" he said. An angry cry went up from the crowd. "We're gonna find his killer! His murder will not go unavenged!" the followers yelled agreement.

"We'll get 'um Newt!" one shouted, above the din.

"Are we together tonight!?" Newt asked.

"Yeah, we're with you Newt!" the Knights clamored.

"Say the pledge!" Newt said.

"Power to The Brotherhood! Power to The Brotherhood! We will keep the white race pure! We pledge to protect our white women against cross breeding! The white race will command! The white Race will prevail!" they cried.

"Go on home to your white families!." Newt bellowed. The crowd murmured, as they went their way. Torches dotted the terrain as they scattered in all directions. Newt's contention was, that the black man was the enemy of the white race. Actually if he had looked honestly within himself or simply looked in the mirror, he could have identified his worst adversary, himself. This shortsightedness continues to reflect bigotry and angry thoughts. Segregation was under fire and yet the old South still haunts us. The reality was disturbing. Politicians then and now play on peoples fears, some with subtlety and others blatantly to be elected. The so called middle class man is much like the Negro. Under the control of men we elect to power.

Newt's brazen effrontery to the city, prompted Aaron to send Laura to stay with her family in New Orleans. In the entry hall to the Manor he hugged her to him, and gently kissed her on the lips, as he smoothed the hair back from her face, Laura pleaded, "Now that we've found each other, I'm undecided about leaving you. Can't you come with me?"

His face changed imperceptibly, as he said, "I'm glad you're going to visit your family. It'll be good for them to see you again. My hands will be full with this Brotherhood unpleasantness."

"All the more reason for me to stay here!" Laura said.

"I love you for that, but I don't want to worry about your safety. These people are killers. I'll probably have to spend a lot of time in Kalb Kove," he said, holding Laura close, her face beneath his chin.

"Aaron, do you think it'll come to killing?!" she asked.

"They've murdered a lot of people," Aaron said.

"It frightens me. You'll be right in the middle of it all," she contended.

"The Knights are in the open. The worst kind of cut throats. Newt held a rally last night in front of the red barn, in Kalb Kove. He was out there for the whole town to see." Aaron said.

"How do you know it was him? I thought they wore masks," she replied.

"He removed his, the gauntlet was tossed, so to speak. We have to act now," he spoke, softly. Laura gasped and moved closer. "I have to go now dear. I'll see you at supper."

"John, when Mrs. Devereaux goes for her visit, have Mother Russell and Amelia moved to the house with the breeze way in the willows. Tell Mother Russell why. She's to know it's for their protection," Aaron instructed.

"Yes sir, your honor. I'll see to it myself."

"There will be light housekeeping and a few meals to cook. I want my wife safe first, understand?" Aaron said. "Yes sir," John said, staring knowingly at the judge in the rear view mirror. He clinched his teeth together, only the muscles of his jaw showed his enmity. Aaron gazed out the car window into another space as the landscape slipped by.

At the Clark County depot that night a young Negro soldier with his arm in a sling stood beside his bag.

Two men appeared from the dark. "Are you Edward Russell?" a harsh whisper asked.

"Yes, I'm Edward Russell," he said.

"You'll come with us," the rasping voice said.

"I'm waiting for the train and I'm not going anywhere with you!" Eddie said.

"You'll come with us, on your feet or laying down, either way, makes no difference to me, boy," the second man said.

"The hell I will!" Edward said. When the men grabbed him, he fought the best he could with a wounded shoulder. "Who the hell are you?! I'm not going one damn step with you!" he jerked, away, gasping for air. The second man hit him with a sap behind the ear. Eddie fell stunned, to the ground.

"Get him to the car. I'll get the bag," the man said, breathing fast. His partner carried the limp soldier to the car and dumped him in the back seat.

In the Devereaux bedroom, Aaron undressed his wife, lightly touching her smooth creamy skin as he guided her to the bed and laid her naked, among the pillows. He trailed kisses down her throat to her shoulders. She laid there and received. Laura had never learned to give. He moved his lips to the valley between her bosom, cradling her breasts in his hands making pointed cones. Her nipples hardened as he fondled them with his warm, wet mouth, stimulating her senses. He dispassionately made love to his wife. Every tantalizing nuance he made, was a thrill to Laura. He tasted her body until she was wild with passion, then he entered her slowly and sensually. Aaron was the best, at tactical love making to satisfy his partner. His penetration sent titillating excitement through her. She uttered cries of pleasure when his strokes went deeper, faster and more jarring. Her satisfaction was complete when he reached climax. He rolled away breathing quickly. She snuggled close, her head rested on his chest, and could hear the steady drum of his heart. When Laura fell asleep, he climbed out of bed, showered and went downstairs where he paced the floor in his study, drinking straight bourbon.

While Aaron and Laura waited for the train the next day, he promised, "I'm sending John and Cora along to help out when you need them. I've made provisions with the bank of New Orleans. This is a letter of credit," he said, giving her an envelop.

"How will you manage!?" Laura asked.

"I can drive myself. The meals at the Country Club are good, the day workers can do the cleaning," Aaron said.

When the train whistle was heard, she became flustered, saying, "Oh that's the train! Aaron must I go!?" he kissed her lingeringly on the lips. The Devereaux Special coach drew along and he helped her aboard. Aaron stood on the platform and watched the train leave.

His day was spent on the telephone, signing papers and organizing his forces. He met with the Town Council to try and resolve the Brotherhood matter. The council was in a quandary. Members panicked, and threatened to leave town.

He drove home exhausted and fell into bed in a troubled sleep. He was awake early the next morning showered and dressed, having coffee when the telephone rang. "Hello." He listened. "We'll need part of the Florida, San Francisco and Detroit Network. I want everything done, yesterday! Get them here immediately by plane, bus or train, any travel method necessary!" he ordered. Aaron listened again and placed the receiver down. He propped a note for Amelia on the hall table, and shrugged into his coat. The legend of the note, "Amelia, I'll be here for a light supper. Leave it in the warmer. Judge Devereaux." On his drive to Kalb Kove he passed the people moving Amelia and her family to the plantation.

Newt had wasted no time gathering forces from around Georgia and nearby states. Strange faces appeared everywhere in the county.

The Network was kept busy, tracking new arrivals.

Aaron visited Tom Lennox in the afternoon. "I'm going home soon for supper and to bed early. We'll have another long day tomorrow," he said.

"You look like you could use a good nights rest. You're right, we'll need all our wits about us until this thing is over. Oh did you hear from Laura?" Tom asked.

"Yes she called today. Help is on the way," Aaron said.

"I hope help is not too late," Tom said.

"I'll see you tomorrow," Aaron said, then stood, stretched the muscles in his back and left Tom's office.

Aaron had undressed when he heard little noises in the bathroom. He slipped into his robe and stood watching Amelia's rounded bottom as she bent over. She straightened and wiped her brow on her sleeve, and was startled to discover him there. She backed away when she saw the lascivious smile on his face. He blocked her way when she tried to pass, pulling her crudely into his arms, crushing her mouth with his. She dropped the cleaning supplies in her struggle to get away. He ripped the front of her dress, overpowered her, and pushed her to the rug on the bathroom floor, then tore off the rest of her clothes; he breathing rapidly.

"Judge Devereaux, please no!" she cried, gasping in pain when he entered her roughly. The encounter was painful and brief. He rolled away exhausted on the floor beside her.

Amelia tried to cover herself clutching her torn dress. "There are clothes in the east wing guest room for you to wear. You'll shower here," he said, and started out of the room. He turned, saying, "When I'm home you'll sleep here those nights. And when we're together, I want your arms around me." He watched her cover herself, "You have a beautiful body but I'm too tired to appreciate it as it should be, I will, later."

"You like my body and you've used it for you own sick desires. It's not right!" she cried.

Aaron held her face between his hands. "Few things in life are right or fair." Then he demanded, "Who was the man you talked with in town a few days ago?"

"I don't know what you're talking about! What man?" she said, frowning, and tried to look away.

His grip tightened on her face, "Across from my office. Who was that man!?" he repeated his demand.

"That was elder James from my church," she said, when memory dawned, and was surprised by the threat in his voice.

"What did you talk about for so long?" he said angrily.

He had her attention; fear overcame her after looking into his eyes, "The church picnic, sir." she said.

"Nothing else? Do you know him well?" Aaron asked. She shook her head.

"You belong here with me. I never want to see you talking to him again, or any man, is that clear?" he said.

She was silent.

He held her chin tighter repeating, 'Is that clear?"

"Judge you're hurting me!" she cried.

"Is that clear?!" he demanded.

"Yes, sir. Judge Devereaux, you're hurting me," she said.

Almost tenderly. "I want to know all about you. What your thoughts are, everything you do," he said, loosening his hold, but keeping his arm around her waist.

She stiffened, and the fire rekindled in her eyes. "That will never happen your honor, because you'll never touch this, my thoughts,"

Amelia said, and tapped her forehead. "This is my territory, and no one is permitted in there!"

"You have Moxie. I like that and I love, your body," he said, laughing. He moved his hands over her cool skin, then hugged her, pulling her pelvis close. "It pleases me. You please me," he whispered and released her. "I'll be home after supper. There's a box in the bedroom closet. I want you bathed and to wear that tonight," he said, then he left.

At twilight, Aaron turned from the window when Amelia came into the room wearing a sheer black negligee. It accented her voluptuous lightly golden body. She went to him and encircled her arms around his neck, laying her head on his chest. The full length of her body kindled his fires of desire. "In Paris you could enjoy life," he whispered, as he lightly ran his fingers tips along her cheek and let her hair down, it fell heavily to her shoulders. He cupped her buttock in his hands and pulled her pelvic against him, then kissed her full lips sensuously, aware of every point of contact, as the fire of lust spread to his loin.

On an embankment opposite the bedroom window, Newt sat with an unlighted cigar clamped between his teeth. From his vantage point on the knoll, he watched Judge Devereaux when he kissed Amelia. And, when Aaron carried her to the bed across the room.

"When the cat's away the 'rat' will play," Newt muttered. The lights were turned off moments later. "I got you now! You Nigger loving son-of-a-bitch!" Newt cackled. Then he left the hillock and drove his pickup truck towards town.

CHAPTER SIXTEEN

Aaron was preoccupied with work, when there was a knock on his office door. Newt popped his head around the door without waiting to be asked in. He removed the cigar from his mouth, and grinned as he walked in the room, like the cat who had eaten the canary. "Got a minute, your honor?" Newt asked.

Aaron was surprised when he looked up from the papers. "Yes ah, come in Newt. What can I do for you?" he replied.

Newt swaggered across the room and leaned with both hands on the desk. There was a knowing look on his face. "No use beating around the bush, Judge. So I'll get right to the point," Newt said.

"I would appreciate that Newt," Aaron acquiesced.

"There's a good view of your bedroom from a knoll in a grove of trees," he chuckled, and made tick tick sounds. "And your wife just left town. Shame on you, yo' honor."

"You know that from your own knowledge?" Aaron asked, nonchalant.

"Believe me, yo' honor that's the truth. I had my eyes full last night," Newt said chuckling, and shaking his head.

Then Newt's face turned from cunning to mean, as he leaned closer, only inches from Aaron's face, saying, "I followed you before you moved that black slut on your property. I saw you drive by her shack, just to look at her." Pausing, Newt said, "Didn't know I saw ya' did ya'?" Aaron listened, toying with the pen in his hand. "I'm surprised at you, and you a judge. Got a taste for dark meat. Now, where did you get that from, yo' honor? Your grand pappy, maybe?" Newt asked, stopping to shake his head, snickering. "I hear tell it runs in the family."

"Did you tell anyone else, Newt?" Aaron asked.

"No, this stays just between you and me, yo' honor. I'll need a judge from time to time in my business," Newt stated.

"What else do you want?" Aaron asked.

"This town. Oh hell, why think small? I want the whole damn county. The Brotherhood will control this town from now on." He shrugged his shoulders, "So that's it, Kalb Kove. You can keep on screwing that black bitch as long as you want to. I'll let you have her, for now," Newt responded, evilly.

"Newt, what can I say?" Aaron said, tossing the pen on his desk.

"Nothing. I got you by the balls and you know it, yo' honor," Newt announced, sarcastically.

"It would seen so, you've got it all," Aaron replied.

"There's gonna be some changes in this town, starting today," Newt said. He turned laughing from the door. "How does it feel to have somebody else in charge, yo' honor? I've got your family jewels in the palm of my hand, and you put them there. Yeah! I've got the power!" Newt made a fist, waving it in the air, before leaving the judges chamber.

A diabolic smile twisted Aaron's mouth. He watched Newt from the window, standing on the sidewalk, his chest expanded, arrogant, pleased with himself. Newt shoved his thumbs in his lapels and rocked back and forth, from heel to toe. He gazed over the town grinning, then walked across the street to his saddle shop.

On a dirt road that bordered the marshland, Jessie Lee and deputy

Sykes looked at the bumper of a pickup truck protruding from the slime of the swamp. The truck with a wench was slowly pulling the pickup out of the mud. As the muck slipped down the sides of the vehicle, Jessie Lee adjusted his hat to shade his eyes, saying, "That looks like ole J.D.'s pickup truck."

"Now we know why his hound dog's been howling all this time," the deputy said. They ambled over when the truck was settled on the bank.

A reporter from the Kalb Kove Express arrived when the truck rested on the shore. He took pictures of the decomposed body of J.D., slumped over behind the steering wheel. "Holy shit, sheriff!" the reporter exclaimed. "I think you have more troubles! Look over there. Isn't that the top of another car?" he said, pointing in the direction of a shiny object in the murky water.

"I think you're right," Jessie Lee said, and yelled to the tow truck driver, saying, "Hey Scooter, get your grappling hooks into that one over there!" The sheriff pointed to a shiny object that protruded from the surface of the watery ooze.

A radio newscaster broadcasting the evening news, said excitedly, "This just in. In 'Swamp Glen' near the town of Kalb Kove, Georgia, today there were some startling discoveries. A number of bodies, in varying stages of decomposition were found in the lake. The authorities aren't sure how many skeletal remains collected there over the years. Reportedly a number of people who disappeared, have never returned to the area. The Georgia State police were on hand throughout the day. It has been alleged 'The Knights of the Brotherhood' may be responsible for most of the dead. We'll update this shocking story as it develops."

Law enforcement from a number of agencies, along with reporters from throughout America roamed the street of Kalb Kove, asking questions, probing for any tidbit of news. The citizens covered their faces and hurried by. The barber shop owner had to slam the door in the news hounds face's. The Depot Cafe along with other businesses, were closed on Main Street. The inhabitants didn't venture out. And the Negroes watched in closed mouth dread; although many were delighted the murders were brought to light. As weeks passed, more skeletons and bodies were dug from the mud.

In Judges Devereaux's chambers, he spoke into the telephone, saying, "Keep a close watch on the situation we discussed, if it get's out of hand take care of it," after barking the order, Aaron hung up. The phone rang almost immediately "Hello?!" he answered gruffly.

"Sweetheart, what is happening there?" Laura's voice assailed his senses.

"I don't have the time to talk right now, Laura. All hell has broken loose. The town is being torn apart. I'll call you when I can," he said, pausing. "Oh, did you keep the appointment with Dr. Swartz?"

"Yes, I saw the doctor and I've made progress. But Aaron, don't you need me there?" Laura asked.

"I don't want you here, not now Laura," anger tinged his voice. "There are too many problems. I can't worry about you too. Stay there until I can call you! State agents are here, and I have to meet with them in a few minutes," he snapped.

"I'm sorry Aaron, but I'm so worried," she said, subdued then was quiet several seconds. "Good-bye dear, call me when you can. Please, take care of yourself."

"I love you Laura. I won't forget, sweetheart. Good-bye, Laura," he said, making an effort to be calm, then slammed the receiver down. He squeezed his tired eyes at the apex of his nose.

The closed sign hung in the window of Newt's saddle shop. The lights were off, except the night light in the back. A man came in; the brim of his hat covered most of his face. "I'm about to close up shop. What can I do for you?" Newt asked.

"I want a special saddle, like this one," the man's voice rasped. He showed Newt a picture of an elaborate saddle. "Do you think you could customize it for me? It's for my wife's birthday."

Newt looked at the picture under the night lights. "That's a beauty, alright," he said, while he examined the photograph. "It might take a while. I could probably have it for you in, say, four weeks unless it's a rush job."

"That long?" the man asked.

"I don't have a helper now, so it'll take a little longer," Newt explained.

The man gave in after several moments, "Okay let's do it. I can wait that long," he said, and looked around the dimly lit shop. "Show me the bridle behind you?"

"Which one?" Newt asked, turning to a rack.

"The one trimmed with silver, near the middle of the rack there," the man answered, pointing.

"You know your bridles," Newt said, moving to the one indicated.

Swiftly the man slipped a looped thong around Newt's throat and pulled it tight. The killer barely had time to twist the ends around his gloved hand, and before he could brace himself for leverage, Newt threw the assailant over his shoulder against the wall. The light was shattered when his body smashed the bulb. Newt's opponent was use to combat situations, and held on doggedly to the garrote. Newt fought violently, straining to throw his attacker off, trying desperately to free himself by clawing into the soft tissue of his throat to dislodge the thong shutting off his life. Newt gasped to breathe.

In the Devereaux bedroom, Aaron made love to Amelia. His breathing was fast, as his penetrations went deeper, and became more forceful. Their sweaty bodies slapped together rhythmically.

While back in the saddle shop, the battle raged. The men knocked over display cases and bridle racks, sending other objects crashing to the walls and floor. The killer held on tenaciously, while being thrown wildly around repeatedly. The leather thong, cut into his gloved hands, as it tightened around Newt's neck. The dying man wheezed for air while his fingers feebly dug at the leather still trying to dislodge the object taking his life, but his efforts were ineffective. Newt's face turned from purple to a sickly gray, as his eyes bulged and his tongue protruded from his mouth.

Aaron's lovemaking neared climax, they breathed in short gasps. His groans came from deep down, as his body hovered above hers, then settled briefly on Amelia. When his breathing was under control, he rolled away, satiated.

In the saddle shop, the assassin was winded, when he placed his foot in the middle of the dead man's back, he held tight to make sure the man was dead. Newt's body settled limply to the floor. His killer tied the special knot in the thong, retrieved the picture of the saddle, hung the closed sign in the window, and left the shop stealthily.

The next morning Amelia stood in front of Aaron, her eyes downcast. "Will you want me here tonight?" she asked.

He raised her face with a finger under her chin, saying, "You have lovely eyes. Always look at me when we talk," he searched her face. "You'll always know when I'm home. The lights will be on, and always meet me with open arms. I like the feel of your body against mine."

"Judge Devereaux, my husband will be home soon, to take us away from here," she stopped speaking in alarm when she saw the coldness in his eyes.

"No one else can have you, not even him!" Aaron said, grasping her shoulders in a vice-like grip. "I'll send you away first!" he snapped, shoving her away. Then he stamped out of the room.

At the Cottage in the willows, Amelia sat forlorn in the breezeway, staring at the river. Her eyes were not focused on the moonlight, as it shimmered on the surface of the waters.

A figure materialized seemingly from no where. He shoved a photograph into her hand. By the light of the moon she saw Eddie, behind bars. He sat on a bunk staring out like a trapped animal, his head swathed in bandages, one arm in a sling. "Say or do nothing, or he dies," the harsh voice spat, and moved into the trees.

Amelia rushed into her bedroom, locked the door, and leaned against it a while staring in horror at the picture of her husband. She pressed it against her bosom. "Stop resisting and shut up! And just take it!" she whispered, vehemently. She turned to the mirror and gazed at her reflection. Then, a new resolve dawned. "You can't do anything, forget everything else. Just keep your family alive!" she said. "Give the almighty judge, everything sexual you've got!" Then she fell on the bed. "Oh God! Can't someone help me!?!" her voice was choked with sobs.

Newt's body was lifted to the stretcher, "Moses sure didn't do that," Jessie Lee said, while he and his deputy watched the undertaker.

"He didn't do Billy Ray either," Sykes answered, drily. "I know that. My problem is who did? Newt's been dead a long time. He's stiff as a board," the sheriff replied.

"It beats me! Who did it, is something for you to figure out sheriff. Whoever did this had a damn tough fight on his hands. This place is a wreck!" Sykes said as they followed the undertaker past the crowd.

"Yeah. Newt didn't go easy, that's for sure," Jessie Lee voiced.

Two state patrol officers stood across from Aaron and presented their credentials. "Be seated. Gentlemen, would you like something to drink, coffee?" he asked, and looked at the identification. "Patrolman Hanson, Sangstrum?"

"No thanks," Hanson said. Glancing out the window, he sat down, saying, "I see you're having your share of troubles now-a-days."

"Yes, the owner of the saddle shop was found strangled this

morning," Aaron answered.

Hanson turned to Aaron, "Judge Devereaux, this won't take long. We're here because of a missing soldier named Edward Russell."

"He's missing?" Aaron asked.

"We were contacted by the War Department to look into the disappearance of this man. Do you know him?" Hanson asked.

"Yes, he's the son and husband of two of my servants.

When did he disappear?" Aaron asked.

"He went on furlough some weeks back. He was last seen at the Clark County Depot, where his trail ran out," Hanson said.

"Russell never returned to camp," Sangstrom interjected. "Nobody, has seen him. We thought with all the bodies found in the swamp, his might be there."

"I would know if he were home. His family lives on my estate," Aaron stated.

"Yes, we know. The station master in Clark County said he saw a colored soldier. He was there one minute and gone the next, just disappeared," Sangstrom replied.

"I'm sorry, I can't help you, gentlemen. Did you speak to our sheriff?"Aaron asked.

"Yes. Neither he nor his deputy could help us. We'd hoped there might be some connection with your problems here. But we'll have to wait until the lake is dredged," Sangstrom continued.

"I'll have the sheriff check for him specifically." Aaron said.

"We'll be in touch," Hanson said, leaving.

The telephone rang early the next morning. Aaron had to reach over the sleeping form of Amelia. The silk sheet partially covered her body. "Hello?" he answered, sleepily.

"Aaron, the news is so awful! Is it time for me to come home?" Laura's voice, assailed his ear.

"No dear, this is not a good time. This is very nasty business," as his eyes roamed over Amelia's body. "I'm not home a lot. I have protection, but men are at a minimum. I'd have to give up my body guards, to cover you," he said.

"But Aaron, a wife's place is at her husbands side at a time like this!" Laura pleaded.

"I don't need you here now, can't you understand that! He snapped. "Keep John and Cora there, until I can sort this mess out. I'll call when it's safe for you to come home. You're precious to me and I don't want you in harms way," he said, convincingly.

"I love you so, Aaron," she replied.

"Yes, and me you dear, more and more everyday," he said.

"Don't forget to call." Laura said, delighted.

"I won't, sweetheart, and don't worry it'll be alright when the press lose interest," he said, placing the receiver down, he lightly moved a tendril of hair from Amelia's face, then rolled her over roughly. His hunger for her was unrelenting.

Amelia awoke with a start, and pushed him away. She stood at the bedside, saying, "Judge, I'm asking you; don't attack me! You can have your way with me. You've proven that I can't fight with you. For once, let me show you how to please me, and no more shoving me around!" Their nude bodies stood inches apart. "Sex shouldn't hurt, please let me show you. I don't like to be handled roughly. Fantasize, treat me gently, make love to me," Amelia said softly.

"Okay show me," he said, savoring the nearness of her.

She moved closer, her arms around his neck. The full length of her body pressed against him, as her nipples hardened, touching his chest. She kissed him fervently on the mouth letting her tongue flick between his lips, arousing him more; the musk of her, captivated him. His hands cupped her hips, then his arms stole around her waist. He drew her close, until their bodies clung. The touch of her cool skin and full mouth sent shocks waves through him. While her hands flowed over his erogenous areas, he guided her to the bed, and laid her among the pillows. He trailed his tongue down her throat to kiss her shoulder, then her breasts. Aaron took the cones of voluptuous flesh in his hands, and tasted first one and then the other. He aroused and titillated her senses.

Her fingers touched and lightly fondled his body. The ache in his loin grew, but he waited. Surprisingly, Amelia was tantalized and thrilled when his mouth tasted every part of her body, until she was consumed with desire. A sigh escaped his lips, when he entered her warm, wet enclosure, it soothed him. His penetration sent exquisite excitement through them, as he made love to her slowly and sweetly. Her movements became faster, as she adjusted her body to receive and meet the impact of his thrusts.

Amelia gave everything erotically, sending his senses to new heights. Her moans of pleasure drove him on, his strokes became stronger. Their jarring climax came at the same time. Aaron made an outcry of release, breathing in gasps as his sweaty body settled on hers momentarily. Then he rolled away exhausted. She jumped out of bed suddenly, and ran to the bathroom. Aaron heard her retching into the toilet bowl. He followed and stood in the door as she flushed the commode.

Amelia went to the sink, rinsed her mouth and bathed her face with a cool wet wash cloth.

"When did this start?" he asked.

"A few weeks ago," she said, softly and dabbed the wet cloth to her face and throat.

"Is this what happens when you're pregnant?" he asked.

"Yes," she whispered.

"I'll have a doctor I know examine you," he said.

She nodded and leaned over the sink.

"Is it mine?" he asked, as a smile touched his lips.

"Who else had a chance?!" she snapped.

"Still the spitfire," he grinned and left.

Amelia burst into tears. She was never allowed to go off the plantation without his knowledge. But his treatment of her changed. He was more gentle. Their sexual encounters never stopped but he was kind-hearted. She grudgingly had to admit, he was a thoughtful lover. His considerations were of her and his child. At times he smiled in the midst of important transactions. Aaron's attitude was different; more subdued, solicitous of her feelings, 'almost loving'.

The telephone in Aaron's office rang one evening. "Judge Devereaux," he answered, listened, then said. "Yes, doctor?"

"All the tests are positive. She is pregnant. Shall I follow her monthly?" the Creole doctor asked.

"Yes. How many months is she?" Aaron asked.

"I'd say twelve to sixteen weeks," the doctor answered. "I'll have her brought to your office every month, in the evening. And doctor, treat her well, she's special," Aaron cautioned.

"Leave it to me. I'll expect her in twenty-one days," the doctor said, as the connection was broken.

Aaron leaned back/ pleased. The telephone rang almost immediately. "Judge Devereaux," Aaron said.

"Aaron, I know you must be busy; you're still in your office." Laura's voice gushed into his ear. Reality, came crashing down for him.

"Laura, ah, I was just thinking of you," he stammered.

"Were you, sweetheart?" she said, pleased. "The news there is so terrible. I'm glad you can think of me."

"Darling, I always think of you, but it's going to take at least another month to dredge the lake. My God! Laura, it's inconceivable the number of bodies and skeletons in that swamp. Some date back probably to horse and buggy days. As a matter of fact, they found a buggy or two," he said.

"Aaron, I've been here almost four months. I worry about you," she said.

"I'm thinking of your safety. If you were here, I'd have one more responsibility. The trial for six of the Brotherhood starts in a few weeks. The State Police are searching for the body of a soldier who might be buried in the lake. When that probe is over, I'll call for you to come home," he promised.

There was an audible gasp from the other end of the line. "A soldier!?" she asked.

"Yes. And there's the possibility of a riot if a Negro soldier's body is found. Things will get very ugly. People from the armed services are here, waiting for the lake to be dredged. I want you to stay there. My hands are too full. Go shopping, go to the theater, listen to some good music, have a party. It'll take your mind off this mess." he paused, then continued, "How're your treatments corning along with Doctor Swartz?" he asked.

"I haven't had a drink in ages, and I feel so healthy. It's seems sinful of me, while you're there in such trouble. Did you have supper yet?" she asked.

"I was getting ready to close the door and go to the Country Club. They're making something special tonight," he replied.

"Aaron It's so late! I'll hang up so you can go have supper. Love you sweetheart," she said in her lilting voice.

"Good bye dear," Aaron said, and broke the connection.

He lingered a few minutes, contemplating his situation.

Aaron was a ruggedly handsome member of the Devereaux clan. Today he appeared rested and vigorous, moving with a spring in his step when he left his office.

CHAPTER SEVENTEEN

There was a knock on Aaron's office door past his lunch hour, then two State Troupers entered. Aaron indicated a seat, and spoke into the telephone. "I will soon Laura, dear," replacing the receiver, saying, "My wife, she's worried, calls every day."

"I'm sorry to interrupt your honor, but we'll be in Savannah for a few days," Hanson said.

"Did you find Russell?" Aaron asked.

"Not yet. Of all the bodies dredged out of the muck and mire, his wasn't one of them. And yet there's no telling what will be brought out of there later," Hanson replied.

"That's a relief," Aaron said.

"His body might turn up somewhere else. I hope not, but you never know," Sangstrorn said, as the troupers stood to go.

"Uncle Sam, doesn't like loosing a good soldier," Hanson interjected, and shook Judge Devereaux's hand. "Thanks Judge for your help. We know you have your hands full, especially with the up corning trial," the trouper said, and left.

The telephone rang in the study at Devereaux Manor. "Hello," Aaron answered. "Yes doctor," listening he sat up straight, "Two shadows? You mean twins?" The receiver squawked in his ear for several seconds. "I'll see to it doctor," he said, placing the receiver down.

Aaron walked to the window, and from his vantage point he watched Amelia cross the gardens on her way to the Manor. He met her at the door. It was his ritual for her to put her arms around him, and they would kiss when inside the Manor. Now she looked up at him smiling, in the circle of his arms, running her fingers through his hair. He hugged Amelia gently, kissing her face and neck, then her mouth, every contour of her warm body touching his. Then he escorted her to the bedroom. "This will be our last night in the manor. Tonight will be special." Aaron planned, saying, "Mother Russell, will sleep in the room with the boys," he tilted her face up. "I'll come to you in the future. Never lock your door, understand? You'll be protected," he said softly.

"Yes, I understand," she whispered, gazing up at him. Aaron shed his robe and removed her clothes slowly, kissing her body. She stood serenely before him as he placed his ear on her lower abdomen and kissed her swollen belly.

Her breasts were more voluptuous he held them in his hands. Her pregnancy, as with most women, gave Amelia a glow. "It's two babies you know, twins!" he said softly in awe.

Aaron positioned her on the mound of pillows, their lips met in a sensuous kiss. Their tongues tasting and darting between open lips. Their bodies clung, as the kiss became more passionate. Gentle hands caressed each others' erogenous zones. Their lovemaking was slow and arousing, as she wrapped her legs around him to hold him closer. Amelia's desires over the months had been heightened. Sex with him was remarkably like an art form, it felt good; afterward she slept snuggled close to him, her face near his chest.

He could feel the warmth of her breathing when he drifted off to sleep. He slept with one of his legs draped over her thigh, and one hand on her buttock. They had reached the ultimate of pagan and the refinement of good sex.

In the court room Judge Aaron Devereaux, admonished the jury. "You were sworn to hear the evidence in a court of Law. You will then make a decision in accordance with the findings. You've heard the testimony in this case. In your deliberations, you will render a verdict. 'If' in your calculations you need assistance, the court is here to instruct you. The jury will retire now. This court is in recess," Aaron said, slamming the gavel down. He left the bench and entered the judge's chambers. The spectators noisily made their way outside.

The state justice systems included a number of lesser courts with limited jurisdiction. They disposed of a modicum of criminal offenses and relatively small civil actions. This encompassed the police and municipal courts in small cities and larger towns.

The jury deliberated into the afternoon. Judge Devereaux was working over a sheaf of papers when the court clerk appeared.

"The jury has reached a verdict your honor," she said. "That didn't take long. Thanks. I'll be right out," he said, looking at his watch, then scribbling something on the page after stacking the papers and storing them in a drawer, Aaron shrugged into his robe and went into the courtroom.

"Hear ye! Hear ye! All rise, this court is now in session. The honorable, Judge Aaron Devereaux presiding," the clerk exhorted. Aaron climbed to his seat above the crowded room. Negroes sat in the balcony and whites filled the lower floor. Six 'Knights of The Brotherhood' the defendants, sat at the table with their lawyer.

"Foreman of the jury, have you reached a verdict?" Judge Devereaux asked.

"We have your honor, the foreman answered.

"Would the defendants rise, and face the jury?" the Judge turned to the foreman. "How say you all on the charge in count one, of burning and depredation of property?"

"We find the defendants on the charge in count one, not guilty, your honor," the foreman replied.

A cheer rose from the crowd on the lower floor. The Negro audience sat in stoic silence. The Judge hammered the gavel down repeatedly for order, saying, "Order in the court! 'Order' in this court!" A modicum of quiet returned among snickers and shuffling feet. "Another outburst like that, and I'll clear the court room!" He looked around the crowd, Mister foreman "How say you all, on the charge in count two of murder in the second degree?"

"We find the defendants on the charge, in count two not guilty, of murder in the second degree!" the foreman shouted.

The judge slammed the gavel down again, until there was quiet. "I thank the jury, for it's time and effort to reach a decision in this matter. The defendants are free to go, and this court is adjourned," Aaron said. The gavel crashed down once more, then he left the courtroom.

There was pandemonium, as rednecks shook hands, hugged and slapped each other on the back. The audience filed out noisily. Cheers rose from the people gathered outside. They milled around the grounds, grouped together in happy little clusters.

Negroes went down the back stairs and out the rear door. They knew there was no fairness for them in the court system. And this time one of their own, J.D., a white man was denied justice. There was little deliberation, the men on the jury remained loyal to the code of the South. A vote for white supremacy to stick together whether they believed in the killers guilt, or innocence.

At Devereaux Manor, Laura had arrived and waited impatiently for Aaron in the living room. She walked from the window that overlooked the tree lined driveway, and back to the couch, chain smoking.

Laura heard his car stop out front, and ran to the window. From her vantage point, Aaron climbed out of his car, then reached across the seat for his briefcase. She ran from the room into the hall. When he opened the front door she rushed into his arms kissing his face repeatedly.

"Oh Aaron, I've missed you so!" Laura cried.

"The house hasn't been the same since you went away," he said, hugging her.

She leaned back in the circle of his arms to look at him. "Darling, you look tired! Now that I'm home I'll see that you get more rest," she said. They walked with their arms encircling each others' waist.

"This has been quite a day," he said. "The trial was exhausting. I need a drink, will you join me?" Aaron asked, as he walked to the liquor cabinet and held up the decanter.

"Scotch?" he asked.

"I'll have what you're having. What happened today?" she asked, lighting a cigarette, inhaling deeply.

"The Brotherhood Six were on trial for the murder of J.D., the moonshine maker, and numerous atrocities across Kalb Kove county. Along with book and church burning and who knows what else," he said, carrying the drinks to sit beside her.

"How awful!" Laura answered.

"I wasn't convinced they committed J.D.'s murder. I'm almost certain they were involved in Moses's death; although there was no proof to support my theory," Aaron stated.

"Whom do you think killed him?" Laura asked.

"I think Newt killed J.D., but we'll never know for sure. He was strangled to death in his shop before the trial started," he replied.

"Don't think about that now. You're here and I'm home! Tonight belongs to us. I want to be in bed in your arms," she proclaimed.

Aaron laughed and took their glasses for a refill. He brought the drinks back, asking, "Now. Tell me everything that happened in New Orleans?"

"It was such fun! I wish you could have been there. I felt so guilty enjoying myself, while you were here with so many problems," Laura replied.

"It's almost over, go on." he encouraged.

"We attended the theaters, visited the French Quarter, just like we did when we were young," she said. He nodded through the whole speech, and watched her animated face. Laura's voice became distant in her confabulation. He observed her while she smoked and drank too much.

"We talked all night just like young girls at a slumber party," she giggled, and Aaron refreshed their drinks.

"Callie had been to Paris, and the fashions are so wonderful! We have to go soon, please!" she pretended to beseech him, then chatted on. Soon her voice faded from his consciousness. He saw the movement of her lips while she talked and giggled.

Her conversation continued through supper. "There was so much gaiety. You had to be there to see the crowds. My old friends from school attended most of the functions." Laura drank steadily, and smoked one cigarette after another." Most of my friends, some I haven't seen since the Cotillion ball, years ago." Supper was over and Laura could barely stand. She slurred, and stumbled, "Oh ho ho hoooo, that last drink was ... ," Laura said. Staggering, she fell into his arms before she finished the sentence. Aaron caught her, and carried her out of the dining room, and upstairs to the bedroom. He deposited her on the bed then undressed her.

Drunkenly she struggled to sit up, but her eyes didn't quite focus. "Sweetheart, it's so good being home for you to undress me and put me to bed. Come to bed with me, I'm ready," she said. Raising her arms to say something else.

Laura fell back into the mound of pillows giggling. "Laura, you get some rest," Aaron said. "I'll be back soon." He walked to the dressing room. Later, when he crawled into bed behind her she snuggled against him. He waited until she had fallen into a sound besotted sleep. Surreptitiously he slipped out of bed, and shoved pillows to her back. He watched her stuporous slumber, then shrugged into his robe and left the bedroom.

In a short time he opened the door quietly to Amelia's bedroom, crept in and gazed at her body in relaxation.

He shed his robe and slipped into bed beside her. She awoke with a start, saying in a whisper, "Judge Devereaux."

"I missed you," he said softly, and kissed her gently on the mouth. "Uummm, you smell so good, so warm. And you taste incredible, how did I get along without you in my life."

"But your wife is home!" she cried in a louder whisper, her eyes wide with dismay.

"She's slumbering the sleep of an evening of drinking," Aaron said caressing her body, touching the mound in her belly. He held her, planting long lingering kisses over her face and mouth. Her arms went around his neck in a familiar way, her body was pressed to his. One of his hands held her bottom, the other embracing her sleep warmed skin as a gentle breeze moaned through the weeping willow trees.

"You were made for love, and I can't get enough of you," he said, softly. And moaned when he achieved climax. The night wore on as they slept. He tipped out at dawn.

In the breakfast room, Aaron was reading over pages of contracts when Laura came in.

"Aaron, why are you working so early?! We'll have to do something about that, and soon," Laura said.

"I have a busy day ahead," he answered.

"I know, I'll have a party and invite people. The whole town needs laughter," she said, as if she hadn't heard.

"That might be a good idea, later, but it's a little premature right now. People are trying to cope with the past months," Aaron replied.

"I'm sorry about last night. It wasn't an enjoyable home corning for you. I'll take care of that tonight," she promised.

"I was tired too. Just having you home was enough," he said softly, Laura's head resting in the curve of his arm. Aaron tilted her face up and kissed her lightly on the lips. He checked his watch then hurriedly shoving papers in his briefcase, saying, "Sweetheart, work calls I've gotta go."

"Will Amelia be here today?" she asked.

He stiffened imperceptibly, then responded, "No, her sentence is over. They had a threat from the Brotherhood, and I had them stay in exchange for washing and ironing. Mother Russell is an accomplished seamstress," Aaron explained.

"Did they find Eddie's body?" Laura asked.

"No, I'm glad to say," he answered.

"Should I talk to them?"

Aaron looked up, his eyes narrow, then he snapped the locks on his case. "Not for a while Laura, Mother Russell is just getting over her sons disappearance. Your visit could dredge up all that ugly mess for her," he reasoned.

"That's true. You know best. I'll wait a while," she replied.

"Good idea. I have to go, works awaiting. Bye Dear." Aaron said, kissing her on the cheek and leaving the room.

She stood smiling, her hand on her cheek.

People across the county listened to the radio broadcast. "Six members of 'The Knights Of The Brotherhood' were found innocent of J.D. Carter's murder. The Knights are a white supremacy faction who espouse the purity of the white race. Carter's body was one of the most recent bodies hidden in 'Swamp Glen'. His faithful dog 'Dodger' alerted nearby residents that something was wrong. We will update the story as it unfolds. This is John Jay. Stay tuned for Ed's Sports Cavalcade." The newscaster ended his report.

"Jay how did, the dog get the name Dodger?" Ed asked.

"J.D. Carter made moonshine whiskey. Dodger was the best dog to sniff out revenue agents; whereby he and his master could dodge the law and make their getaway," John said.

In the Devereaux dining room Laura went to the door, and looking over her shoulder seductively, said softly, "I'm for bed, won't you join me?"

"I'm right behind you," Aaron said, gulping his wine.

He followed her, turning off the lights. Laura was in bed when he came out of the dressing room, nude. Aaron dove into bed beside her and pulled the covers over their heads. There was lots of movement and laughter under the sheet. "Oh Aaron! You're so naughty!" Laura giggled.

In the early morning light, Laura sat in the middle of the bed holding the sheet over her bosom. Aaron turned at the dressing room door, his eyes playing a trick in this light.

He imagined Amelia sitting there. Aaron's smile froze on his face.

"Aaron? Darling? What's wrong dear? Aaron!" Laura called. Her voice saying his name penetrated his mind.

"What? What did you say?" he asked

"You had such a strange look for a moment. You frightened me! What's wrong?" she asked, alarmed.

"Nothing dear. You're so lovely sitting there in the soft light. I was speechless for a moment," he said in an affable manner.

"You silver tongued devil! I should go away more often, to hear such courtly declarations," she said, looking away with pretended coyness.

"I just realized, how much I missed you," he said, then went into the bathroom.

Laura leaned back on her mound of pillows to luxuriate in the warmth of his words.

In Aaron's office later the intercommunication system buzzed, "Yes Trudy?" he said.

"Your call to Paris, sir," Trudy stated.

"Thanks Trudy, put it through please."

"Hello, my friend!" a Frenchman's voice said.

"Jacque! It's good to hear your voice again."

"To whom do I owe the honor of your call after such a long time?" Jacque asked.

"I have a situation here that's very special to me. I need the same help as my grandfather," Aaron explained.

"An affair of the heart!" Jacque said laughing, "I am at your disposal, my friend! When can I expect the arrival?"

"I'll expedite matters in the next few weeks. You'll hear from me," Aaron answered.

"I will await your instructions," Jacque said.

"The Devereaux's can always depend on your discretion. I may come myself this time," Aaron suggested.

"The arrangements will be made when you're ready. Will everything be the same as with your grandfather?" Jacque asked.

"Yes, there will be two small packages too," Aaron stated.

"Not a problem, Monsieur."

"Thanks Jacque. I'll call you soon, good-bye my confrere," Aaron said smiling, he placed the receiver down.

Aaron was leaving, but stood in the breezeway of the cottage. "Your honor! I can't go to Paris! Judge, this has to stop!" Amelia pleaded. "You have a wife, and I'm pregnant with your children. What more do you want?" she cried.

Laura peered cut the bedroom window toward the cottage in the willows. She saw Amelia struggling with Aaron.

He was holding Amelia by the shoulders, saying, "You'll go where I send you. The twins are mine, they belong with me, and I will never let you go!" Aaron said, "Despite your pregnancy I can't get my fill of you." She fought to free herself. He bent her backward as his hands roamed familiarly over her swollen body. His mouth crushed her lips in a grinding kiss. "You'll leave in two weeks, aboard the Devereaux Clipper," he said fervently.

In the Devereaux bedroom, Laura shocked, flattened her back against the wall, breathing in short gasps, then she stumbled out of the room. In moments she opened the door to the study with shaking fingers. At the liquor cabinet she gulped bourbon straight.

Aaron found her hours later, slumped over the arm of the couch. He came in and looked down at her in distaste. "Drunk again," he uttered, then carried her upstairs.

Laura stayed in bed the next day with a cool cloth on her forehead.

"Supper is ready are you corning down?" Aaron asked. "I'm not feeling well, you go on," she said.

"I'll have Cora save your supper in the warmer," he said, leaning toward her.

"Thanks Aaron," she said, turning quickly away.

He pulled the covers over her shoulders and turned off the lights, then left the room.

Laura lay there staring into the darkness, then started to cry. When he came to bed her back was turned. In the night he quietly climbed out of bed and shrugged into his robe.

Laura's eyes were open as she listened to his movements.

He leaned over the bed, she closed her eyes feinting sleep. The latch clicked as he closed the bedroom door. Waiting for several moments, she stood by the window, moving into the shadows when Aaron walked into her sight on his way to the cottage. She watched his progress when he moved from tree shadows to pools of moonlight. He arrived at the cottage and she saw the dim light from the open door when he entered Amelia's bedroom.

Laura had one drink after another, until she passed out across the bed.

Cora cleared the breakfast table as Laura came in. "The Judge left early, but he'll be home for supper," Cora said.

"Thanks Cora. I'll have toast and black coffee."

"Is that all you're having chile? Not enough to keep a bird alive," Cora said.

"That's all for now Cora. I'm not hungry."

"Yes, Miz. Devereaux."

Laura sat and gazed out the window. For weeks she walked around the house like a wraith, pallid and haggard. She drank herself into a stupor by afternoon. However in spite of all the liquor she consumed, the hurt, anger, loathing and a plethora of other emotions, coursed through her mind.

When watching her gulp her drink, Aaron said. "I don't like the way you're moping around and drinking. Laura it's eight o'clock in the morning, for God's sake!" he continued and felt her forehead, then took the drink from her hand. "No more of this until Dr. Crane takes a look at you." Then he held her by the shoulders. She looked at him with a listless, vacant stare. Aaron shook her gently, saying, "Promise me, no more drinking." She didn't answer. "Laura, promise me!" he shook her again, with more force.

"Yes Aaron, I promise," she said, with her eyes focusing apathetically on him.

"The doctor will be here today," he said, then kissed her cheek and left. She moved toward the liquor cabinet as if it beckoned to her.

Laura had deep-seated emotional conflicts, and used liquor as a relief from her tensions and anxieties, to the point of endangering her health. She was aware that she should not take the first drink, and should try for abstinence, Dr. Swartz had said so in all of her sessions. Unfortunately this was not always possible for Laura.

As Aaron was driven to work that morning, he ordered, "John, stop by Dr. Crane's. I want to talk to him."

"Yes sir, Judge Devereaux." A short time later, John stopped in front of a white, not ostentatious Southern home.

Dr. Crane's driver had maneuvered his car out of the driveway. They stopped along side the other car. The doctor and Aaron rolled their rear windows down.

"Good morning, doc."

"Morning, Aaron, what brings you out this way?"

"It's Laura. She's not herself," Aaron answered.

"What seems to be her problem?" the doctor quizzed.

"She's drinking too much, for one. Not eating, maybe she's coming down with something," Aaron explained.

"I'll drop by, after I see the Sanders boy," Doctor Crane said.

"Let me know what you find?" Aaron said.

"I'll do that," the doctor said, and drove away with John following.

Aaron's private telephone rang that afternoon. "This is Judge Devereaux."

"Aaron, Dr. Crane."

"Yes, Doc," Aaron said, waiting.

"I saw Laura, and you're right. There's something seriously wrong," Doctor Crane acknowledged.

"What?" Aaren asked.

"I need some tests, in a controlled environment. It's plain to see she's run down, and needs nourishment," the doctor, stated.

"Your hospital?" Aaron asked.

"Just for a few days, bring her tomorrow morning," Doctor Crane instructed.

"She'll be there. What time?" Aaron said.

"Nine o'clock. I'll call the hospital to expect her," the doctor answered, then the connection was broken.

Laura spent the next seven days undergoing, tests, xrays, and other studies. She fought having anything done, and pleaded with Aaron to take her home. During her stay she was gripped with Delirium tremors because of her bodies craving for alcohol. She had to be restrained to her bed for tearing her intravenous feeding tube out repeatedly.

When she came home a week later, Laura would lie listening to

Aaron pace the floor in the study.

He'd stopped at intervals to peer out the window. Eventually, Aaron slumped morosely in a chair, drinking Bourbon straight from the bottle.

A week went by and Laura roamed around Aaron's study. As he worked she had a glimpse of an envelop from "Embassy Steamship Lines". She waited for him to tell her about a trip. Alcohol no longer had the desired effect, her mind was clear. She watched Amelia as she went about her daily activity. Her body had grown more cumbersome. Mother Russell was adept at making full 'A-line' dresses to cover the pregnancy. Laura had a feeling of ambivalence toward the other woman while another week went by and still nothing was said about the steamship tickets.

Aaron's compulsion grew, and his nightly visits were extended, lasting until morning. He would get into bed with Laura in the early morning hours. but the scent of Amelia clung to him. Laura agonized through the days, drinking heavily. One afternoon she set her drink down with determination, and went to the desk. The drawer with the steamship tickets was locked. Using a letter opener she pried the drawer open. Then she shuffled through the folder that dealt with the twins Amelia was baring, and one with Laura's name on the cover. The first page was headed 'Hemstead Institute, For Country Living'.

"Commitment papers! Oh Aaron no!" she lamented.

Then she heard John's voice outside, saying, "Do you want me here early, Judge Devereaux?"

Laura scrambled to get the folders back in the drawer.

"Make that nine o'clock," Aaron answered. "John bring my briefcase from the back seat, please."

Laura dropped a folder, and papers scattered on the floor. Desperately she picked them up. The front door slammed, then silence. She closed the drawer, then rushed across the room and picked up her drink just as Aaron came in the door. He saw her there, and pecked her absentmindedly on the cheek. "Laura are you feeling better?" he asked, and went to his desk, laid his briefcase on top, opening the mail, and never noticed the pry marks on the desk drawer.

"Want a drink? To join my party?" Laura asked.

"No thanks, too early and you go easy on that stuff," he said.

"Not too early for me, ne'er too early," she said, making a face when she gulped her drink, and turned toward the window. Amelia was in the breezeway of the cottage with two little boys. Laura looked at Aaron, absorbed in a document. She left the room, he never noticed. Laura's mind and eyes were clear.

At the cottage she knocked. Amelia opened the door to find Laura standing there. She started to close the entry.

"No, don't close the door. I'm here to help you," Laura said, quickly.

"Why would you want to help me?" Amelia asked suspiciously. she was hesitant, but opened the door wider.

"First of all, I know you can't help yourself out of the situation you find yourself in. Can you?" Laura asked, gently. Amelia started to speak. "Let me finish. This is the South. And you're caught in a web, where you and your whole family can be wiped out in an instant." Fear covered Amelia's face. "Don't be frightened of me. We're both trapped in this mess. Me, because I still love him," Laura said, softly.

"How can I trust 'you'?" Amelia asked, her voice hovering near tears.

"The difference between us is our color, and because of cross-breeding, that isn't much difference anymore. My husband wanted a son and he'll do just about anything to have one, or two in this case." Amelia inadvertently touched her swollen belly. "Don't panic. I've seen the doctor's reports." Amelia's eyes grew wide, even more afraid. "Oh Aaron doesn't know I've seen them. In addition, I know he leaves me to sleep with you at night. You're having twins, something I could never do for him," Laura said, and smiled sadly.

"I tried to fight him off!" Amelia replied.

"I know. Before I go, there's one other thing I'm sure of. You and your family will be alright in the near future. I have money and I'll see to that," Laura said, approaching Amelia, she held Amelia by the shoulders. "Do you think you can keep my visit a secret? He'll be back you know," Laura warned.

"Yes, Mrs. Devereaux," Amelia answered.

"We have far too much in common for you to call me, Mrs. Devereaux. I'm Laura to you, we're members of an exclusive sisterhood, of a sort," she said, and started out the door.

"Laura, ... my husband Eddie, is missing too!" Amelia said, breathlessly.

"I'll try to find him. It's getting late, I'd better get back," Laura said. Amelia burst into tears. They hugged each other briefly, then Laura left the cottage.

CHAPTER EIGHTEEN

The doctor's face was grave. "I'll come right to the point, Laura has lung cancer."

Aaron sat listening to Doctor Crane in the Country Club Bar. "Does she know?" Aaron asked, momentarily speechless.

She might be suspicious. Most people with a terminal illness have a feeling something is wrong. I wanted to tell you first," the doctor replied.

"Is that why you suggested the 'Hemstead Institute'?" Aaron asked, toying with his drink.

"Yes. I suspected cancer; however I wanted to get her off the booze and cigarettes. She's killing herself at an alarming pace," the doctor continued.

"The drinking I suspect, is because of the loss of our children," Aaron explained.

"Possibly that, but it could be a combination of many things," Dr. Crane replied.

"I don't want her to know," Aaron said, emphatically.

"What will you tell her about the pain when it starts?" the doctor asked.

"I'll cross that hurdle, when I get to it. Is that all? Hell! That's enough," Aaron exclaimed, very disturbed.

"Aaron I know this is a bitter pill to swallow, but that's the way life is. We take the bad with the good," Dr. Crane said.

"I'll have to go now," Aaron said, "Are you sure there's no, hope?!"

"There's always hope," Dr. Crane answered. "There's no indication the cancer has spread from the initial sight. That's why we should get her to the Hemstead Institute for therapy. We may be able to add years to her life."

"That will be a battle getting her to go," Aaron replied "The fight will be up to you. I don't envy you that one bit," the doctor answered drily.

Aaron walked slowly out of the bar. His shoulders were stooped, like an older man.

Aaron found Laura, passed out on the couch. He looked down at his wife, noticing how ashen her color was. She appeared pitifully thin. There were tiny lines near her eyes and around her sensitive mouth.

Lines he hadn't noticed before. Tenderly picking her up, he carried her upstairs.

"No! Don' wanna go! You can't send me! I don' wanna go any ... whhheeere," she cried out. But the sentence trailed off when she lapsed into stuporous sleep.

Aaron sat in the dim light of the living room. A bottle of Jack Daniels in his hand, and drank from the bottle. He walked over to gaze up at Laura's portrait, above the hearth, then leaned his head on the mantel. "She doesn't deserve this!" he said, bitterly. Angrily he banged the bottle down on the table and left the room, slamming the front door.

Three nights later, 'The Knights Of The Brotherhood' met between the hills. The new leader stood on his flat rock.

"Ya'll know me, Jed Potter," he yelled. "We're here tonight about our dead Brothers. We know who killed Billy Ray and Newt!"

"Yeah, them damn uppity soldiers!" one member shouted, followed by a hubbub of agreement from the crowd.

"They did it, alright!" they all yelled.

"They're having a meetin' over in that Nigger church! We're going over there and burn 'em out! Now! Tonight! You with me!?" Jed incited.

"Yeah, we with you Jed!" the crowd clamored.

"Come on, let's get the black sons-a-bitches! They got guns, so come armed!" Jed instructed, while they tramped off into the woods.

Later in front of the church, Jed yelled, "Burn 'em out!" While his men torched the cross.

One member was poised to throw his torch when a shot rang out from the church. He fell in his tracks, and the others scattered for cover.

"We can't burn 'em out! Kill the black bastards!" Jed bellowed. There were shots from the church, and return fire from the Knights. People were falling wounded, others were killed. Brush fires spread, houses were ablaze, the populace ran and screamed in terror.

Deputy Sykes burst into the sheriff's office out of breath, saying, "Sheriff!" and swallowed to catch his breath. "Sheriff! A race riot! Over by the 'Beaver Darn Church'! Them colored soldiers and 'The Knight's', they shootin' it out!"

"What!" the sheriff bellowed, almost falling over backward.

"It's bad! Better call the State Police! We can't do nothing!" Sykes said, trying to catch his breath.

Jessie Lee grabbed the telephone and dialed, then waited impatiently.

When the operator came on the line, he shouted, "Lois, get me the State Police! Quick!"

Outside, the townspeople had joined the fight. Amid the gun fire; breaking glass, curses and running feet were heard.

"Come ooooon! Come ooonnnn!" the nervous sheriff prompted. "State Police! This is sheriff Jessie Lee, over here in Kalb Kove!" There was a squawk at the end of line. "Yes! Kalb Kove! We got trouble over here! A race riot! People shootin' each other! Houses burnin' ! The towns on fire! My deputy and me can't handle it! We out numbered!" he yelled, then listened, and slammed the receiver down.

"What did he say!" Sykes asked.

"For us to wait inside, they're on the way! Turn off the lights, for God's sake!" Jessie Lee said, They stood to either side of the window peering out.

The telephone rang in the Devereaux bedroom. "Hello?" Aaron answered, and listened. Suddenly he sat up in bed. "What?! When did it start?" he barked, and rolled out of bed. "I'm on my way!" He slammed down the receiver and dressed hurriedly.

"What happened, Aaron?" Laura asked.

"The one thing I've feared all along, a race riot. Stores are on fire, most of the houses in the flats, and in town are burning," Aaron answered.

"Oh no!" Laura cried.

"Have John bring the car around, while I finish dressing," he said, then changed his mind, "No! I'll drive myself."

The racial riot had gone beyond civil disobedience. The ferocious and detestable nature of the fighting was distinctive because of the savagery, barbarism and years of pent up fury. Hand to hand battles raged on for days. Black and white men lay injured, some fatally in the street.

A house with several little black children was blown up, killing them all. Judge Devereaux, Tom and Doctor Crane worked along with other merchants and citizens carrying the wounded and dying to common shelters.

The State Patrol, National Guard and the Kalb Kove Sheriff, were out-manned and out-gunned most of the time. When the new leader of 'The Brotherhood' was killed, the rest of his group scattered to the hills.

Aaron would usually arrive home late at night, and make sure Laura was asleep before he left for the cottage in the willows. It was near

Amelia's delivery date, and he spent most nights blatantly in the cottage with her. He needed the closeness and the feel of his children when they moved in her swollen belly.

Laura watched when he went to the cabin in his spare time. She had found a purpose, a resolve that was stronger than drink; although she never gave it up. She had the strength to control it, most days.

Laura sat behind Aaron's desk during the last days of rioting. John was across from her, his head down. "John, I know you told the Judge things about Amelia. You helped keep one of your own in bondage.

"But Miz. Devereaux, I never... !," he started to say.

"Don't bother to deny it. You did! Now you'll help her get away, and if you tell Aaron, I'll personally have you jailed, or worse. I'll shoot you myself!"

"Yes Miz. Devereaux." John said.

"That's all for now. I'm making the arrangements, and remember, not one word to the Judge. Is that clear, John?"

"Yes Miz. Devereaux, it's clear," he said, walking out of the room, closing the door softly.

In a radio broadcast a day later, the announcer said, 'Law enforcement has stopped the race riot in Kalb Kove. It took the joint efforts of law agencies. The death toll is unknown at this time, many are dead or wounded. The leader of this faction of the white supremacy group, was killed. His followers have fled to the marshland. It was alleged that the Brotherhood started the riot. Jed Potter, it's new leaders death was the turning point in the conflict. We will update this very volatile episode in the life of Kalb Kove."

Outside the cottage, the next dark night in 1952, Amelia, heavy with the pregnancy, urged John, "We have to hurry!"

"Just a few more things to put in the boat," he said.

In the back garden of the manor. Aaron got out of the car and went toward the cottage.

Laura watched anxiously from the bedroom window, gulping her drink.

"Hurry! Judge Devereaux is coming!" Mother Russell said, running from the back door. John grabbed the two boys, and rushed to the boat.

"Oh Mother Russell!" Amelia said, in an agonized whisper holding her abdomen as a contraction seized her.

"Lord! Is it time Chile?" Mother Russell asked anxiously.

Amelia dropped to one knee with the next contraction. "John! John! Come get this chile! She's having labor pain!" Mother Russell said, in terror.

Aaron walked along, coming closer. John picked Amelia up and carried her toward the boat. When another contraction seized her, she tried to hold back her cry of agony.

John put Amelia in the boat, moving the boys further back, then helped Mother Russell on board.

Aaron stepped upon the porch and opened the door to the bedroom. He entered and looked in the small bathroom. Then he heard someone trying to start an engine, and turned toward the sound.

John tried nervously to start the motor. In desperation he checked everything he could think of, and tried again.

Aaron was on the path between the cottage and the river.

He started to jog when he saw who was in the motor boat.

"Hold on there! John!" Aaron yelled, as he ran along the path and onto the pier.

The engine caught, just as Aaron reached the edge of the water. The boat roared away with Amelia screaming in pain.

Mother Russell covered her to keep her warm.

"John! Come back here!" Aaron barked, but was left standing in consternation. He turned and hurried back to the Manor. Laura came into the study while he rummaged through his desk.

"Are you looking for these?" she said, and dropped the file on the desk. He was surprised as he looked down at the folder. "Amelia, did get away?" Laura asked, as she poured a stiff drink.

"You helped her!?"Aaron asked.

"Yes, I helped her. I know you conceived those babies in our bed. She had to sleep here with you while I was away. It's a family tradition, right? Grandfather to grandson?" she charged. "Amelia couldn't help herself so I saved her, from you, Aaron!"

"You had no right to send them away!" he shouted. The veins stood out in his neck. His face was suffused with blood. Aaron's anger was apoplectic when he moved around his desk.

"I have every right, Aaron! This is my life too!" she corrected.

"Where did they go? To your brothers? I'll find them!" he bellowed.

"You can't love her nor your children, or you would never have held them captive," Laura argued.

"They're mine! You had no right!" Aaron barked.

"I beg your pardon, the 'Barren-ess', I believe you once said, has every right Aaron," she retorted.

He raised his fist as if to strike her, when suddenly the blood drained from his face, one leg buckled and Aaron collapsed to the floor. His breathing was labored and made strangling sounds and had problems swallowing. His color was a pasty gray.

Laura dropped her drink and ran to Aaron touching his throat. "Aaron! Oh my God!" she screamed and rushed to the telephone, dialing, waiting anxiously. "Dr. Crane! It's Aaron! He's collapsed! Hurry doctor, hurry!" Laura slammed the receiver down and went back to Aaron, yanking a throw and pillow from the couch. She put the pillow under his head and tucked the throw around him, and sat on the floor rocking him in her arms, waiting.

In the local hospital, Dr. Crane explained to Laura hours later, "Aaron had a stroke that effected the left side of his brain. It in turn showed up on the right side of the body in paralysis and an interrupted speech pattern."

"He's young! Only 'old' people have strokes!" she exclaimed.

"It's probably because of all the tensions over the last few months," the doctor said, shrugging. "Too much pressure. The body can only take so much, stress can kill you."

"What can we do? Will he get better?" she asked.

"I've made arrangements for him at the Hemstead Institute. They have a good record for rehabilitation in cases of this sort; moreover Aaron's a young and strong man. He has a chance to regain some speech and movement. Just how much we can't predict," Dr. Crane answered.

"Poor Aaron. It's all my fault," Laura paused, then said, "How soon can we take him there?"

"His company plane can have him there tonight," Dr. Crane suggested.

"I'll make the arrangements," Laura said, jumping at the chance to be helpful.

"Good. I'll see that he has nurses and a doctor on board with him. I can meet you there tomorrow," he said and hurried out.

"It's all my fault," she whispered. Laura stood in his hospital room forlorn, holding Aaron's limp hand to her lips. "Don't worry sweetheart. I'll be with you, all the way," she promised. The only other sounds in the room were the hissing of oxygen and the mechanical breathing of the respirator. The heart monitor beeped incessantly in the background.

While at the Hemstead Institute he had a surreptitious night visitor. Aaron was annoyed because he couldn't formulate words correctly, his speech was garbled. His mouth was twisted grotesquely to one side. Frustration was mirrored in his eyes, with the realization that his body had failed him when he needed it most.

The rasping voice whispered. "I'll talk for you, nod if I'm right." Aaron nodded his understanding, clutching the hand of a loyal confidant. "You want me to find them?" Aaron nodded. "Bring them back?" Was the next question. Aaron frowned and shook his head vigorously. "Watch over them? Take care of them?" He squeezed his hand and nodded. "The job is as good as done." Aaron breathed a sigh of relief, then grabbed his friends arm again. His smile twisted his once handsome face to one side. His expressive eyes spoke volumes.

A year later, Aaron sat in a comfortable chair toying with his cane. His activities were limited and frustrating.

Laura sat beside him. saying, "You're the only man I've ever loved, and ironically I still do. I'll be here, at your side, 'til death do we part," she said. He turned and looked at her with a desolate stare. Still not able to answer clearly, he refused to speak when others were around. His anger was directed toward himself, because his body was still failing him. Laura continued, "Aaron, your dark side has always intrigued me; does that make me a masochist?" She turned to look at him, "So my darling, when you were evil you were wretched." There was a long pause as she looked out over the plantation, then continued, "You'll never see your sons you know, not soon anyway. I've made provisions for them and Amelia, with our money. There's more than enough and they deserve the help," Aaron gazed at her in surprise. "You didn't know I had the strength and the knowledge to accomplish it, but I find I'm a smart woman." He looked away to hide the twinkle in his eyes. "Oh, I didn't tell you, but Amelia had identical twin boys. And as near as I can tell they look exactly like you. It's a pity you won't have any contact with them, at least for a while.

I know about my cancer, Dr. Crane explained it all to me." Aaron had a far away look, as her voice came into his consciousness from a distant. Laura said, "I'll keep you up to date. In fact I can start now," she took an envelop from her pocket. "These are the first pictures as per, Amelia's and my agreement. Oh and by the way, she and Edward, her husband, 'you remember her husband' they're doing fine." She spread the photographs on the table at his elbow. "Now, my next surprise. I've exchanged the steamship tickets on 'Embassy Lines', We're going to Switzerland for your rehabilitation and treatment for me," he shook his head. "We'll be gone for a long time." She looked around and spread her arms to indicate the whole plantation. "This place and the business will run without you, there are Devereaux's in control. The arrangements have been made, we leave in a week. Enjoy the pictures," she said, leaving him alone.

He stared with pride at his sons as they tried to walk, slept, laughed, at meal times with food over their faces, and playing in the snow. Amelia was there caring for them all.

Aaron had a fluttering feeling in the pit of his stomach as he looked at her photograph.

CHAPTER NINETEEN

While the years passed, changes in the country slowly evolved. In 1955 Montgomery, Alabama, Rosa Parks, too tired, refused to give up her seat to a white man, thus the bus boycott.

Malcolm X's new and excitingly radical ideas were aired on nationwide television and radio.

Martin Luther King Jr's, 'I have a dream' speech was also aired.

John Fitzgerald Kennedy, said, "Ask not what your country can do for you, but what you can do for your country."

Astronauts walked on the moon. 'One small step for man and a giant step for mankind'.

Then the Assassinations. These threads were woven through the fabric of time in America.

A television newscaster reported, "Laura Devereaux of Kalb Kove, Georgia died of metastatic cancer. Judge Aaron Devereaux brought his wife's remains home for the final services. The judge was also recuperating in Switzerland from several debilitating strokes, over the past twenty years."

On an afternoon in 1976, graduation exercises were well under way. Amelia sat proudly in the front row of the audience, watching her younger sons. Stanton and Stanley Devereaux-Russell march across the stage and receive their diplomas. Their carriage was erect, as they moved to friendly applause. Her older children arrived late, but were on hand to congratulate the new graduates.

A surreptitious watcher, observed them from a distance. As the mother hugged her sons, the siblings laughed and talked in pantomime, slapping each other on the back. The family walked happily from the auditorium, as the crowd disbursed.

In the study at Devereaux Manor, Aaron answered, the telephone, saying, "Hello, Judge Devereaux here." His speech was halting but clear, his hair was touched with gray. An older voices rasped in his ear, "Hello, Judge."

"Good morning, ole friend. Do you have news for me? What did you find?" Aaron asked.

"Eddie Russell was the first black judge in Pittsburgh. He died last year," the voice stated.

"What about the rest of the family, the twins, my sons?" Aaron asked.

"The older brothers are professional, and the twins graduated recently. Their mother works as a counselor."

"The same city?" Aaron asked. The old excitement stirred inside him, with the anticipation of seeing Amelia again.

"Yes, they live in the Eagle Rock district," the voice answered.

"Stay well old friend. I'll contact you when I arrive," Aaron said.

"Yes Judge," the voice replied.

Aaron walked over to stare at the album of his sons' pictures. Stanton and Stanley in the stages of their growth.

"I've missed so much, too much," Aaron said, touching the latest photograph and straightening the picture.

On a clear night in a restaurant garden, the Russell family celebrated. They raised their glasses in a salute. "Here's to the newest graduates, may their years be prosperous," Amelia said.

Aaron sat in a secluded corner and from his vantage point, saw everything that transpired.

His sons were across the narrow space: and yet the distance was like a great chasm separating them.

While the family talked in happy pantomime, Aaron appreciated the beauty of the moment. Then he started to make his way toward the exit.

Amelia looked up and had a glimpse of Aaron, as he went out the door. Her smile froze on her face.

"Mom? What's wrong mom?" Eddie Jr. asked.

Her smile broadened when she turned back to her children, saying, "I thought I saw someone I knew, just my imagination." The families jovial mood continued as Amelia took a second look at the exit. A frown creasing her brow momentarily. She shook her head and turned back to her family.

Warmth spread through Aaron while he watched Amelia come closer and sit beside him. The muted fragrance of her provocative perfume assailed his senses.

"I thought that was you in the restaurant," Amelia said.

"Yes, I was there. Even before Laura died, I've followed Stanton and Stanley's progress. Did you think I wouldn't?" he answered.

"I'm glad you didn't try to contact them," she replied.

"No, I didn't, not that I wasn't tempted. So I waited. Now I'm talking to you, first," he said.

"They're intelligent young men," she said.

"Yes, I'm aware of that," Aaron said. There was a long uncomfortable silence that followed. Then he continued, saying, "Thanks for the pictures over the years; even though I didn't deserve the consideration."

"I made Laura a promise, it was the least I could do. I'm sorry about her, she was a good person, with a lot of class," Amelia said, softly.

"Laura didn't deserve to die that way. She was tortured with the pain in the last years. The end was heartbreaking. I really did love her," Aaron confessed.

His eyes devoured Amelia's face, her eyes, her sensuous mouth. Everything he had taken as his right was unchanged.

The years had treated her well. She had to look away from his scrutiny. "I should have taken you to Paris," he whispered.

"I was there with my family, before my husband died. We enjoyed the tour," Amelia replied.

"Will you tell my sons about me?" he asked.

"Your sons are aware of their origin. They wanted to know about the 'Devereaux' in their names. My husband and I explained everything to them," Amelia said.

"I hope you were kind," Aaron quipped.

"They know the simple truth," she replied. "May I meet them?" Aaron asked, hesitantly.

"I'll ask," Amelia said, giving him a photograph. "This will be the last." The picture showed the twins as men, with broad smiles, curly dark hair and green eyes just as most Devereaux' before them.

Their hands touched and she recoiled. "May I hold your hand?" he asked, as she withdrew farther. "It can't hurt. This is, a public place." She reluctantly extended her hand. He covered it with both of his. "There was a time in your captivity. I never knew when," he said, and stopped to look into her eyes. "You became the most important person in my life." She started to speak, Aaron stopped her, saying, "Please, let me finish. If you can find the strength. I'm asking you to forgive me for causing you so much suffering."

She looked at him levelly, and replied, "Over the years, I've put that episode in the past. My husband understood, and was the most help. You see, he was a prisoner too," she took her hand from his. "I'll never forget it happened. One has to live with adversity. But I can't let it control my life." She stood, asking, "Where can I reach you? To tell you if the boys will see you?"

"Thank you. I'm staying at the Essex House, room nineteen thirty," Aaron answered. Amelia nodded and walked away.

Her slender figure moved regally away. "I love you Amelia," Aaron whispered softly, as she walked across the park, and out of his sight. He was shaken by their encounter.

In a Federal courtroom, in nineteen seventy-nine, the Negro foreman of a jury read the verdicts. An angry murmur ran through the audience, where five white men stood at the table with their attorneys. "We the jury, find the before mentioned members of 'The Knight's Of The Brotherhood' in count one, of the indictment, guilty of murder, in the first degree." Flash bulbs flared, newsmen scribbled frantically, and angry cries of protest rose from the audience. The judge on the case had difficulty maintaining order.

When order was restored, the foreman continued, saying, "We find, 'The Knights Of The Brotherhood' in count two as listed in the indictment, guilty of terrorism, and of conspiring to violate the civil rights of minorities."

Pandemonium broke loose in the courtroom.

The federal Judge banged his gavel repeatedly for order. He shouted, over the din, "Order in the court! Order, in the court! I will have 'order' in this courtroom!" His gavel sounded until there was order, "Another outburst like that and I'll clear the courtroom, is that understood?!" glaring around the courtroom. "Will the foreman please complete the reading of the verdicts?"

"Yes, your honor. We the jury find 'The Knights Of The Brotherhood' in count three of the indictment, guilty of using explosives and fire in the commission of a crime and the interference with housing rights, your honor."

"Would the clerk please poll the jury?" the judge instructed.

Later a newscaster reported, "The Knights Of The Brotherhood's conviction led to a landmark settlement of over seven million dollars. The money is to be used by the 'Movement For Non-violence' to assist victims of this sort of crime."

The same city park in suburban Pittsburgh, on another day. Two young men, a true mixture of the races, identical twins, walked across the park toward Aaron. After twenty three years he sat in awe while they came nearer, his sons. If he had never seen his sons before there was no mistaking their lineage.

They shook hands and sat across from Aaron, their conversation was carried out in friendly pantomime lasting for nearly two hours.

THE END

Epilogue.

Bondage, this is a rare perversion of men in which another individual is bound for sexual or other personal gratifications of the captor. The crucial element is the helplessness of the enslaved. Aaron, a man of power created a state of bondage for Amelia that held her and her family captive in an unrelenting social structure.

Sometime in life, roles change and the captor will become the captive.

An addendum: The state of Mississippi passed into law the Emancipation Proclamation in March, 1995.

            DEVEREAUX FAMILY TREE   1868-1976

                1868 HENRI DEVEREAUX
                      *   LIZZETTE ROGET-DEVEREAUX
                    *   *
                   *   *
                  *   1869 ETIENNE DEVEREAUX
After the death   *   *
of Lizzette   *   *
Late 1870   *   1891 ETIENNE DEVEREAUX
                *   *   CAROLINE RAVELL
               *   *   DEVEREAUX
HENRI DEVEREAUX   *   *
    YMANI 1871   * * * * * *   *
        *   1891 *   *** NICHOLAS 1892
        *   ETIENNE DEVEREAUX   *   DEVEREAUX
        *   MYRIAH VANDER VOORT   *
        *   *   *
        *   *   1919 NICHOLAS DEVEREAUX
        *   DANIELLE '93   ELIZABETH ASHLEY-SAMUELSON
        *   *   *   DEVEREAUX
        *   JULIANNA '94   *   *
* * * * * * * *   *   *   *
*   ROGER   '92   *   *
*   AaRON DEVEREAUX * 1924
JEAN-CLAUDE DEVEREAUX 1872   *   *
JEAN-PIERRE DEVEREAUX   *   ABIGAIL DEVEREAUX 1921
ROBERT DEVEREAUX   1873   *   *
DENISE DEVEREAUX   1874   *   *
                              *   NO CHILDREN
                             *   Actress
                            *
                1949   AaRON DEVEREAUX
                      *   LAURA COULTER-DEVEREAUX
                     *   *
                    *   *
                   *   *
                  *   *
                 *   NO LIVE BIRTHS
AaRON DEVEREAUX *******
    AMELIA RUSSELL   1952
                     *
  Twin   *
  boys   *   Caroline died 1927
  Born 1953   *
        ****
          *   *
          *   *
          *   STANLEY DEVEREAUX 1976 met father Aaron
STANTON DEVEREAUX

        ETIENNE DEVEREAUX MARRIED MYRIAH VANDER VOORT ON THE
EUROPEAN CONTINENT 1897